"Miles wouldn't betray us, betray you, that way."

Something bleak closed over Trent's anger, and he pushed Sarah's hands away as if he couldn't stand to touch her anymore. "If you think that, you're even more naive than I thought you were. Anyone is capable of betrayal. *Anyone.*"

"Not Miles," she insisted. "I don't mean to hurt you. But I'm here, and I intend to stay until I find out the truth."

His dark, winged eyebrows lifted slightly. "And if I tell you you're not welcome here?"

"Then I'd say that you don't own St. James Island. Not all of it, anyway."

Something, perhaps faint, bitter amusement, crossed Trent's face. He moved toward the door. "You may be surprised."

"You can't force me to leave."

Trent pulled the door open, then paused, a dark silhouette against the rectangle of sunlight. "Goodbye, Sarah. I don't expect I'll see you again."

MARTA PERRY

has written everything from Sunday school curriculum to travel articles to magazine stories in twenty years of writing, but she feels she's found her home in the stories she writes for Love Inspired.

Marta lives in rural Pennsylvania, but she and her husband spend part of each year at their second home in South Carolina. When she's not writing, she's probably visiting her children and her beautiful grandchildren, traveling or relaxing with a good book.

Marta loves hearing from readers and she'll write back with a signed bookplate or bookmark. Write to her c/o Steeple Hill Books, 233 Broadway, Suite 1001, New York, NY 10279, e-mail her at marta@martaperry.com, or visit her on the Web at www.martaperry.com.

LAND'S END
MARTA PERRY

Steeple
Hill®

Published by Steeple Hill Books™

STEEPLE HILL BOOKS

Steeple
Hill®

ISBN 0-373-87372-7

LAND'S END

Printed in U.S.A.

The Lord is my stronghold, my fortress and my champion, my God, my rock where I find safety, my shield, my mountain refuge, my strong tower.
—*Psalms* 18:2

This story is dedicated to Christine Teisher, with much love. And, as always, to Brian.

ONE

Years ago there had been no bridge to the island, and it had slept in haunted isolation. Now two lanes of concrete spanned the sound, carrying Sarah Wainwright quickly from the Georgia coast to St. James Island. Too quickly. She wasn't ready.

Perspiration slickened her hands against the steering wheel. She couldn't stop, couldn't pull off, couldn't turn around. The bridge funneled her inexorably to the one place in the world she didn't want to be. The entire past year hadn't been enough time to prepare herself for what awaited her on St. James.

The island appeared, a green, insubstantial smudge against a clear May sky, and Sarah's stomach lurched. St. James—home to an uneasy, volatile mixture of local Gullah fishermen and the rich incomers who'd turned one end of the island into a private enclave for the wealthy and powerful.

St. James had been Sarah's home, too, for six short months. Then betrayal and tragedy sent her fleeing back to her native Boston.

Fleeing unsuccessfully. She'd discovered, since the anniversary of Miles's death in April, that she couldn't outrun grief. It hung, persistent, on her heels, hampering her every step, demanding her constant attention. Demanding that she face it here, on St. James. Her stomach gave another protesting spasm as the car wheels rolled off the bridge and onto the island.

Live oaks, shrouded with Spanish moss, canopied the road. Sarah shivered in spite of the heat. Haunted.

I don't believe in ghosts, Heavenly Father, but no other word fits.

St. James was haunted by its own past, and now haunted by *her* past, too, and that of the husband who'd died here—died in an apparent lovers' tryst with his employer's wife.

The lobby of the St. James Inn was shuttered and cool, its only inhabitant the manager, leaning on his desk. Sarah caught the expression of shock mingled with avid curiosity that crossed his face at the sight of her, quickly replaced by his professional welcoming smile.

"Dr. Wainwright. This is a pleasant surprise. We weren't expecting you." He glanced nervously at the desk computer and patted his thinning hair. "Were we?"

"No, you weren't." She'd known instinctively it would be a mistake to announce her coming.

She smiled, wishing she remembered the man's name. It would give her a fraction more leverage. Obviously he remembered hers. The island had probably talked of little else for months.

"I'm sure you can find a room for me." The inn mainly housed overflow guests from the big houses, and they both knew May wasn't the high season.

"Why…um…" He punched a few keys on his computer, clearly hoping for inspiration. Sarah knew exactly what he was thinking. What would Trent Donner want him to do? "Does—does Mr. Donner know you're coming?"

Nobody on St. James, conceivably nobody in Georgia,

crossed Trent Donner with impunity. Sarah's stomach lurched again. Sooner or later she'd have to face him. Was she a coward for hoping it would be later?

She managed a cool smile. "I thought I'd surprise him. I'll go out to Land's End tomorrow."

Maybe it was the casual mention of the Donner estate. Something eased in the manager's face. "Why don't we give you the suite you had the last time you were here?"

A lady never shows her feelings in public.

Her grandmother's maxim, drilled into Sarah from birth, stiffened her spine and kept a smile frozen on her face. Knowing what he must, how could the man assume she'd want the suite she'd shared with Miles when they'd first arrived on the island?

"That will be fine."

She tried to put herself on autopilot to get through the next few minutes. Fill out the registration card, exchange comments about the weather. Follow the bellman, tip him, don't think about staying here with Miles when they'd first arrived on the island.

Finally the door closed behind him, and she was alone in the quiet room with its cool white shutters, bamboo furniture and four-poster bed. Staying here was no worse than staying in any other room. No place on the island would be free of memories.

That was why she'd fled, wasn't it? And that was why she'd come back.

Her parents hadn't seemed surprised at Sarah's abrupt decision to return to the place of Miles's death. Duty loomed large in six generations of New England virtue, and they clearly felt Sarah had left duty unresolved, racing home the day after Miles's death, hiding from reporters, evading even her friends.

But then, her parents had never believed Miles Wainwright could be guilty of betraying both his marriage and his employer by having an affair with his employer's wife. Or by dying with her. Not Miles Wainwright, descendant of his own six generations' worth of Puritan values.

She hadn't believed it either, in spite of overwhelming evidence that Miles had, indeed, had an affair with Lynette Donner and died with her in a gas heater accident at the cottage where they'd met. She hadn't believed, couldn't believe, what Lynette's husband so obviously did.

For weeks, maybe months, Sarah's mind had winced every time it came too close to the thought of Miles and Lynette together. If she didn't think about it, it didn't happen.

Over time, the anguish and grief receded to a dull, hollow ache, only flaring painfully when unexpectedly jostled, like a deep wound beginning to skin over with tender, fragile flesh. Work had helped. She'd taken on emergency room duty at the hospital, grateful for the killing schedule that let her fall into bed, exhausted enough to sleep, every night.

Eventually she could actually look at the possibility of Miles's betrayal for more than a moment at a time. Look at it, assess it, bring reason to bear.

And find that she still, more than a year after the fact, didn't believe it. Miles—loyal, upright Miles—was not a man who'd betray his marriage and his employer. He *wasn't*.

To the weight of her faith in Miles, Sarah added faith in her own perceptions. *I couldn't not have known that Miles was deceiving me, could I, Lord?* If her perceptions were that skewed, the earth was no longer solid under her feet.

So she'd come back to St. James. Everyone—Lynette's husband, the police, the coroner—everyone was wrong. Whatever Miles had been doing at Cat Isle that day with Lynette, he wasn't having an affair. Somewhere on St. James there were answers, and this time she wouldn't run away. This time she wouldn't leave until she found them.

A knock shattered the stillness. The manager, having forgotten something in his nervous haste? She smoothed her linen slacks, wrinkled from travel, and opened the door. And confronted Trent Donner, filling the doorway with well over six feet of fury, all of it radiating directly at her.

"What are you doing here?" He surged inside on the words. Sarah stumbled back a step or two, heart hammering against her ribs. Trying to keep him out would be as futile as trying to stop the tide.

"The manager called you," she stated flatly.

She should have known he would do that. She should have been prepared, instead of standing here with her mouth dry from shock. She'd forgotten the aura of power Trent brought with him into a room, as if everyone and everything rotated around him.

"Of course." Trent dismissed the man with a negligent gesture.

Sarah found her temper at the unconscious arrogance of the man. Good. One always needed an edge in dealing with Trent Donner, and anger seemed to be the only edge she had.

"Why shouldn't I be here?" Answer a question with a question. Catch your breath. Slow your pounding heart.

"I'd think that would be obvious." Trent's voice was hard, incisive, with an edge of mockery. He took a swift step forward, and the afternoon sun crossed his face, lighting the harsh angles of cheekbone and jaw.

Sarah drew in a breath. The last time she'd seen him, it had been across two motionless bodies and the wreckage of too many lives. His normally impassive face had been etched with pain, grief and a kind of hopeless rage.

Now the lines seemed permanently engraved, turning the strong planes of his face into a marble mask. Only his clear gray eyes were alive, blazing with feeling. With fury. Her heart jolted, sickeningly. She was trapped by his presence.

"I didn't…"

Sarah heard a faint waver in her voice, stopped and swallowed. She could face drug overdoses and multiple fatalities in the E.R. She could face him.

"I'm sorry if my being here upsets you, but I do have ties here." She forced herself to meet his fierce gaze calmly. "My husband died here."

"I hardly need a reminder of that." His voice, normally deep, roughened and deepened still further. Shared pain flicked past the anger Sarah held like a shield, catching her on the raw.

That elemental pain must be the only thing they shared. She wanted, suddenly, to comfort him, and knew in the same instant that she was the one person who never could.

Perhaps he saw her wince, perhaps he only heard the revelation in his own voice. He paused, another feeling quarreling with the anger.

"I'm sorry." He brushed a strand of black hair from his forehead with a swift, economical movement, and she saw that his hair was touched now with white at both temples. The year had aged him, as it had her. "I've never had much in the way of manners." His mouth twitched in what might have been a smile. "I'm forgetting myself. How are you, Sarah?"

The reluctant concern in his voice disarmed her, touching something that seemed to reverberate to the timbre of his voice.

"I'm…all right. I went back to work. That helped."

"At Boston General?"

She nodded, vaguely surprised that he remembered the name of the hospital where she'd interned before she'd moved south and married Miles. But Trent had always had an encyclopedic memory, as well as an unerring ability to rearrange odd pieces in unexpected ways. That gift that had fascinated Miles's more prosaic intelligence.

"How is Melissa?" His daughter would be twelve now, a crucial age for a girl. How had she coped with the tragedy?

Trent's face tightened, if marble conceivably could. He'd never looked his nearly forty years, until bitterness and grief etched their mark on him. "She's all right."

The shortness of his answer told Sarah Melissa was not all right, and fresh pain gripped her heart. Poor child. She'd had problems enough before tragedy had shattered all their worlds.

Well, little though she'd wanted to see Trent today, he'd given her the opportunity to get on with what she had to do. "I'd like to see her…"

"No!" Trent's eyes blazed, and her heart lurched into overdrive. She'd always felt something wild lurked under that expensively tailored gray business suit, and now it seemed about to surface.

"Trent, just hear me out." What could she say that would make him listen?

"I don't want you anywhere near my daughter." A muscle twitched at the corner of his mouth and was ruthlessly stilled. "I don't want you anywhere on St. James at all."

The momentary truce was over, the brief span of shared emotion banished. Sarah stopped attempting to control her anger. When Trent had been Miles's employer, she'd had to be polite to him. That constraint didn't exist anymore.

"Or anywhere in Georgia? I'm not sure my whereabouts is your concern."

"It is when it affects me. When it affects my daughter." The words shot at her like bullets. His hands knotted into fists and then unwound with what appeared a superhuman effort.

"Don't you think I'm affected by being here?" Hurt edged her voice. "I had to come."

He shook his head, as if to clear it. "I know you're as much a victim of what happened as we are." He clearly tried hard for a reasonable tone. "I'm sorry for you. But your being here will only stir up things that are better left buried."

"Better for whom? Not better for me!" If only she could make him see. "Don't you understand? I've spent a year trying to bury the past. It can't be done. I can't leave it alone until I know what really happened."

For the space of a heartbeat the words hung in silence between them. Then Trent made a sudden, violent motion that sent Sarah back a step.

"Is that what this is all about?" His hands shot out to grasp her wrists, and he looked as if he'd rather have them around her throat. "You want to dig it all up again, make us relive it. For what? So you can satisfy that strict Puritan conscience of yours? That's it, isn't it? You have to prove to yourself that you're not to blame."

"No!" Sarah felt her pulse pound against the warm hard grip of his hands. He was too close. She was suffocating, as if his pain and anger drew all the air out of the room. "This isn't for me. This is for Miles. I don't believe it. I've tried, and I can't believe it."

"Try harder." Eyes blazing, he thrust his hard face toward her. "It happened."

Sarah had a sudden vivid image of a wolf, eyes gleaming, closing on its prey. People said Trent Donner never forgot and never forgave. She could believe it.

"No." Stubbornness seemed her only refuge against his intensity. "Miles wouldn't betray us, betray you, that way."

Something bleak closed over Trent's anger, and he pushed her hands away as if he couldn't stand to touch her anymore. "If you think that, you're even more naive than I thought you were. Anyone is capable of betrayal. *Anyone.*"

Sarah rubbed her arms, chilled in spite of the sunlight slanting through the open windows. She hadn't prepared enough, obviously, for Trent's reaction to what she intended to do. Maybe because she tried so hard not to think of him at all.

"Not Miles," she insisted. "I don't mean to hurt you, or Melissa. But I'm here, and I intend to stay until I find out the truth."

His dark, winged eyebrows lifted slightly. "And if I tell you you're not welcome here?"

"Then I'd say that you don't own St. James Island. Not all of it, anyway."

Something, perhaps faint, bitter amusement, crossed Trent's face. He moved toward the door. "You may be surprised."

"You can't force me to leave."

Trent pulled the door open, then paused, a dark silhouette against the rectangle of sunlight. "Goodbye, Sarah. I don't expect I'll see you again."

Trent hadn't taken more than a few steps from Sarah's room when he spotted Ed Farrell lounging on the patio, probably within earshot of the open windows. Plant security wouldn't have sent Farrell to serve as Trent's driver-cum-bodyguard unless he'd passed all their stringent tests, but the man still annoyed him. Farrell's curiosity grated on Trent's nerves in much the same way his harsh New Jersey accent grated on his ears.

"Bring the car around. I'm going home."

"Yes, suh."

One of Farrell's more annoying habits was this attempt to assume a Southern drawl. Maybe he thought the drawl, the paunch and the sunglasses made him into the media version of a redneck cop. It didn't.

"And in future, stay with the car unless I tell you otherwise."

Farrell's stolid face showed no emotion except mild stubbornness. "It's my job to protect you."

"I'm in no danger from Dr. Wainwright."

No physical danger, anyway. He stalked toward the car, ignoring Farrell's quick dance to get there first and open the door.

Small, slender, blond, Sarah looked as fragile as a piece of fine china. When he'd grasped her wrists, his fingers had entirely encircled them—like holding a child's small bones within his grasp.

He slid into the car. Nothing else about her was childlike, however. Not the warm, peaches-and-cream glow of her skin. Or that steel structure she called backbone.

Sarah Wainwright reminded him of someone, and for a moment he couldn't think who. Not Lynette. That was certain. His hand tightened into a fist, and he deliberately relaxed it. Lynette had been all fireworks and talent and temperament.

Contained, self-possessed Sarah, with her single-minded devotion to medicine, was not remotely like Lynette. He'd been alternately annoyed and amused by Sarah once.

His head moved restlessly against smooth gray leather as the car took the winding, narrow road to Land's End. Amused. Annoyed. *Attracted*. The word gave a bitter edge to his thoughts. He'd never have acted on that feeling, of course. Unlike Lynette.

He'd handled the news of Sarah's presence badly. If he

hadn't already been beat from three days' worth of meetings in San Francisco followed by the red-eye back to Savannah, he might have coped more rationally. He'd called the house to check his messages, intercepted the news that she was at the inn and barged in without thinking.

Once he was in the room with her, it was too late to think. The complex feelings she sparked in him hadn't left space for thought. It hadn't seemed the time for civilized niceties, but a few of those might have gotten him further.

Or maybe he shouldn't have gone near Sarah at all. He could have let Derek handle the situation. His half brother's easy charm had smoothed difficult patches more than once.

The car rolled past the security gate, one of those unfortunate necessities of life for corporate heads. He might be willing to take chances with himself, but he wouldn't take chances with Melissa.

His heart clenched at the thought of his daughter. Sarah posed no physical danger, but her very presence on the island was still a threat. A threat that would have to be dealt with.

He got out of the car onto the shell-encrusted drive, suddenly realizing who Sarah reminded him of. His grandmother. Just as tiny, just as iron-willed, she'd immigrated from Ireland, headed for New York and ended up, most improbably, the wife of a dirt-poor shrimper on the Georgia sea islands.

Sarah, with generations of New England upper-crust breeding behind her, probably wouldn't appreciate the comparison. But Mary Elizabeth O'Neill Donner had had backbone, too. Once she'd made up her mind to do something, she never turned back.

Trent paused for a moment on the veranda, letting the breeze that accompanied the rising tide cool his face. His pulse slowed in rhythm with the roll of the breakers and the undulating wave of the sea oats on the dunes.

The house he'd worked with the architect to design spread accommodatingly on a narrow strip of land between ocean and salt marsh, its pale yellow, shallow wings built in true Low Country style to catch every breeze. He'd been happy here once. Maybe he could be again.

But not until he got rid of Sarah Wainwright.

Geneva Robinson waited in the foyer, ready to take his briefcase and hand him an iced glass of her raspberry tea.

"Did you have a good trip this time?" The housekeeper's voice retained the melodic, singsong cadence of Gullah, the language born on the vast rice plantations that once covered the Low Country.

"So-so." Trent shrugged out of his jacket, stretching. He'd probably sleep better tonight if he took one of the boats out. Get the smell of cities and airplanes out of his lungs and replace it with the lush, fecund aroma of the salt marsh. "Is my brother here?"

Geneva shook her head. "Mr. Derek hasn't come in yet."

She called him Trent when they were alone, but his brother was always Mr. Derek. He'd never known why. "What about Melissa?"

"In her room." Geneva's smile faltered, and he saw the worry in her eyes. "That child's hardly been out of her room since you left. I tried to get her to call her friends, but she wouldn't."

The burden of Melissa's unhappiness settled over his shoulders, weighing him down like a hot, humid Georgia day. "I'll see what I can do." They both knew he could probably do very little, but he had to try. Had to pretend his being here might make a difference.

He took the wide, shallow staircase two steps at a time. Music boomed from behind the closed door of Melissa's room, rattling the panels. Trent grimaced. If he could understand the words, he'd probably be appalled. He tapped twice, then opened the door. "Melissa?"

His daughter shot bolt upright on the bed, swinging a startled, angry face toward him. "Can't you knock?"

If he took issue with every rude thing she said these days, they'd never talk at all. "I did." He felt as if he mouthed the words. He gestured toward the speakers. "Will you turn that down, please?"

Melissa snapped the switch and silence fell. Trent's eardrums still throbbed. Now was probably not the time to discuss hearing loss.

"What have you been up to while I was gone?" He hated his inability to carry on a simple conversation with this child he loved and didn't understand.

"Nothing." Melissa crossed her arms over her chest defensively. "School's out. You're not supposed to have to do stuff when you're on vacation."

"See any of your friends lately?" Every interaction with Melissa turned into a game of Twenty Questions.

She shrugged, a curtain of brown hair swinging forward to hide her face. It was becoming a characteristic posture. "No."

"Wouldn't you like to invite some of the girls from school over?" He hated the desperate note in his voice.

"I just want to be by myself. Okay?" She did look up then, hazel eyes darkening. She glared pointedly at the door.

He valued privacy himself too highly to argue. "No, I guess not." He said it quietly, because the only other choice was to shout, and shouting just drove Melissa deeper into the shell she'd constructed around herself, like a conch hiding in its beautiful labyrinth. "I'll see you at dinner."

He closed the door and stood for a moment, hand resting on its panel as lightly as if he touched his daughter. He'd like to believe this was normal behavior for a twelve-year-old, but he couldn't. How much damage had they done, he and Lynette, to the child they'd created? How much more waited for her?

He straightened, hand dropping from the door. Sarah Wainwright might not intend harm to Melissa, but that didn't mean she wouldn't cause it. And that was something he intended to prevent. No matter what he had to do.

Sarah lay across the bed, staring at the shadows cast by the lazy revolving of the ceiling fan. Images flickered in the shadows. Miles's face, glowing with excitement when he told her about the offer to become second in command of Donner's conglomerate of software and engineering companies.

"I owe it all to you, Sarah. If you hadn't pushed me to blow the whistle on the scam in the Atlanta office, Donner would never even have remembered my name."

She'd been surprised that she'd had to push. Even if the rot at Donner Enterprises had gone all the way to Donner himself, exposing it had been the right thing to do.

Miles had seen that, once she pointed it out. Donner hadn't been involved, and his appreciation of Miles's integrity had taken a tangible form.

Brilliant, creative, iconoclastic… Every word applied to Trent Donner was a superlative. Trent had risen from poverty to parlay a shoestring operation into a multimillion-dollar empire. Miles's appointment as his assistant had been a plum, but it had meant a move to the isolated, moneyed environs of St. James. Trent preferred to run his empire from the island, flying—as need took him—to Atlanta or Singapore. His assistant had to be on call twenty-four hours a day.

Of course she'd been happy for Miles, but moving meant

leaving behind her position at the pediatric clinic in Atlanta. Where was she going to practice medicine on St. James?

That had worked out, after a fashion. She'd found an emergency room position at a hospital in Savannah, the closest city. It was only part-time, but before she had time to grow restless, she'd discovered another opportunity, right on St. James. The island had been without a clinic of its own.

The wealthy, in their private compounds, didn't need one, but the several hundred native sea islanders, clinging to their Gullah culture while coping with the influx of outsiders, did. She'd never been able to see a problem without feeling it her duty to solve it.

Trent had been the obvious choice to put money behind her idea. She'd begun to enjoy her clashes with him on the subject, and he'd finally donated the building so they could start the clinic. And then after six short months, their world exploded.

Trent's embittered face formed against the shadows. Did the pain show as clearly on her face as it did on his? A man who hated to show his feelings, he must despise every line, resent it every time he looked into a mirror.

Unbidden, another image of Trent's face sprang into her mind. His eyes glowing with laughter, then surprised by attraction, silhouetted against the dark green shadows of a garden. They'd sensed the feeling at the same moment, recognized it in each other. And turned away, as guilty as if they'd acted on the impulse.

No. Sarah slammed the door of her mind on that memory. She had to concentrate on the mission that had brought her here.

The truth about Miles and Lynette is buried on St. James, Father. You've brought me back, and I won't leave until I find it.

TWO

Sarah paused in the entrance to the inn's dining room. After a quick, quiet meal, she'd tumble into bed. Tomorrow she'd figure out what her first step had to be, now that Trent had made it clear she could expect nothing from him. Thank goodness the dining room, like the lobby earlier, was nearly deserted.

Not quite. She saw the couple at the table by the window, heart sinking. What perverse luck had led her into a meeting with Trent's closest neighbors? It was too late to retreat. Jonathan Lee was already on his feet and coming toward her.

"Sarah Wainwright! We didn't know you were back on the island. It's good to see you, honey." Jonathan took her hands and kissed her cheek.

Was it good to see her? She had no idea where the Lees stood in relation to respecting Trent's wishes that she leave.

"I just arrived. It's good to see you, too. And Adriana." She smiled at Jonathan's wife, who hadn't left her chair.

Jonathan drew back and studied her, his round, merry face, like a sophisticated faun's, growing solemn. "It doesn't look as if being back agrees with you."

Sarah shrugged, not sure how much his perceptive, sometimes malicious, black eyes picked up. "Mixed feelings, I suppose. Please greet Adriana for me."

She tried to disengage herself, but Jonathan had a firm grip on her hand. "Tell her yourself. Have dinner with us."

If she tried to make polite conversation, she'd probably fall asleep in her dinner plate. "Another time."

Jonathan shook his head. "You can't eat alone your first night back. Besides, Adriana's dying to talk with you."

Sarah was swept to their table on the tide of that Southern charm Jonathan dispensed with such enthusiasm. He played the role of Southern gentleman with so much flair, one could never quite tell if it was real or exaggerated.

The waiter produced another chair, and she ordered the first special he mentioned, trying to organize her thoughts. This meeting had fallen into her lap. If anyone knew what had gone on with Trent after she'd left the island, the Lees did. She'd better shake off her fatigue and use this opportunity.

She glanced up to find herself the target of two pairs of eyes, Jonathan's brightly curious, Adriana's bored. At least she supposed it was boredom. Adriana was always perfectly made-up, her dark hair swept back from her strong-featured face, her clothing a perfect example of retrained elegance.

Jonathan leaned toward her, pixie face warm. He must be a good ten years older than Trent, but he had a perennially youthful air. His interest in everything about everyone balanced Adriana's coolness.

"Has it been a bad year?" He grimaced. "Of course it has. Scratch that question, sugar. Tell us what you've been doing."

An account of her recent life shouldn't have lasted through the serving of the she-crab soup, but Jonathan managed to spin it out through the main course with questions and comments.

Sarah was still wondering how she could tactfully introduce the subject she wanted when the talk turned to island society, and Jonathan said Lynette's name at last.

"Everyone misses Lynette." Adriana's spoon chinked against the china cup. Candlelight cast shadows across her face. "I'm not sure I even want to have our party this year."

"Of course we will." Was that an edge in Jonathan's voice? His black eyes bored into his wife, and Sarah had a sense of meaning under the words. "Our party always kicks off the summer. Everyone will be disappointed if we cancel."

"Not everyone." Adriana toyed with her spoon. "Trent's turned into such a recluse, he probably won't come anyway."

"A recluse?" Adriana's comment seemed to bring Trent's frowning presence to the table.

Jonathan's eyes darkened. "I wouldn't call it that. After what happened, naturally he didn't go out much."

"I hear he's neglecting the business." Adriana's brows lifted. "Escaping on his boat and letting his brother run things."

"I'm sure Derek's not taking on anything important," Jonathan said. "He's not a heavyweight at business."

Adriana shrugged, dismissing Trent's brother. "The way Trent's acting, anyone would think he and Lynette had been devoted to each other, instead of fighting all the time."

"I hadn't realized they were having problems." She'd seldom seen Trent and Lynette, but she'd been busy with her work. Or maybe she hadn't cared enough.

"I don't suppose you knew Lynette well." Adriana's tone implied that Lynette would hardly have chosen her for a friend.

"No, I didn't. But obviously people think my husband did." Sarah put the blunt statement out and waited for a response.

Jonathan shook his head, looking shocked at her frankness. "I'm sure no one believes—"

"Don't be stupid, Jonathan." Adriana sounded scornful. "That's what everyone thinks. What other explanation is there?"

Adriana didn't care whether she hurt your feelings, but she was privy to gossip that Sarah would never hear. Gossip that she now *needed* to hear if she wanted to uncover the truth.

"Did people suspect they were involved before the accident, or just afterward?" She ignored the pain.

"Well, I heard—"

Jonathan's hand closed over his wife's. "Please, Adriana. Let's not repeat gossip. It can only be hurtful."

"I'd rather hear it than wonder what people are saying behind my back."

He shook his head, and under the sympathy in his face she saw determination. Jonathan didn't want her to hear the talk. Was his concern based on his ideas of what constituted polite conversation, or was there really something out there he thought too painful for her to hear?

"Both you and Trent lost a great deal." He patted her hand sympathetically. "Some things are better left unsaid."

She didn't agree, but she subsided. She'd probably pushed as much as she could for the moment.

At least she'd learned something. Jonathan wouldn't talk, but Adriana would. She had to find a way of seeing her alone.

She slid her chair back. "Please excuse me. I'm afraid I'm exhausted from the trip. Maybe we can get together again soon." She stood, looking at Adriana as she said the words, and thought she saw a flicker of understanding in her eyes.

"Oh, honey, of course." Jonathan got up. "Don't you forget now, we're here if you need anything."

Anything but the truth. Well, she could get around that. Trent might think he could stop her, but people would talk. No matter how painful, that was better than silence.

She walked into the lobby feeling more hopeful than she had an hour earlier. But it didn't last. The lobby now held something that hadn't been there before—her luggage stood forlornly against the desk.

The manager wore an expression of mixed embarrassment and determination. "I'm sorry, Dr. Wainwright. I'm afraid we have to ask you to vacate your room."

Sarah stared at him, her mind as blank as she knew her face must be. "What on earth are you talking about?"

He shuffled a sheaf of computer printouts on the desktop. "This is very embarrassing." He looked everywhere but at her. "The entire inn is booked for a business meeting."

Cold rage stiffened her spine. "Let me guess. This business meeting… It wouldn't be Donner Enterprises, would it?"

"There'll be no charge for the room, of course, or for your dinner." He attempted a smile, fastening his gaze somewhere over her head. "Maybe you'll come back another time."

"And if I did? Would you find the inn full again?"

For a moment his eyes met hers and he was a human being, instead of Trent Donner's tool. "I'm sorry." He spread his hands out helplessly. "There's nothing I can do."

"Sarah?"

She turned, realizing that Jonathan and Adriana had come out of the dining room. Jonathan stared at her bags.

"You're not leaving already, are you? You just got here."

"Not willingly. The manager has suddenly discovered that all the rooms have been booked by Trent's company. In other words, Trent is having me evicted."

She probably shouldn't be so blunt. They were Trent's friends. She couldn't expect them to side with her.

Jonathan turned on the manager. "Dunphries, you can't ask Dr. Wainwright to leave at this hour of the night."

The man reddened. "I don't have a choice."

"You mean you're afraid to make one." Jonathan's black eyes snapped. "Donner provides a lot of your business."

"It's not his fault." She remembered Trent's stinging accusation. "I was naive not to expect it. I'll go elsewhere."

The manager cleared his throat. "I understand Mr. Donner booked all the rooms on the island for this business meeting."

She'd underestimated Trent. She wouldn't make that mistake again. "It looks as if I'll be sleeping on the beach tonight."

"Don't be silly." Adriana's entry into the conversation startled Sarah. "You can stay in our guesthouse."

Sarah could only hope her mouth didn't gape. Adriana had barely spoken two sentences to her in the time she'd been on the island. Why on earth was she extending an invitation now?

Jonathan smiled. "Of course. That's the perfect solution." He reached for Sarah's bags. "Come on. You're coming home with us."

"Trent won't be very happy with you."

"It won't hurt Trent not to get his own way for once." Jonathan picked up her bags. "Our car's out in the lot."

She'd better stop protesting, or they might change their minds. "I have my car, so I'll follow you."

The manager sprang to open the lobby door for them, probably with a sigh of relief. She'd blame him, but she knew the power Trent wielded here. He was the one who deserved her anger, not people who depended on him for their livelihoods.

Adriana fell into step with Sarah. "Don't worry about our relationship with Trent." Her voice was cool and light, almost amused. "Your staying with us won't make it any worse."

That seemed fairly ambiguous. What was Adriana thinking? "It's very kind of you."

"Not at all." That definitely was amusement in her tone. "Your presence might make life more…interesting."

Interesting.

She weighed Adriana's words later as she followed their car down the black, winding road. Streetlights were nonexistent on the island, and street signs rare. You either knew where you were going at night, or you got lost, just as she felt lost in the tangle of ambiguities and hidden meanings in nearly everything that had been said tonight.

What was Adriana up to? She hadn't invited Sarah to stay based on her ideas of Southern hospitality. Still, staying with them should open some doors to her. Whatever Adriana's motives, she had to be grateful for that.

He ought to feel pleased. The problem presented by Sarah Wainwright had been taken care of.

Trent leaned back in his leather desk chair, looking over the computer to the wide windows. A silvery moon rode low on the ocean, sending a path of light toward the shore.

He didn't feel anything of the kind. He couldn't rejoice that Sarah was ending an exhausting day by driving off the island to the nearest motel. She'd have to go all the way to the interstate to find one that wasn't inexplicably full.

No, he wasn't pleased, but he was satisfied. He'd done what he had to do. Some would say he'd been ruthless, but that was because he did what other people only thought about. Sarah Wainwright would not open up the busy lines of gossip again.

In the long run, he'd done her a favor. She'd have found more grief if she'd stayed here.

Faint music filtered through the study door he'd left ajar. Derek must be playing the piano in the living room, since Melissa had already gone up to her room. He wasn't sure whether to be glad or not that Derek was at his suite of rooms here instead of at his waterfront apartment in Savannah.

Trent's first instinct, after Lynette's death, had been to have that grand piano of hers chopped into firewood. He hadn't, of course. Melissa had her mother's talent, and it wouldn't be fair to deprive her of that solace.

Besides, he hadn't wanted to do anything that might detract from the explanation he'd given for Lynette's and Miles's presence at the cottage together. He'd asked them to check out the cottage for possible expansion. That was what he'd told the police, the press, anyone else who dared ask. The police were satisfied that it was an unfortunate accident with the gas heater and only too glad to have a rational explanation for their presence. End of story.

Maybe people didn't really believe that story, but they pretended they did. No one would dare suggest anything else in his hearing, or in Melissa's. Or would they? He'd like to believe he'd protected his child from the speculation, but he'd never be sure.

He tilted his head back against cool leather, letting the music soothe his frazzled nerves. He'd done what he had to, all along the line. And if he spent sleepless nights raging at God over this betrayal—well, that was no one's business but his.

Sarah thought there was another answer, but she was wrong. He'd accepted that, and she'd be better off if she did, too. Her face formed in his mind—the clear green eyes that weighed and assessed everything, the determined set to her mouth, that stubborn chin. Sarah wouldn't give up easily.

That conviction ruffled his thoughts. He'd gotten her off

the island. Word would get around that it wasn't wise to talk with her, even if she came back. She hadn't been here long enough to make many friends who'd help her—only the people she'd recruited to help at the fledgling clinic.

Derek had been as close to her as anyone. Maybe Trent had best close that gap.

He shoved back the chair and went down the flight of stairs from the loft to the living room. His half brother played with his eyes shut, lost in the music. With his features relaxed, he had a strong resemblance to their mother—the same curly brown hair and full lips. Music had been a bond between him and Lynette, one Trent had never shared.

"Derek." He leaned against the piano. It was a piece of furniture, nothing else. He could stand here without remembering the hours Lynette had spent playing it.

Derek played a final chord and then glanced at him, eyes curious. "What's up?"

"Did you hear that Sarah Wainwright was on the island?"

Derek whistled softly. "No. Why would she come back?"

"She has some crazy idea that Miles and Lynette couldn't have been involved." He hated the words. They tasted of betrayal. "She wanted my help to prove it."

Derek played a random chord or two. "You told her no."

"Of course I told her no." Irritation edged his voice. He shouldn't have to explain that to Derek. "What did you think? That I'd welcome her and jump right into an investigation?"

"Guess not, when you put it that way. Still, you've got to feel sorry for the woman. She must be hurting."

"Poking into the past isn't going to heal that hurt." He ought to know. "I'm doing her a favor by shutting her down before she starts."

"She probably doesn't see it that way."

"Maybe not, but she doesn't have a choice."

"From what I remember about Sarah, I'd say she isn't one to take no for an answer. Where is she staying?"

"Gone." He clipped the word. "She was at the inn."

Derek filled in the rest. "You sent her packing."

"Yes." She'd be gone by now. He ignored the faint trace of regret at the thought.

"Well, I guess that's taken care of, then." Derek lifted his brows, his brown eyes questioning. "Isn't it?"

"You knew her as well as anyone. She might contact you."

"And you want me to do what?"

"That should be obvious." He suppressed a flicker of irritation. "Close her down."

"Kind of rude, don't you think?" Derek's long-fingered hands moved on the keys, picking out something harsh and dissonant.

"You can pretty it up any way you want." His voice was equally harsh. "Just don't tell her anything to encourage her."

"You're the boss."

He frowned at Derek's flippant tone. But Derek, no matter how he felt, would cooperate.

A step sounded on the tile floor, and he turned to see Farrell, the driver-cum-body-guard, standing just inside the door, his heavy face impassive.

"Well?" He'd left the man at the inn to confirm that Sarah went on her way.

"Thought you'd want to know."

"Know what?" The only thing he wanted to hear was that Sarah had left the island.

"Doc Wainwright. She left the inn, but she didn't head for the mainland. She moved into the guesthouse at the Lees'."

Derek played something ominous and threatening, like a storm coming up at sea.

"Stop it," Trent snapped at him.

Derek lifted his hands from the keys. "It sounds as if Sarah didn't do what you expected. How enterprising of her."

"She will." His jaw tightened, and he turned toward Farrell. "That's all. You can go."

She would. No matter how enterprising she was, Sarah wouldn't find any answers here. He'd see to that.

Sarah rubbed the back of her neck as she turned into the drive at the Lees' seaside villa. "Tara with hot tubs," some local wag had called it. Jonathan stopped in front of the pillared portico, she stopped behind and he then came and slid into the front seat of her car.

He pointed. "Just go round the end of the house."

Oleander branches, thick with blossoms, brushed the car as Sarah pulled up to the guesthouse. The architect had given up on antebellum design here—the cottage was a typical Low Country beach house. Its wide windows had shutters that could be closed against a storm. Between it and the main house, a turquoise swimming pool glowed with underwater lights.

Jonathan heaved her bags from the car. "You feel free to use the pool anytime you want. That's what it's there for."

Sarah followed as he unlocked the front door and switched on lights.

"I'll just put these in the master bedroom. You make yourself at home. You ought to find everything ready."

Sarah dropped her shoulder bag on a glass-topped coffee table. Pale cream walls, pale beige Berber carpeting, glass everywhere. The bright cushions on the white wicker furniture were the only splash of color, other than the seascapes on the walls. A living room with dining area, tiny kitchen, two bedrooms, two baths… This little retreat for extra guests was more than comfortable.

Sarah glanced out toward the pool, remembering how it had looked a year ago at Adriana's party. Twinkling white lights had festooned the trees. Everywhere there had been flowers, music, laughter, the clink of china. All of island society had been there. The heavy scent of magnolias in an isolated corner of the garden filled her mind.

No. She wasn't going to remember.

Jonathan came back, handing her the key. "Come up to breakfast anytime you like." His black eyes warmed with sympathy. "Honey, you look plain exhausted. Tomorrow we'll talk about your problem with Trent. Okay?"

Sarah nodded, her throat tightening at his kindness. "I'll do that. Jonathan, I can't thank you enough…"

"Don't." Something she couldn't read moved in his eyes. "I'm not sure we're doing you a favor." He kissed her cheek lightly. "Good night."

Jonathan's advice was good, but Sarah wasn't sure how to follow it. Once ready for bed, she couldn't settle. She turned down the peach spread on the king-size bed, fluffed the pillows, switched on the bedside lamp. Still she felt restless, uneasy, physically and emotionally exhausted but unable to rest.

Finally she wandered into the kitchen, switching on the light. The tea canister was stocked with herbals, so she filled a mug and popped it in the microwave.

A dose of chamomile tea, to be taken at bedtime. Her grandmother used to recite the line from Peter Rabbit whenever Sarah, visiting her at the big house on Beacon Hill, struggled to get to sleep.

Something rattled over the soft hum of the microwave.

Sarah paused, spoon in hand. What was it? Something inside the cottage, or out? She listened.

Somewhere an owl called. Beyond the owl she could just make out the muffled murmur of the surf. The main house was between her and the ocean, but that must be what she'd heard.

When she and Miles first arrived on St. James, she'd wake up sometimes, tense, listening, and then realize that it was the quiet that had wakened her.

The water boiled. Sarah added the tea bag and a little sugar. When she lifted the mug to her lips, the aroma of the chamomile teased her nose, reminding her of home. Reminding her how far away, how alien, this place was.

Nonsense. Only tiredness made her think that. In the morning, her prospects would look better. She'd have to reassess her plans. She'd hoped that Trent would be, if not happy to see her, at least cooperative.

He must have had some reason for accepting so readily the idea that Lynette and Miles were lovers. Had there been something Lynette said or did that convinced him she was having an affair? If so, he clearly didn't intend to tell her.

On to Plan B. She'd talk to Adriana to get the local gossip.

Then there was Trent's half brother. Derek had always been kind, and always less afraid, less in awe, of Trent than everyone else. The difficult part might be getting to him without letting Trent know it, but she'd manage.

And she had to see the police reports. Her parents were right; she'd run away too quickly. She hadn't the faintest idea how thorough the investigation had been. Surely there were other people she could talk to, other avenues she could explore.

Sarah put the mug down, realizing she'd been standing there, staring blankly at the black rectangle of the window.

Thinking about what she had to do wasn't making her more relaxed, it was making her tenser.

The sound again. Sarah froze. That hadn't been the distant rumble of the surf. That gentle rattle…she knew what it was. Something, perhaps an unwary step, had rattled the crushed shell that surrounded the guest house. The hairs lifted along her arms as if a chill wind had blown into the room.

Animal? Human? No one should be outside the guesthouse with the elaborate security Jonathan had installed. It must be an animal. She was letting stress fuel her imagination.

She switched off the light, ears straining. Nothing. Darkness pressed against the window glass, seeming as palpable as a hand, but there was nothing else. She was being ridiculous.

A footstep. Just outside the window a step fell on the tabby walk. Something, maybe a hand, maybe a sleeve, brushed the wall inches away from her.

THREE

Stifling a gasp, Sarah slipped away from the window. No one should be out there. If Jonathan had returned, he'd knock on the door. She moved, step by careful step, out of the kitchen, trying to think where the telephone was. Maybe she was over-reacting, but she'd rather be safe than sorry.

Her pulse jolted. She hadn't noticed whether Jonathan had locked the door when he'd left.

Please, Lord. I'm probably being ridiculous, but be with me.

Heart thudding in time with the prayer, she started across the darkened living room. Maybe there was no reason to fear, but she'd still make sure the door was locked before whoever was outside could reach it. She strained for the faintest sound that would tell her where that person was.

Shadows distorted the furniture. There'd been a glass-topped coffee table, hadn't there, somewhere between the kitchen and the entrance?

Her shin cracked against the table, and her breath caught at the pain. All right. A few feet more to the door. Arms out-reached, she touched a panel just as she heard the telltale crunch of shells outside. Her fingertips brushed a dangling chain. She caught it, snapped it into place.

She stood for a moment, hand on the door, listening. Nothing. The pounding of her heart slowed. She was locked in. Now find the phone, call the main house.

Back across the living room, bumping into the table once more. The phone must be in the master bedroom. Why didn't she remember?

She paused in the door to the bedroom. Naturally she'd left the light on here, and the drapes were open. The lamp was on the bedside table.

And there sat the telephone, also on the bedside table. She had no choice but to cross the room, in full view of anyone standing outside, to reach the phone.

Quickly, before she could think too much, she raced to the table, snapped off the light and sank to the floor in blessed darkness, pulling the telephone down with her. The lighted receiver listed the house code. She punched the button.

"Hello? Sarah?" Thank goodness Jonathan picked up.

Now that she heard his voice, she felt foolish.

"I heard someone outside the guesthouse just now. Should there be someone in the grounds?"

"Sugar, I should have told you a security patrol checks the grounds during the night." His voice was warmly reassuring. "We're pretty safe here on the island, but you never know. It must have been one of the guards, but let me check. I'll call you right back."

Phone in her lap, Sarah sat against the bed, shivering a little. She'd have to turn the air conditioning down, but she didn't intend to move from this spot until Jonathan called back.

She lifted the receiver almost before it stopped ringing, feeling as if she already knew what she'd hear.

"I should have told you." Jonathan sounded rueful. "The security guard made his rounds by the guesthouse just about the time you called. Said he saw the lights go off, but didn't think anything about it. He didn't spot another soul anywhere."

"I feel like an idiot. I'm so sorry I disturbed you."

"Not at all. You try and get a good night's sleep, okay?"

That seemed highly unlikely, but she agreed.

Once he'd hung up, Sarah crossed to the window and pulled the drapes closed with a violent jerk on the cord. She felt irritated, embarrassed and more than a little foolish. It would be amazing if she got to sleep before dawn.

Sarah struggled to get her eyes open, aware of sunlight beyond the cream drapes. She fumbled for the bedside clock. Nearly nine, and she'd planned to get an early start today. At least she'd slept, and last night's alarm was a half-forgotten dream.

Once she'd showered and dressed, Sarah looked up the telephone number for the Donner house in her small personal directory. She sat on the edge of the bed for a moment, staring at the phone. If she called, how likely was it that Trent would answer?

If anyone else answered, she could simply ask for Derek, without giving her name. She punched in the number quickly, before she could change her mind.

"Donner."

Sarah stopped breathing. Okay, she definitely didn't want to talk to Trent this morning.

"Is anyone there?" The words snapped, tinged with irritation.

Carefully, holding her breath as if he might identify her by the slightest exhalation, Sarah hung up.

Well, that little exercise showed that she was in no better shape to deal with Trent than she had been yesterday. She'd try again later. It must be possible to get through to Derek without Trent knowing about it. The man was powerful, not omniscient.

She walked to the main house through air so wet it felt like a sauna. May on the island was like August in Boston.

French doors fronted on the patio, and Jonathan sat with coffee and a newspaper in a sunny breakfast room beyond them. He sprang to his feet when she opened the door.

"Good morning." He laid aside the paper and pulled out a chair. "Sit down and have some breakfast with me."

She slid into a chair. A smiling maid appeared, setting a wedge of melon in front of her and pouring coffee.

"You look better today." Jonathan sounded as satisfied as if he were personally responsible.

"I'm sorry about calling you last night. I shouldn't have bothered you."

Jonathan waved her concern away. "Not at all. You did the right thing." He held up a section of newspaper. "Do you like to hide behind the paper at breakfast, or would you rather talk?"

"Actually, I'd like to talk." He had been frustratingly circumspect the previous night. Maybe if he understood what she was after, he'd feel differently. "About why I'm here."

He put the paper down on the glass tabletop, folding it neatly, not looking at her. "Forgive me for saying so, but this seems like the last place in the world you'd want to be."

"In some ways, it is." Sarah frowned down at the scrambled eggs that had appeared in front of her. "A year ago, I never expected to come back."

"Anyone would feel that way."

"So you can't help wondering why I'm here." She couldn't quite manage a smile.

"Only if you want to tell me."

She didn't, but she had to if she were to get his help. "I finally realized I couldn't accept what happened and move on.

The truth is, I don't believe it." Sarah dropped the spoon to the saucer, its tiny clatter accenting her words. "I don't believe my husband was having an affair with Lynette Donner."

"Maybe it's easier for you to feel that." Jonathan's voice was very gentle. "You loved him."

"You're very sweet and tactful, Jonathan." But she'd rather have honesty than tact. "It isn't that I think our marriage was so perfect, Miles couldn't fall for someone else."

"Then what?" He didn't look at her, and she sensed his discomfort.

"Miles. The kind of person Miles was. Honest, honorable. All those boring, typically New England virtues."

Puritan, Trent had said. There was nothing wrong with that.

"Even the most honorable man might succumb to attraction."

"Miles wouldn't betray his marriage vows. And he wouldn't betray his friendship and respect for Trent."

"Anyone can make a mistake."

Her lips tightened. "You sound like Trent. He thinks anyone capable of betrayal. I don't."

Finally his eyes met hers. "So you've come back to do what?"

"To find out," she said promptly. "If I'm wrong, I have to know that. If I'm right, then Miles had some other reason for being at the Cat Isle cottage that day. I intend to find out what it was."

"How, I wonder, are you going to do that?"

She took a deep breath. "I thought you might help me."

For a moment, his expression froze. Then, quite suddenly, he laughed. "Honey, no wonder Trent's trying to get rid of you. With you set to go prying, he's afraid he won't be able to keep things locked up anymore."

She blinked. "What do you mean?"

"Power. The most blatant use of power I've ever seen." He chuckled. "Didn't you wonder why the papers didn't have a field day with that story?"

"I thought they did." Even the Boston papers had run it.

"Not like they could have. Trent gave out his version of the story and then he stonewalled those reporters. So did the local police. He called in every favor anybody in the state owed him to keep a lid on the story. Tragic accident—that was the verdict at the inquest and only a few scandal rags dared to print anything else. The story died for lack of fuel to feed it."

"People still talked. They must have. Not even Trent could control that."

Jonathan shrugged, lifting his coffee cup. "I suppose so, but for the most part, the islanders rallied around. No one wanted Melissa reading about her mother's affair in the paper." He stopped, reddening slightly.

In other words, he believed Miles and Lynette were lovers. "Hurting Melissa is the last thing I'd do. She's already been hurt enough. But I've got to know the truth."

"And just what part did you see me playing in this?"

Something about his expression encouraged her. "I thought you might run a little interference for me. I tried to reach Derek this morning, but Trent answered the phone."

"And you don't want him to know for fear he'd forbid Derek to speak to you." Jonathan shrugged. "That might not stop Derek, but I agree it'll be easier if Trent doesn't know. Okay, I'll try. Anything else?" He looked as if he fervently hoped not.

"I need to talk to Guy O'Hara. He was Miles's closest friend here. I can do that myself." Sarah swallowed. This was the hard part. "But I need you to take me over to Cat Isle in your boat."

"Cat Isle." Jonathan's eyes filled with dismay. "Sarah, are you sure you want to go over there? Wouldn't it be better to…

Well, not give yourself so graphic a picture? It's not as if there's going to be evidence of anything at this late date."

Of a romantic tryst. That was what he meant. "Maybe it does seem a little morbid, but I've never been there." She'd only read about it, in one of the stories Trent hadn't been able to quash. "I can rent a boat at the marina, but people will talk."

He shoved his chair back. She could see the "no" forming on his lips.

"You don't have to rent a boat. Jonathan will take you."

She hadn't heard Adriana come in. She stood at the mahogany sideboard, pouring a cup of coffee, elegant in white pants and a white silk shirt.

"I don't think that's a good idea." Jonathan didn't look particularly happy with his wife's intervention.

"Why don't you want to go there?" Adriana turned, balancing the cup between her fingers.

"It's not that I don't want to go." Jonathan's face tightened. "I just think it'll be needlessly hard on Sarah."

"On the contrary." Adriana sounded oddly satisfied. "We ought to help Sarah. It's time the truth came out."

Sarah held her breath. Jonathan stared at his wife a moment longer. Finally he nodded.

"We'll have to go on the tide. Meet me at the boat dock around three."

"Thank you." She wasn't sure what else to say.

Jonathan gave her a rueful smile. "Don't thank me. I'm not doing anything good for you. And I hope I'm not going to live to regret it."

"I'd like to speak to Chief Gifford, please. My name is Sarah Wainwright."

The officer behind the gray metal desk looked barely old

enough to be out of high school. He nodded, and Sarah thought she saw a faint flush behind the freckles on his cheeks.

"Yes, ma'am… I mean, Doctor." He lurched from the chair, banging his foot on the metal wastebasket, and flushed a deeper red. "I'll tell Chief Gifford you're here."

Sarah looked after him. His name plate said R. Whiting, and the name seemed vaguely familiar in a way the face didn't. She frowned. She was letting her mind ramble, when what she needed to do was concentrate on Chief Gifford.

Him she remembered… a short, cocky, bantam of a man with a barrel chest, given to florid gestures. He could tell her details no one else could about the investigation. If he would.

"Dr. Wainwright!" Gifford bounded across the office to shake her hand. "This is a surprise. What are you doing back here?"

The surprise seemed a little overdone. Surely he'd heard by now she was back. "I have a few things to clear up here." Leave it vague, and she might get more out of him, although Trent would have spoken to him by now. "If I might have a few minutes?"

"Of course, of course." He gestured expansively toward his office. "As much time as you like." He glanced briefly at Whiting. "Bobby, you get that filing done yet?"

"I'm on it, Chief." His eyes were on Sarah, almost as if he wanted to say something to her. "Right away."

"See you do." Gifford ushered her to the straight-backed visitor's chair in his office. He closed the door and then bounced back into his own seat, which creaked in protest. "These young fellas think police work's like what they see on the TV. Got no idea somebody actually has to do the filing." Shrewd hazel eyes, belying his good-ole-boy manner, zeroed in on her face. "Now then, what can I do for you?"

"You may remember I left St. James very soon after my

husband's death last year." She'd prepared the opening. Where the conversation went after that was up to him. Or possibly to Trent. "I never found out what your investigation showed."

"Now, ma'am, you don't want to go making yourself unhappy by raking all that up again, do you?" His pale eyes were so opaque she couldn't tell whether that was concern or a warning. She might get farther by interpreting it in a positive light.

"I appreciate your concern, Chief Gifford, but I want to know. I do have that right, don't I?"

Gifford leaned back and the chair protested. "I surely don't object to talking to you about it, but I don't want you to get all upset."

Sarah managed a tight smile. "I think enough time has passed that I can talk about it, and there's so much I don't know. I don't even know who found them. I was off the island that day, and didn't know anything was wrong until I got back."

The police car had been waiting when she drove across the bridge, coming home from a shift at the hospital, prepared to work another four hours at the clinic as a volunteer. The officers had flagged her down, told her there'd been an accident, taken her to her fledgling clinic, where one of the volunteer retired physicians she'd recruited had been on duty.

The officer mentioned Cat Isle, but it wasn't until she'd burst into the room and seen Trent's ravaged face across the two white stretchers that she realized Miles hadn't been alone.

"Well, that's not much of a mystery," the chief said. "Mr. Donner called us when his wife wasn't back to get ready for some dinner party. One of the boats was missing, so we divvied up the places she might have gone. Whiting and I drew Cat Isle. We found the two boats, then we checked the cottage and found them."

That was why Whiting's name seemed familiar. She must have heard it at the time.

"It was too late when you got there?" She tried to say the words without letting her mind touch on what they'd found. She'd treated carbon monoxide victims. She knew too much.

Gifford nodded. "Whole place was filled with gas."

"From a space heater. I remember."

"Probably never would have been enough concentration of gas in a place like that, except that Mr. and Mrs. Donner had remodeled it. Made it tight enough to use all year long—and tight enough to hold the gas." He shook his head sadly.

It had been a cloudy, wet day, she remembered, with a sharp wind blowing and a tropical storm threatening. "It seems odd they'd go there on a day like that."

"Begging your pardon, ma'am, but I reckon they had to take what opportunities they could get. With you away…"

Of course that was what he'd think. She swallowed hard. "What were they doing when the gas overcame them?"

Gifford looked a bit scandalized, but he answered. "Miz Donner, she lay toppled over on the sofa, like she was asleep. Wainwright lay on the floor. The medical examiner said it looked like he'd hit his head on the coffee table when he fell. Could be he knocked himself out before he knew what was happening."

She hadn't known that, and she should have.

"What about Mrs. Donner? Did she have any injuries?"

He shook his head. "Nothing. Looked like she just drifted off."

There was another question she had to ask. "Everyone assumes my husband met Mrs. Wainwright there because they were lovers. Did you find any evidence of that?"

Now he really did look shocked. "No, ma'am. This office never said any such thing. Fatal accident, that's all we said."

"Yes, I know." She tried to read Gifford's expression. "So you didn't really conduct an investigation into what they were doing there."

Gifford's chair teetered for an instant and then came down squarely, and his relaxed pose vanished. "We investigated. Miz Donner come in one of the Land's End boats. You husband rented a fifteen-footer from Clawson down at the marina. There was no evidence of any foul play. Mr. Donner said he'd mentioned to them that he'd like their opinion on expanding the cottage. He figured that was why they'd gone there." His eyes narrowed. "Are you saying we didn't do our duty?"

"I'm concerned that the investigation was closed so quickly. I know Mr. Donner's an important person—"

Gifford's hand came down on his desk with a thump. "That's got nothing to do with what happens here in this office, and I don't take kindly to you suggesting otherwise."

"I wouldn't dream of saying that." But it was what she thought.

He wasn't mollified. "I've tried to answer your questions as best I can. Nobody tried to hide anything about the way your husband and Miz Donner died. We just tried to protect the living as best we could."

And you should be grateful, his tone implied.

"I wasn't suggesting any laxity on your part, Chief Gifford." Not at the moment, anyway.

"I've told you everything I can." Gifford stood up. "Now, if you'll excuse me, I've got work to do."

Sarah rose, too. "I'd like to talk to Officer Whiting."

Gifford swelled alarmingly, his neck turning a rich maroon. "Whiting doesn't speak for this department. I do. He has nothing to say to you."

He stalked to the door and threw it open. "If I were you, ma'am, I'd go back up north before St. James brings you more trouble." His lips moved in what might have been meant for a smile. "The Sea Islands can be dangerous places for people who don't belong here."

The small boat nosed away from the dock cautiously. Hitting the channel, deep now because of the high tide, Jonathan accelerated. The roar of the motor and the wind rushing through her hair made conversation impossible, and Sarah was grateful.

Jonathan, face drawn tight with distaste, clearly thought this a bad idea. Maybe it was, but that didn't change her mind. It was ridiculous to assume she'd ever stop imagining what the place looked like. She might as well know.

A dolphin lifted from the water in a perfect silver arc, and her breath caught in her throat. She'd nearly forgotten the unexpected moments of sheer beauty the island provided. Sunlight was warm on her shoulders, accentuating the golden haze that gleamed from sand and sea oats. No wonder these were called the Golden Isles.

Jonathan throttled back and pointed. For hundreds of years oyster shells had washed up into a barrier ridge, separating the sound and the salt marshes. Along the ridge, fifty or more brown pelicans sunned themselves. Startled by the boat, they took off, skimming the breakers and squawking their dislike.

It took only minutes to reach their destination. Cat Isle was hardly big enough to be called an island—a few acres of tangled vines, hoary old live oaks draped funereally in Spanish moss, scraggly pines. As far as Sarah knew, Trent's cottage was the only building of any sort.

Jonathan idled up to the crumbling dock. The weathered gray boards were adorned with moss.

"Does Trent own the whole island?"

He nodded, tossing a line over an upright. "Bought it from me, as a matter of fact. We never came here much, but it's easier access from Land's End—you can take a kayak down the creek when the tide is right."

She nodded, trying to fix the geography in her mind. Land's End was nearly surrounded by water, with the ocean in front, the sound to the south and the marshes and creek running behind it.

"Trent completely remodeled the cottage, but Lynette didn't like it. She said the place made her nervous. She—" He stopped abruptly, shutting down as sharply as the boat's engine had. "Go ahead." He jerked his head toward the path. "I'll wait here."

She'd expected him to go with her, but maybe it was just as well. She didn't need anyone to see her reaction to the place. She scrambled up on the dock, getting a green smear on her khakis in the process, and started toward the cottage.

The path, surrounded by lush, overpowering green undergrowth, nearly lost itself several times. This was her dark image of the islands, the gloomy, mysterious depths of maritime forest, only a step or two from the sunlit water.

The scent of honeysuckle enveloped her, deepening like incense as she moved farther from the dock. With a wary eye out for snakes, Sarah pushed along the path until it widened into a clearing.

Weathered a gray-green like the dock, the cottage seemed to grow out of the forest. It had a rustic charm, if she could divorce herself what had happened here. But if Lynette disliked the place so much, why would she choose to meet anyone here, especially a lover?

She pushed hair back from her damp forehead. That wasn't right, anyway. Whatever Miles had been doing here, it wasn't making love to Lynette Donner. If she couldn't believe that, nothing in her life made any sense.

She grasped the door handle and pushed it open. She stood for a moment, eyes adjusting to the gloom. Abruptly a wave of distaste washed over her. What was she doing here?

Like an echo of her thought, the voice came from within the room. "What are you doing here?"

With a queer, cold twist in her stomach, she turned. The shaft of light from the open door cast harsh shadows on Trent's rigid face.

"A stupid question, isn't it, Sarah? I already know what you're doing here. You're looking for more grief, and you've found it."

FOUR

Trent didn't know which emotion was stronger at the sight of Sarah—rage or shame. Rage that she was here, or shame that she, of all people, had caught him here?

"You just can't listen to me, can you?" He took a furious step toward her. Rage, definitely.

The shock that had filled her eyes at the sight of him faded. She squared her shoulders, as if determined he'd find no weakness in her.

"I want to see where it happened. I have to."

"You're trespassing." If his tone was any sharper, he'd cut himself. "Get out."

Her mouth firmed. "I have a right to see where my husband died, trespassing or not."

"It won't do you any good. There's nothing to see here." *Nothing but betrayal.* The thought burned like acid.

She studied his face, as if she'd see behind the words to the feeling. She wouldn't. He didn't let anyone in.

"Why are you here, then?"

The rage flashed along his nerves again, and he fought it back. "That's none of your business."

She shook her head, her pale hair moving like silk on her

shoulders. "We're the same, Trent. You came here for the same reason I did. To try and make sense of what happened."

"If we're alike, then neither of us should come here. There is no sense in it."

He wanted to deny the despair in his voice. It was a weakness, this failure to put Lynette's death behind him. He didn't tolerate weakness, not in the people who worked for him, not in himself. Certainly not in himself.

I tried. You know I tried. Why couldn't I make her happy?

God didn't give him an answer. He never did to that question.

He took a breath, forcing himself to calm. "I'm sorry for your pain." He gestured to the cottage he'd once thought would be a peaceful retreat for him and Lynette. "Believe me, I've looked, but this place doesn't have answers. It's just a shell."

She moved slightly, as if he'd given her a respite from the tension. "Did you come here often? Before, I mean."

Before their lives exploded.

"I thought we would, but it didn't happen. Lynette—" He swallowed. "She was enthusiastic about fixing the place up when we first bought it, but she soon gave up. She didn't seem to like it here."

"Someone made it comfortable." Sarah touched the back of the leather sofa that faced the fireplace.

"My housekeeper." His voice sounded strangled to his ears. "She ordered the furniture."

Did Sarah know Lynette had died on that spot? Pain twisted inside him, as fresh as if it had happened yesterday—racing to the cottage when the police called, bursting in the door, heart pounding as if it would explode from the pressure.

Gifford and a couple of his officers had straightened at the sight of him. They'd stepped back, averting their eyes, as if it were indecent to look at him at such a moment.

No. He wouldn't remember the rest of it. He wouldn't let that image back into his mind.

The fury surged through him again. This was Sarah's fault. He was here, remembering, because of Sarah.

He stepped toward her, driven by blind anger. His leg brushed the table next to the sofa, and the small glass vase on it wobbled. His fingers closed on the vase—tight, tighter, until it should snap in his hand.

With a quick, hard movement he threw it. It smashed against the logs that lay ready in the fireplace, the sound a shocking punctuation to his thoughts.

Sarah jerked back, her green eyes darkening like the ocean on a stormy day. "Trent, don't—"

He couldn't be here with her any longer without losing control. He grasped her elbow and propelled her toward the door. "You're going. Now."

Maybe she recognized the futility of protesting. She let him usher her out the door, across the porch, down the steps. He rushed her down the path toward the dock, brushing through overgrown branches of crepe myrtle and tendrils of Spanish moss, dozens of Low Country scents released by their brusque passing.

He charged onto the dock and came to an abrupt halt. It hadn't occurred to him to wonder how Sarah had gotten to the cottage. Now he knew. Jonathan's four-passenger jet boat bobbed on the swell. Jonathan stared at him, shock and apprehension on his face.

He gave Sarah a final push toward the boat. She slipped on the mossy planks, and Jonathan extended his hand to help her. Without looking back, she stepped lightly onto the rail and down to the deck.

Maybe he'd frightened her. He hoped so.

"Trent, I'm sorry if this has upset you." Jonathan's tone was grave.

"Upset?" He was aware of an urge to punch something. Or someone. "Why would it upset me to know that my friend is going against my wishes behind my back?"

"I understand how you feel."

"Do you?" His eyebrows lifted. "I doubt it."

Jonathan's patrician face seldom showed anything so raw as embarrassment, but he seemed to wince. "No, I suppose not. But Sarah has feelings, too. Her loss is as great as yours."

The impulse to deny that astounded him and gave him pause. He'd been giving lip service to Sarah's loss, but had he really considered how the tragedy had affected her? She and Miles seemed to have a happy marriage—happier than his and Lynette's, in any event. And she still believed in Miles.

It didn't matter, he thought at some level, and was instantly ashamed. Of course Sarah's grief mattered. But he had his child to protect, and that one fact outweighed everything else.

He had to say something. He looked at them. Jonathan wore a slightly chiding air. Sarah's eyes were dark with pain, but she stared back at him steadily, as if to say that she wouldn't give in. That this wasn't finished between them.

He wouldn't apologize again. "You've seen the cottage. That will have to be enough for you, Sarah. Go back to Boston and get on with your life."

She didn't respond. She didn't have to. Sarah wouldn't give up.

That was the first thing he'd learned about her, back when she was nothing more than his new assistant's slightly inconvenient wife. He'd soon learned she was much more than that. She'd nearly driven him crazy over that clinic idea of hers, and probably the real reason he'd resisted it so long had been because he'd enjoyed butting heads with her.

Jonathan, apparently realizing there was nothing to be gained here, turned the ignition. The sound of the motor sent a brown pelican lifting from the water. The jet boat backed slowly away, the gulf widening between boat and dock.

The gulf between him and Sarah had widened that night at Adriana's party, when a half-serious, half-laughing quarrel had, as suddenly as summer lightning, sparked into awareness. They'd both recognized it in the same instant, both turned guiltily away.

He watched the figures in the boat grow rapidly smaller as Jonathan accelerated, throwing up an emphatic spray. Determination hardened inside him.

Sarah had to leave St. James.

Sarah turned the car off the main road onto a narrow lane, wincing as overhanging branches slapped the windshield. The rays of the setting sun slanted through the trees, dappling the lane ahead of her with alternating patches of sun and shade.

Jonathan had reluctantly given her the directions to Haller's Tavern, and he hadn't offered to go with her. Maybe because he knew she'd refuse, or maybe because he was already tiring of her and her quest.

Jonathan's attitude toward her had changed after that encounter with Trent the previous day. She could hardly blame him. He was Trent's friend, unless she'd ruined that with her interference.

That friendship had always surprised her a bit. There didn't seem much common ground between the idle patrician and the self-made man, and now—

Now, according to Adriana, Trent had turned into a hermit,

rejecting all invitations. Sarah seemed to see again the bitter lines in his face as he swung toward her at the cottage.

At the very place where Lynette and Miles had died. She could hardly be surprised that his bitterness had surfaced there. Why had he been there? Did he go often, torturing himself with memories?

There's so much pain between us, Heavenly Father. I'd help him if I could, but it seems impossible.

She didn't want to cause Trent more pain, but she had to know the truth.

And what if this truth is all there is, a small voice in the back of her mind inquired.

Her fingers tightened on the steering wheel as she negotiated a bend in the road, splashing through puddles left by the afternoon's rain. Well, if all her searching only proved that what people already believed was true, somehow she'd have to learn to live with it. But not until she was sure.

Which led her to Guy O'Hara. He'd been one of the engineers on some project Trent had been pursuing. He'd been as close to a friend as Miles had made on the island in the short time they'd been there. If Miles had confided in anyone, it would have been Guy.

Lights glinted to her left, and the road, apparently giving up its forward momentum, widened into a parking lot. Already several cars and pick-ups dotted the area in front of the low cement block building. No attempt had been made to blend into the surrounding landscape—it looked like a roadhouse, and that's what it was. Still, the lush growth of the forest made inroads on it, softening the hard blocks with tendrils of green and gray that would inexorably cover it if not cut away.

She parked and turned off the ignition. Guy had rejected

her suggestion that he come to the cottage or meet her at the inn. He'd insisted on this place.

Maybe he preferred not to be seen with her where Trent would hear about it. Or maybe he knew something and wanted the security his own turf provided when he talked to her.

She got out, scoffing at her own reluctance to go inside. She'd learned to take care of herself a long time ago. She'd go inside, find Guy and get this conversation over with.

When she pulled the sagging metal door open, a blast of country music and a wave of cigarette smoke enveloped her. Holding her breath, she stepped inside. Faces turned toward her instantly, as if they all swung on the same pivot. She glanced around quickly. Guy wasn't there.

He'd said eight, and it was that now. She'd have to wait, and she'd be less conspicuous sitting at a table than standing in the doorway like a deer in the headlights. She took one close to the door, yanked out a chair and sat down. The jukebox segued into another plaintive song of lost love, heads turned away from her again, and the bartender jerked his head in what might have been a greeting.

"Get you something, ma'am?"

"An iced tea, if you have it."

He nodded, wiping a glass out with a towel that looked as if it had never known bleach.

He brought the filled glass to the table. She laid a bill beside it. "Has Guy O'Hara been in yet?"

He shook his head. "He comes most nights, but not yet tonight. You're welcome to wait." He jerked his head toward the bar. "Don't you mind the boys. They can be a mite mouthy, but nobody acts up in my place."

Had she been looking that apprehensive? Apparently so. She managed a smile. "Thanks. I appreciate it."

He headed back to the bar. She took a gulp of the tea and nearly choked. She'd forgotten the Southern habit of making sweet tea, laced with enough sugar to turn it into syrup. Hopefully Guy would show up before the combination of sugar and caffeine had her bouncing off the walls.

Forty-five minutes later, Guy still hadn't shown. The room had gotten progressively more smoky, the music louder, the crowd larger. Two of the men at the bar stole glances at her and nudged each other. In a moment one of them would work up enough courage to come over, and she'd have to deal with him.

A wave of disgust went through her. If Guy intended to keep this meeting, he'd have been here by now. She shoved her chair back, dropped some change onto the scarred tabletop next to the cash and pushed back out the door, letting it clatter shut behind her.

The sweet, close aroma of the Southern night closed around her, and she took a deep breath. This had been a singularly unprofitable evening. Annoyance flickered. What was Guy playing at, making an appointment and then failing to show? Had Trent somehow anticipated this and frightened him off?

Or was there a darker answer? If Guy knew something about Lynette's and Miles' deaths, someone might not want him to talk to her. But that was making an assumption that someone had something to hide. Trent's only interest seemed to be in protecting Melissa and himself from further gossip.

She wove her way through the dark shapes of cars, shells crunching under her feet. A footstep sounded behind her, and she glanced back. No one. The hair lifted on her arms. No one had come out of the tavern behind her—she'd have heard the blast of music if the door had opened. But someone was there. Someone who had halted when she had, sheltering behind one of the parked vehicles.

Heartbeat accelerating, she scurried toward her car, key out and ready. It was probably nothing, but she'd feel better when she was in her car, the doors locked. She'd—

She stopped, staring at her car. It seemed to sag listlessly. No wonder. All four of the tires had been slashed.

For a moment she stood, raging silently. Then common sense kicked in. Whoever had done this could still be nearby. The thought of that footstep sent her scrambling into the safety of the car. She couldn't drive away, but she could lock the doors and call the police.

It took fifteen minutes by her watch for the police car to pull into the lot. In that time no one came out of or went into the tavern. She might have been alone in the world. But someone had been there. Someone who'd slashed her tires in a mute, pointed warning. Who had an interest in doing that but Trent?

She unlocked the door as the uniformed officer approached.

"Miz Wainwright?" The beam of his powerful torch swept from one tire to another. "Looks like you got yourself in some trouble here."

She got out, facing him. He was older than the young patrolman she'd seen at the station, his face lined with resignation, as if he'd seen everything there was to see and no longer thought he could make a difference.

"Someone slashed my tires while I was inside."

He glanced toward the tavern. "Seems like a funny place for a lady to be."

She stiffened. His implication was clear. Her troubles were her own fault, for coming to such a place. "I was supposed to meet a friend here. I assume it's against the law to slash my tires, no matter where I happen to park."

"Yes, ma'am, it sure is, but I doubt I'll be able to find out who did it. Folks who frequent Haller's don't confide much in the cops. Still, I'll try." He gestured. "Maybe you'd like to wait in the patrol car. I'll give you a lift home, and you can have the garage come out and take care of your car."

She didn't have much choice. She climbed into the front seat of the patrol car, not caring to sit in back like a felon. She caught a glimpse of the interior of the bar as the officer swung the door open. The faces turned toward him didn't look particularly welcoming.

He was back in a suspiciously short time. She rubbed her forehead. Or maybe she was the suspicious one, creating enemies where they didn't exist. She had enough real ones that she didn't need to invent any.

She tried to muster a smile as he climbed into the driver's seat. "Any luck?"

He shook his head, turning the ignition key. "No, ma'am. They was like the three monkeys, you know. See no evil—"

"I know," she said shortly. He was clearly amused at his own joke. "So you didn't find out anything."

"Well, Joe Findley did say he saw a car pull in and then out again quick, but Joe'd been hitting the bottle pretty hard. You don't want to pay too much attention to what old Joe says."

She wasn't as quick to dismiss it as he was. "Did this Joe say what the car looked like?"

He shrugged, his shoulders moving uneasily as he pulled back onto the road. "Said it was a big car. A big gray car."

A big gray car. Like Trent's Rolls. Had he thought of that, dismissed it so quickly because he didn't want to tangle with Trent?

Words bubbled up, but she suppressed them. It would do no good to argue with the patrolman. The person she needed to confront about this was Trent. And that probably wouldn't do any good, either.

By the time the patrol car swung into the driveway at the Lee house, she felt too wiped out to confront anyone about anything. With any luck, Jonathan and Adriana would never know she'd come home in a police car.

The car stopped in front of the cottage, and she slid out with a word of thanks. The cruiser rolled quickly away, leaving her alone in the still night. The cop hadn't had to ask her where she was staying. He'd known. Probably everyone on the island knew by now. St. James was Trent's fiefdom, and she'd best remember that.

She unlocked the door and stepped inside, sagging with weariness. She'd have to call about the car. Switching on lights, she crossed to the bedroom. She'd call from the phone there.

Kicking off her shoes in the doorway, she took one step into the room and stopped. Her stomach clenched as if she'd been punched.

A hurricane might have swept through, ripping apart everything it passed. Clothes, makeup, everything she'd brought with her had been strewn over the furniture, ripped and crumpled. Nothing had been spared.

It took several minutes for the shock to subside enough that she could start thinking. Then she realized the desolation extended only to her things. Nothing that belonged to the Lees had been touched.

She picked up a coral cotton sweater. It had been one of her favorites. Not any longer. A jagged tear rent it nearly in half. She dropped it as if it burned her fingers. It had been cut. With a knife.

A shudder rocked her, and the room seemed to shift. A knife. Probably the same knife that had slashed her tires had slashed her clothing, too. The sheer malevolence of the act twisted inside her. How could anyone—

Not anyone. The sick feeling escalated to active nausea. Trent. Trent was the only one who wanted her off the island. The slashing of her tires at the tavern could have been a random act of vandalism, aimed at no one in particular. This couldn't. This was deliberate. Ugly and deliberate.

She pressed her hand against her stomach, trying to still the waves of nausea. She had to think. Had to decide what to do. Tell Jonathan?

She supposed she must, but she shrank from what would inevitably follow. He would call the police, but what could or would they do?

The doorbell jangled, and her hand dropped away from the phone. Probably Jonathan. If he'd seen the police car, he'd come to find out what was going on. She'd have to show him.

She crossed the living room quickly. Nothing had been touched here, because nothing in this room belonged to her. The intruder must have realized that.

How had he gotten in? She hadn't noticed any sign that the door had been tampered with. Obviously Jonathan's security wasn't as good as he'd thought. Either that, or someone in the Lee household was involved. No, she couldn't believe that.

Her hand closed on the knob, cool against her palm. She turned it, swung the door open.

It wasn't Jonathan. It was Trent.

For an instant all she could do was stare at him. Then fury swamped her, sweeping away the sick hopeless feeling and replacing it with bright, bracing anger. She lifted her head and glared at him.

Before she could stop herself, she blurted, "What is it, Trent? Weren't you content with destroying everything I brought to the island? Did you have to come and survey the results of your handiwork? Did you need to see for yourself?"

FIVE

Trent could only stare at Sarah. She might as well be speaking a foreign language for all the sense her statement made. He lifted an eyebrow.

"I suppose you know what you're talking about. I certainly don't."

He'd come here prepared to offer an inducement for her to leave—he'd answer her questions, and he'd make the police turn over all the reports. He hadn't come so she could accuse him of whatever it was that had her cheeks flushed and her eyes bright with anger.

Sarah planted her fists on her hips, looking as if she'd rather use them on him. "Your innocence is a bit overdone. If you think this will make me leave, you're sadly mistaken."

He'd seen the flash of anger in her eyes before, when they'd argued about the clinic, but she'd never been quite so outspoken. Because he'd been her husband's employer then, he supposed. Now she probably felt she had nothing to lose.

She hadn't invited him in, but he stepped over the threshold anyway. Her anger was affecting him, and he couldn't have that. He needed a level head when he dealt with her.

"I repeat—I don't know what you're talking about. Maybe

you'd explain first, so I know what it is I'm supposed to have done."

For a moment longer she glared at him. Then she whirled and headed toward the bedroom door. "This way."

He followed, close on her heels. Reached the door, stopped, looked. And felt a wave of revulsion strong enough to rock him back on his heels.

"Sarah, I'm sorry. When did this happen?"

She didn't answer. She just looked at him.

"Oh, right, I forgot. I'm supposed to have done this, so naturally I'd know when it happened." The anger he felt that she thought him capable of this was probably irrational. "You can't seriously believe I'd do this."

"You'd have me kicked out of my hotel at a ridiculous hour of night, leaving me homeless, you'd have my tires slashed, but destroying my belongings is a line you wouldn't cross. Hmm, why don't I buy that?"

She might have a point, but— "What are you talking about? When were your tires slashed?"

For a moment he thought she wouldn't answer. The gaze from those green eyes was hot enough to scald.

"Tonight," she said shortly. "An hour or so ago, while my car was parked outside Haller's Tavern."

"What were you doing there?" He seized on the one piece of information he understood. "That's a rough crowd."

"I can take care of myself."

"Apparently not, if someone slashed your tires." The image that evoked was too vivid. A startlingly strong wave of protectiveness swept through him.

Ridiculous. He couldn't afford to feel protective toward Sarah, of all people. And she certainly wouldn't welcome it from him.

"I didn't need to worry about the rough crowd, did I? The trouble came from another source."

It was a good thing she managed to irritate him with every other word. It counteracted that absurd sense that he ought to take care of her.

"I did not slash your tires."

"You were seen."

"What?" That punch came out of nowhere.

"Your car, anyway. The big, expensive gray Rolls. So either you did it. Or he did." She jerked a nod, glancing past him toward the living room door that still stood open. "It's the same thing, isn't it?"

He turned. Farrell lounged in the doorway, watching them. The man wore an odd, avid expression that turned his stomach. It couldn't be true. But even as he thought the words, he realized he wasn't sure.

He crossed the room in a few long strides, propelled by… what? The need to prove her wrong? Or the fear that she was right?

"Is that true? Did you do this?" He swept a hand toward the chaos behind them in the bedroom.

Farrell straightened at his approach. "No, sir. I don't know what she's been telling you, but I wouldn't do anything like this. That'd be breaking and entering, destruction of property. I draw the line at that."

"Do you?" His voice went soft, cold. He recognized that evasion for what it was. "You wouldn't come into the cottage, but you'd slash Dr. Wainwright's tires?" Small wonder Sarah had sneered at his attempt to separate one action from another. He felt the same way.

Farrell darted a glance from him to Sarah and back again.

"Not saying I did anything, but maybe Miz Wainwright ought to be more careful where she goes."

Something about the snide tone went right through the control he'd thought he had. His hands shot out and grabbed the man's shirt almost before he realized what he was doing.

"*Dr.* Wainwright," he snapped. "You refer to Dr. Wainwright in a respectful way, understand?" His grip tightened. "Now tell me the truth, before I—"

He stopped, appalled. Was he really offering the man violence? He let go. Sometimes it seemed his anger had been bubbling beneath the surface since Lynette died. This act had brought it surging out.

Farrell took a careful step back, straightening his shirt. A sulky look replaced the sneer.

"Not saying I did, but what if I had? Maybe I prowled around outside here, just to keep an eye on things. Maybe I messed with the tires. So what? The cops won't be interested."

He could only stare at the man. Farrell had admitted it. He'd actually slashed Sarah's tires, and he stood there acting as if it were all in a day's work.

"Why?" The fury returned, full force, and he clenched his fists to keep from grabbing Farrell again. "Who told you to do such a thing?"

Farrell looked at him blankly. "You did. You wanted her gone. It was my job to make that happen. I only did what you wanted me to do."

Sarah wasn't sure how to take what she was seeing. Trent's shock and anger seemed real enough, but she didn't believe for a minute that she could accept anything he said or did at face value. He was too good at hiding his feelings.

"Let me understand this." His voice had dropped until it

was a low, even pitch, but that didn't make it any less deadly. His tone was so icy that it was a wonder Farrell didn't stiffen into a frozen block. "You heard me say I wanted Dr. Wainwright to leave the island, so you thought that gave you carte blanche to commit criminal acts to make that happen."

Farrell moved restlessly, his gaze evading Trent's. Hardly surprising—she wouldn't want to meet those frigid eyes, either.

"I just did what I thought you wanted me to do," he mumbled.

"Wrong on all counts, but I suppose that's what I should expect from an incompetent imbecile."

Farrell's head snapped up at that. "Hey, I—"

"Quiet." Trent still didn't raise his voice, but he didn't need to. His scorn could flay a person without that. "You're fired. Get out of my sight and off my island."

"But—"

Trent extended his hand, palm up. "Give me your keys."

"Listen, I didn't mean anything. I thought I was doing what you wanted me to do." He glanced at her. "I'll apologize to Miz—Dr. Wainwright. But you can't fire me just like that."

Trent moved slightly, as if he'd block the man from looking at her. "I don't tolerate criminals in my employ. The keys." His tone left no room for argument.

Farrell stared at him for a moment longer, looking baffled. Then he yanked a ring of keys from his pocket and thrust them at Trent.

"That's not the end of this. I got rights."

"You broke the law. Consider yourself lucky not to be under arrest."

Trent turned away, giving the door a nudge. It shut in Farrell's face.

Sarah sucked in a breath. For a moment she'd thought

Trent would actually hit the man, his fury had been so palpable. And the way Farrell had looked…

"Maybe you should call the police," she said. "He might—"

"I don't need the police to deal with a coward like Farrell." Trent's gaze met hers. "But I suppose I have been a little high-handed. You certainly have every right to press charges against him. I hope you won't, for obvious reasons, but I won't stand in your way."

But her anger had disappeared sometime in the past few minutes. All she felt now was distaste, and an urge to have this business behind her. "That would only generate publicity that neither of us wants."

She thought there was relief in his gray eyes, but she couldn't be sure.

"I'll make restitution for your losses, of course."

"You don't need to. It wasn't your fault."

His eyebrows lifted. "I'm glad you accept that. Nevertheless, it's my responsibility. Farrell was in my employ. I'll take care of it."

She was too tired to go on arguing about it. She wanted to fall into bed and sleep for ten hours straight, but she had too much to do to indulge in that luxury.

"All right. Whatever you want." She pushed her hair back from her forehead, trying to think what to do first. "If you'll excuse me, I've got to clean up this mess."

She expected him to leave, but instead he followed her to the bedroom. He bent to pick up a pair of slacks.

"What are you doing?"

"I said I'd take responsibility for this."

She took the slacks from him, shaking them out. They were crumpled, but at least they'd escaped the knife. "There's nothing you can do here." She certainly didn't want him picking up her clothing.

"I have to help." He stood there, looking oddly hesitant. That had to be a first, for Trent Donner not to know what to do.

"You can figure out how I'm going to explain all this to Jonathan. He was already unhappy enough with the situation."

She picked up a sleep shirt. It had been slit from neckline to hem. A shudder ran through her. No, she definitely didn't want Trent to help. She dropped it into the wastebasket.

She glanced at Trent. He stared at the wastebasket, an odd expression on his face. He caught her watching him and produced a half smile.

"As far as Jonathan's concerned, you can just blame me."

"It wasn't your fault. And Jonathan already hates being on the outs with you."

"It was my fault." His face tightened. "I should have realized what kind of man Farrell was. I should have been more careful what I said in front of him."

"People in power have to be careful of what they wish for. Someone might try to make it come true." She wondered if he really understood the amount of power he wielded.

"Is your car still at the tavern?" he asked abruptly.

She nodded. "It wasn't going anywhere on four flats. I'll have to call a garage."

"I'll take care of it." He pulled a cell phone from his pocket. "I can do that, at least." He stepped into the living room, and she heard the murmur of his voice, giving orders.

Trent was used to giving orders, used to having them obeyed. Doubt flickered. Could she really accept that he hadn't known what Farrell was up to?

He reappeared, pocketing the cell phone. "That's taken care of. I've been thinking about what's best for you to do.

Assuming you are still determined to stay on the island, that is?" He raised his eyebrows.

"You can assume that, yes."

"Then I think you should move to Land's End."

She could only stare at him. "Move to Land's End," she repeated. Trent's compound, a combination of home and business headquarters, occupied one entire end of the island. "But—why would you want me to do that? You're the one who had me thrown out of my hotel."

"You're not going to let me forget that, are you?" The sudden warmth of his smile took her breath away.

"No. I mean—" She tried to regroup. "Unless Jonathan decides I'm too much trouble, I'm fine here."

He frowned. "You're not safe here. That should be evident."

"With Farrell gone, I'm not in danger."

His frown deepened. "Farrell didn't admit to having done this."

"Did you think he was telling the truth?"

"I don't know." He sounded reluctant to make the admission. "But I don't want to find out the hard way."

"What about your daughter? How will you explain my presence?"

"We often have people staying at the house. Melissa is used to that."

She looked down at the crumpled blouse she held. A knife had slashed it, just as a knife had slashed her tires. Surely Farrell had done both, whether he admitted it or not. If not—

If not, someone else had a reason to want to scare her off. A chill seemed to settle deep inside her. That would imply that there was more to Miles's and Lynette's deaths than she'd imagined. No, she couldn't believe that.

"No one else could wish me ill."

"I hope so, but your return has stirred up a lot of memories." He looked as if the words left a bad taste in his mouth. "There may well be other people who'd be just as happy if you left St. James. No one appreciated being hounded by reporters day and night for weeks on the off chance they knew something."

The bitterness in his voice told her who'd been hounded the most. She'd escaped so quickly that she hadn't thought about what it must have been like on the island when the story broke.

"I guess I didn't realize how bad it was. Or that people here would blame me for it."

He shrugged. "Not blame. But maybe be eager for you to leave before some enterprising reporter learns you're here and decides to revive the scandal."

"Hardly to the extent of vandalism, surely." That chill moved through her again.

"A scandal brings out the worst in some people." His face darkened. "They gossip, they write ugly letters." He sounded as if he'd experienced both. "It's a small step from that to active vandalism."

"Even if you're right, Jonathan has security precautions."

He smiled faintly. "Not like mine."

The unconscious arrogance of the words annoyed her, but he was probably right. No one could get into Land's End unless Trent wanted them to. The only danger to her there would come from inside.

"Even so—"

"Sarah, little though I want you here, if you're determined to stay, I intend to protect you. I can do that more efficiently at Land's End."

"Are you sure you don't mean you can control me more efficiently there?"

"I doubt very much that anyone can control you." He sounded as if he found that cause for regret. "Let's say it will serve two purposes. It will keep you safe, and it will let me keep a wary eye on you. What do you say?"

Instinct told her to reject the idea, but he was offering her the very access she needed most. It would be uncomfortable to stay at Land's End, certainly, but what was that compared to what she might gain?

Apparently impatient with her hesitation, he frowned. "If you're worried about the proprieties, you needn't be," he said shortly. "Both my housekeeper and my secretary live in, along with several other staff members." But not a replacement for Miles, she'd heard. Apparently, he'd decided not to trust anyone else that much again.

"And your daughter."

His hand shot out to firmly encircle her wrist. "One thing. If you come, you'll leave my daughter alone. I won't have you questioning her."

His fierce concern seemed to surge through his touch. He cared so much for Melissa.

"No, of course not. I understand." She took a breath, praying she was making the right decision. "All right. I agree."

The answers she sought were at Land's End if they were anywhere. So that's where she would go.

Trent pressed a remote control on the dashboard of the Rolls, and the high iron gates to Land's End opened smoothly. Silently. Sarah tried to quell a trickle of apprehension that shivered down her spine.

The car moved through the gateway and onto a tabby drive that glowed whitely with crushed shells in the beam of the headlights. She glanced back, to see the gate close behind them.

Trent shot a sideways glance at her. "Having regrets already?"

"No." She wasn't, was she? "I just felt as if the gates should close with an ominous bang."

"I'll see if I can arrange that." His words were light, but his mouth tightened. "I'm afraid security is an unpleasant necessity of life."

"For people like you, you mean."

This time the glance was distinctly annoyed. "For everyone. Don't tell me you don't take reasonable precautions when you walk to your car in a deserted parking lot after working a night shift at the hospital."

"That's different."

"Not as far as I can see. I'm just trying to keep my family safe."

His family. Was he thinking of Lynette? He hadn't been able to keep her safe.

No matter how Trent rationalized it, the high fences and security cameras made his home a fortress. Perhaps Lynette had begun to see it as a prison.

The drive, emerging from the avenue of live oaks draped with Spanish moss, opened into a wide sweep in front of the house. Light spilled from the windows onto the veranda that spanned the width of the house, and geraniums rioted from the concrete planters on either side of the steps.

It looked welcoming. It should feel welcoming. But as Sarah slid out into honeysuckle-scented night air, she reminded herself that looks could be deceiving. Trent had brought her here not because he welcomed her presence, but because he wanted to control her, just as he controlled everyone else who came within his orbit.

She wasn't going to let him do that to her, but she'd have

to be on her guard every minute, because it was as natural to Trent as breathing.

He came around the car with a suitcase in each hand. "Go ahead." He nodded toward the door. "Geneva has a guest suite ready for you."

Sarah searched her memory for the rest of the name as she mounted the steps. The tall, stately Gullah woman who stood in the open doorway was Trent's housekeeper. They'd met before. Robinson—that was it. Geneva Robinson. She ran Land's End with what seemed effortless efficiency.

"Welcome, Dr. Wainwright. Please come in." The woman stepped back as they approached, ushering Sarah into the cool, gracious hallway. Square white tile gleamed underfoot, drawing the eye in an unbroken sweep to the graceful lines of the curving staircase.

It was a beautiful entry to a beautiful home, one that might have appeared in a Southern homes magazine, if not for Trent's distaste for publicity. On either side of the hallway, arches led to the formal living room and dining room. She half expected Lynette to come sweeping through the archway, hands outstretched in welcome, her beautiful, vivid face lit with the smile that enslaved every man she met. She'd seen Lynette in action on the several occasions she'd been invited for dinner.

Sarah pushed the thought aside. Lynette no longer filled Land's End with the imprint of her capricious personality. Something had taken its place, but she wasn't sure what. The house seemed to wait, as if it wondered, too.

"Would you care for something to eat before you retire, Dr. Wainwright?"

Her stomach roiled at the thought of food. "No, thank you, Mrs. Robinson. It's good to see you again. I hope you're well?"

"Fine, thank you." Sympathy flickered in the woman's dark eyes. "I'll show you to your room."

"I'll do that. You go to bed." Affection filled Trent's voice as he spoke to the housekeeper, but his smile slid away as he turned to Sarah. "This way." He headed for a set of French doors that opened from the rear of the hallway onto a patio.

She followed him, glancing around. She'd been here, too, at a dinner party Lynette had held. The patio had been lit by torches whose reflections danced in the clear water of the swimming pool.

The house was U-shaped, stretching out wings on either side of the pool. Trent headed to the right. "The guest suites are on this side. Geneva has put you in the blue suite."

"And the other wing?" Most of the windows there were dark, but a few lights glowed behind drawn shades.

"Those are offices and rooms for staff who live in."

"There are a lot of people in and out of Land's End."

He stopped in front of another door and set the cases down while he unlocked it. "No one gets into Land's End that I don't want to be here." Something grim sounded in his voice. "You don't have to worry about your safety here."

The door swung open, giving her an excuse to avoid answering that comment. She wasn't worried about who came and went at Land's End. She was wondering which of them might know something, and which would be willing to talk to her.

Geneva Robinson? She'd sensed sympathy from the woman, but her loyalty to Trent might be so ingrained that she wouldn't speak, no matter how much she might sympathize. Perhaps Joanna Larson, Trent's secretary. Miles had always said she knew everything that happened here.

Never mind. Someone would have seen something, would

know something, about any relationship between Miles and Lynette. About what would have sent them to the cottage. She just had to find that person.

"This is lovely," Sarah said as she entered the room. Someone—Geneva, presumably—had left the lights burning in the suite. White wicker furniture shone against blue walls, and the quilt on the queen-size bed echoed the blue and white colors in a geometric patchwork instead of the more predictable floral design.

Trent followed with the suitcases, which he set down. "Get a good night's sleep. The morning will be time enough to deal with things."

"My car, you mean. Did you have it towed someplace? I'll have to arrange to pick it up."

"I gave orders for it to be left at the garage. You won't need it here."

Her stomach lurched. The lovely room would turn into an elegant trap if she were not careful. "No," she said distinctly.

He gave her an annoyed frown. "What do you mean? There are plenty of cars here. Someone can drive you anyplace you want to go."

"And report back to you on where I've been and who I've spoken to? I don't think so." Their truce had been brief.

"Fine. I'll give you the keys to a car. You can drive yourself."

"I'd prefer to have my own car back." Absurd, perhaps, to feel she didn't want to owe him for the use of a car when she was staying in his house, but she'd feel more independent driving her own each time she left Land's End.

His frown deepened. "Have I mentioned lately how stubborn you are?"

"Several times."

"Very well." He clipped off the words. "I'll have the tires

fixed and the car brought here. It will be ready for you in the morning."

She didn't doubt it. There were obvious benefits to the kind of power Trent wielded. "Thank you." She could breathe again. She'd avoided one of the dangers of being here by staking out her independence so clearly. If Trent respected that, they'd get through this.

He turned as if to leave, but stopped at a panel to the left of the door that was nearly hidden by the sweep of draperies. "This controls the room's security, and it can be set independently. No unauthorized person can get into Land's End, but this will give you added assurance. Come here, and I'll show you how to set it."

The blade of a knife gleamed for an instant in her mind. Yes, she'd be very happy to have her own security system. She crossed to stand next to him, peering at the array of switches and lights disclosed when he flipped the panel's door open.

"When you're in and planning to stay, just hit this switch. It activates the system. When you're going out and want to leave the alarm on, touch this one and go out, pulling the door shut behind you."

"And when I want to get back in? How do I keep from alarming the whole house?"

"Unlock the door with this key, then come right to the control pad and punch in the code—five-seven-one-eight."

"Right here?" She leaned closer, intent on the keypad.

He caught her hand in his and touched it to the keys lightly. "Touch the numbers. That disarms the alarm. Do it quickly or it'll go off."

"Right." The word came out a bit breathlessly. He was too close, his grip too firm. The warmth of his touch was doing odd things to her self-control.

She took a step back. "Thanks. I understand. I'll be careful."

Very careful. In her pride at not having given in to his control, she'd forgotten about another danger—one that might prove an even greater threat if she weren't careful.

SIX

He'd made a mistake in bringing Sarah here. Trent frowned at the bowl of roses on the hall table as he came down the stairs the next morning. His foul mood had no effect on the pink roses—they perfumed the air with no respect for his temper.

Like Sarah, who also had no respect for either his temper or his wishes. And now he'd saddled himself with responsibility for the woman. He must have been crazy. He'd overreacted, but even now his stomach tightened at the memory of that vandalism of her things.

He had to take responsibility for that. Farrell had been in his employ, and the buck stopped with him. Still, that overmastering fear for Sarah's safety had been irrational. Farrell, whether he admitted it or not, must have been responsible for that campaign against Sarah. Farrell was gone, so she was safe. There was no reason for her disturbing presence at Land's End.

It was too late to change that now. He paused in the hallway, touching the roses lightly. Lynette had always insisted on fresh flowers in the house, and the staff continued to follow her orders, even though she was gone.

Too late. So many things were too late. He'd have to make the best of Sarah's presence until she gave up this foolish quest and went back where she belonged. At least having her here meant he could keep tabs on her.

He walked quickly to the breakfast room. Breakfast was set out buffet-style on weekdays so that his staff could serve themselves. Lynette had always had her meal in bed, saying the process reminded her too much of a bed-and-breakfast, but he'd felt providing breakfast a small enough perk to offer people who were willing to work in such an out-of-the-way place.

At the moment the room was empty except for one person. Sarah sat alone near the window. Her head was bowed, as if she were asking for a blessing on the food, and the morning sunlight that poured through the window turned her pale hair to gilt.

He wouldn't stand and stare at her. He crossed quickly to the coffee urn, annoyed that the woman made him feel uncomfortable in his own home. He filled a mug and turned. She was watching him.

It would be ridiculous to follow his first impulse and sit as far from her as possible. He had to treat her with the same courtesy he'd show any other guest. That was another result of his ill-considered invitation. He crossed to her, carrying the coffee, and sat down.

"Good morning. I trust you had a peaceful night."

She nodded. "Just fine." But dark shadows were like bruises under her eyes.

"You don't look it."

That surprised a smile out of her. "Thanks. That's just what a woman wants to hear first thing in the morning."

"Sorry. I didn't mean—well, you know what I meant."

She studied the coffee as if she saw something important in its murky depths. "I haven't slept well since I've been back on the island. Understandable, I guess."

Since he hadn't slept well for about a year, he could understand, but he didn't intend to admit it. "What are your plans for the day?"

Her head came up, her green eyes filled with suspicion. "Why do you ask?"

He set the mug down, harder than he'd intended, and the coffee sloshed dangerously. "I was just making conversation, Sarah. Not starting an inquisition."

"Of course," she said, doubt lacing the words.

Why did she persist in thinking the worst of him? He wasn't an ogre—just a man trying to protect what was his.

You weren't able to protect Lynette, a small voice in his mind reminded him.

All the more reason to protect his daughter. He couldn't let Sarah's presence stir up doubts in Melissa. He'd set up the official line—that Lynette had died in a tragic, innocent accident. No one on the island would dare to suggest anything else, but Sarah had always been incalculable. She was not beautiful, not compliant, not willing to follow anyone's lead.

She was everything he disliked in a woman, which made the attraction she held for him all the more incomprehensible.

He rejected the thought. Sarah was nothing to him. He simply had to be sure her presence didn't affect his daughter.

He heard Melissa's light step on the tile and looked toward the doorway. Melissa came through quickly, her momentum carrying her several steps into the room before she saw who was there. She came to an abrupt halt, staring.

"What is she doing here?"

He rose. Now was obviously not the time to correct Melissa's manners. Her small face was rigid with anger, and her fists pressed against her jeans.

"Dr. Wainwright is going to stay with us for a few days. I

know you're surprised to see her, but she had to come back to the island to take care of some business."

He could only hope Sarah caught the warning in his voice. That was all Melissa was to know about her presence.

His daughter sent him a contemptuous look. "I knew she was back. Everyone does. I want to know why she's in our house."

His peripheral vision caught a glimpse of Sarah's fingers, curled so tightly around her spoon that they were white. Don't say anything, he commanded silently.

"Sarah has had some trouble since she returned. She's staying at Land's End because she'll be safe here."

"Safe!" Melissa's mouth seemed to tremble for an instant before it took on the contemptuous smile he'd grown to dislike. "She'll be safe here. This place is as safe as a jail."

She spun around and darted toward the door, her long dark hair whipping like a flag in the wind.

"Melissa, sit down and have some breakfast."

But she was already gone. He heard the swinging door to the kitchen swoosh with her passing.

"I'm sorry." Distress filled Sarah's voice. "She shouldn't miss her breakfast because of me. I'll leave."

"Forget it." He sank back into his chair. As usual, his daughter had made him feel inept and incompetent. "She'll eat with Geneva, and Geneva will explain the situation to her." Better than he could.

"I never intended my coming to hurt her."

That empathy of hers could be a weapon against Sarah, but he found he didn't have the heart to use it. "It's not just you. Melissa's that way with everyone these days."

"She's at a difficult age. I seem to recall being a monster at twelve and thirteen."

"You?" He lifted an eyebrow, oddly comforted. "That's hard to believe. I always pictured you as the perfect child."

"I tried to be." There was an odd note in her voice that made him want to ask why. Before he could, she went on. "Has she talked to anyone about her mother's death? A professional, I mean."

Guilt tightened until it threatened to strangle him. "My daughter doesn't need a therapist, if that's what you mean."

His tone would warn off anyone else, but Sarah seemed to be the exception. She raised that clear green gaze to his face.

"I'd recommend some sessions with a counselor for any child who lost her mother so traumatically. Or possibly your pastor." Her voice took on a professional tone. "All the adults in her life were dealing with their own grief."

He pinned her with a glare that should silence her. "My daughter doesn't need a therapist. Just leave her alone."

Sarah didn't look cowed. She studied him for a long moment and nodded. Pushing her chair back, she paused, hand resting lightly on the pale pink tablecloth. "I'm going to the clinic this morning," she said, and walked quickly out of the room.

So Sarah trusted him with her destination. One step forward with her—two steps backward with Melissa. Grief and guilt gnawed at his stomach.

How am I going to protect both of them? You tell me that, because I sure don't know the answer.

Sarah watched the gates to Land's End slide closed behind her in her rearview mirror. She was free of the place for a short time, at least. She hadn't realized how much Trent's guarded enclave had affected her until she was outside. She could breathe now.

She drove down the narrow road, her gaze flickering to the rearview mirror again. The drapery of Spanish moss seemed to stir at her passing and then swing down, hiding Land's End from view, like Brigadoon vanishing into the mist. She was alone and back in her car. Outside those walls she might be free, but she was also vulnerable. The danger had probably been banished from the island with Farrell, but it made sense to be on her guard.

Like Melissa? That poor child was certainly guarded enough—all wrapped up into a prickly bundle ready to repel anyone who got too close. She'd always felt sympathy for Melissa, caught as she'd been between her beautiful, erratic mother and her overprotective, powerful father.

Her own childhood circumstances had been entirely different, but still, she'd known what it was like to try to live up to overachieving parents.

Lord, please show me how to help that child. I can't help but feel You've put her in my life again for a reason.

Trent wouldn't welcome her help for Melissa. His quick rebuff of her comment about a counselor showed that. As always, he thought he could control everything and everyone.

Or maybe not. That expression of his when Melissa had stormed out of the breakfast room had been just like that of any baffled, befuddled father of a twelve-year-old daughter. Girls turned into different creatures at that age, even if they hadn't suffered the traumatic loss of a parent.

The private lane that led only to Land's End opened out onto the main road. Main, and only. Everything on St. James was off this two-lane stretch of macadam. At this end were the gracious houses of the wealthy.

She passed Jonathan and Adriana's gate. She should call and thank them again. Trent had ushered her out so quickly the previous night that she hadn't done a good job of that. Still, she'd sensed relief under Jonathan's protestations. He'd been happy to be relieved of so troublesome a guest.

The road swung through the small commercial district. She wouldn't find much to replenish her wardrobe here—she'd probably have to run to Savannah to do that. Her reluctance to leave the island now that she'd gotten here was surely irrational. Trent couldn't very well close the bridge to keep her off.

A wide, shallow curve appeared ahead of her and she slowed, putting on the turn signal. Straight ahead the road crossed the bridge to the mainland, but the moment she turned onto the side road, she was in a different world.

Live oaks, crepe myrtles and the dense stands of loblolly pines crowded in on either side. Silvery swags of Spanish moss draped the road, sometimes low enough to brush the top of the car. The maritime forest edged onto the roadway, as if it would eat up the intrusive strip of concrete.

The small houses that appeared now and then, tucked into their quilt-size gardens, looked ramshackle in comparison to the mansions at the opposite end of the island, but they'd been here longer, blending into their surroundings like the wild deer disappearing into the forest.

A neat sign marked the turnoff to the clinic, and the sight reassured her. At least the clinic had survived her departure. It had been barely up and running when she'd left, with a full-time Gullah nurse, a handful of volunteer retired doctors and a building Trent had grudgingly donated.

Guilty feelings descended. She'd left them in the lurch when she'd run from the island, but surely they'd understood. She'd written to Esther Johnson, the nurse who'd been their only paid employee, but Esther's reply had been brief to the point of curtness. The clinic was fine; that was all she'd said.

Now she'd see for herself. She pulled into the shell-encrusted parking lot and stopped, blinking, hardly able to believe her eyes.

The building had nearly doubled in size. What had been an uncompromising square of concrete block with peeling paint and a rusted tin roof was now a long, low rectangle. The new roof was red tile, and the building itself had been painted a mossy gray-green that blended into its surroundings.

The clinic hadn't survived her leaving. It had thrived.

She got out of the car slowly, still hardly able to believe what her eyes were telling her. She'd had to fight and scrape every inch of the way to get the clinic off the ground, but it apparently soared without her.

The tan door had St. James Free Clinic lettered on it in gold. She pushed the door open and stepped from harsh sunlight to a cool, quiet room lined with chairs.

"I'm sorry. The clinic doesn't open for another half hour. Would you like to wait?" The young woman behind the counter, wearing a colorful head scarf and dangling gold earrings with her lab coat, was a stranger to Sarah.

"I'm not a patient." It was oddly disconcerting to be unknown in a place where just a year ago she'd been an important part. "I'm Dr. Wainwright. Is Esther Johnson in?"

"I'll see." No expression crossed the woman's face, but she had the sense that recognition had flickered briefly in her dark eyes. She picked up a phone, pressed a button and spoke softly, turning away from Sarah.

Not quite the welcome she'd been looking for, but what could she expect? Life had moved on without her. Only she and Trent remained trapped in the lingering memories of their shared past.

A door behind the counter opened, and Esther Johnson

swept through, moving with that quick grace that had always reminded Sarah of a bird on the wing. If Sarah hadn't known she was sixty, she'd have put Esther's age at anywhere between thirty and forty. That smooth brown skin didn't age, and her eyes were bright with intelligence and interest in everyone.

Except, it seemed, Sarah Wainwright. Esther stopped at the counter, looking at Sarah without expression. "You're back."

What was she to say to that? "It's good to see you again, Esther. You're looking well."

We were friends once, Esther. Did I lose that completely when I ran away?

The woman inclined her head, accepting the words as a queen might accept the praise of her subjects. Well, Esther was the queen here, she supposed. If anyone was responsible for the growth of the clinic, it would be Esther.

The silence was becoming unnerving. "The clinic looks wonderful. You're obviously doing well."

"Yes."

She forced a smile. "I knew you'd do a wonderful job. Do you have a minute to show me the new addition?"

Esther didn't bother consulting her watch. "I'm afraid not. I have new volunteers coming in for an orientation."

The rebuff was like a slap in the face. She had to take a breath before she could speak calmly.

"I know how scarce good volunteers are. I could work a few shifts while I'm on the island, if you're shorthanded." And perhaps find her place again, if she got back in the comfortable professional role she knew how to fill.

"Thank you, but we don't need any additional help at the moment." If Esther had held up a sign saying, *You're Not Wanted Here*, she couldn't have been any clearer.

She had let them down, leaving the way she had. Obviously

Esther, at least, didn't intend to forgive her easily for that. Guilt reared its head. She'd cut and run without a thought for the trouble she'd left behind on St. James. How did she begin to apologize for that?

"Esther—"

The outside door burst open, and a teenaged boy shouldered his way in, supporting another boy whose arm hung limply at his side. His face was terrified and tear-stained.

"You gotta help Joey. He run his bike right into a car."

Sarah started for the injured boy, but before she could take a step, Esther had rounded the counter and moved in front of her, issuing crisp orders to the other woman.

"I'll help—" Sarah began, but already someone pushed a gurney into the hallway, a doctor loping along behind it.

She recognized Sam Drake's lean, bony frame and shock of snow-white hair. Sam had been one of her first recruits, admitting under pressure that spending every moment of his retirement on the golf course had begun to pall.

"Hey, Sarah. Nice to see you, stranger." He gave her a quick wave before turning to the patient. The rest of the team rolled into action, just as she'd trained them. With a minimum of fuss the patient was whisked off to an exam room, his friend taken care of and she was left standing uselessly in place.

Nice to see you, stranger. Sam hadn't meant anything offensive. Not like Esther, with her coldness. But his attitude had shown her the truth nonetheless.

She wasn't needed here. Maybe she'd once been an important cog in the machinery, but now she just observed, ghostlike, with no part to play. She didn't belong.

Dinner at Land's End was, apparently, a command performance. Sarah sat across from Melissa at the linen-covered table, uneasily aware that the simple skirt and top she'd found in one of the island shops that afternoon didn't measure up.

Across from her, Joanna Larson, Trent's secretary, wore the neutral beige suit that seemed to be her uniform for day or evening. She had barely nodded when Sarah spoke to her, turning instead to Trent with a question about some correspondence. If her suit was no more suited to the atmosphere than Sarah's attire, it apparently didn't bother her.

Candlelight shone on white linen, reflected in crystal, made tiny flame points on the heavy silver. The mahogany furniture of the formal dining room was hand-carved in a rice pattern—a reminder of the rice culture that had once ruled the vast plantations of the sea islands.

Rice, indigo, sea island cotton had taken their turns as the favored cash crop for the plantation owners, and they'd all had one great need—the slave laborers who'd come from West Africa to produce the crops and build their own culture and their own language.

That culture still existed in uneasy partnership with the encroachment of the outside world, and the man seated next to Melissa exemplified that. Robert Butler was an MIT-educated, gifted engineer. Butler could be a success anywhere, but Trent had brought him back to his roots.

That could be a problem for some people, but Robert seemed unaffected. He switched easily from joking with Geneva in Gullah to a technical discussion with Trent that was equally incomprehensible to Sarah.

Trent sat at the end of the table, more at ease than she'd seen him since her return. His gray eyes lit with amusement as he responded to something Robert Butler said. Perhaps Trent enjoyed playing the role of patriarch. Everyone at the dinner table depended on him. Except her.

Perhaps it wasn't fair to think of Robert Butler as a dependent. He could probably name his own price to work for one of Trent's competitors, if he wanted to do so. Derek, on the other hand, didn't have that luxury. As Trent's half brother, he filled a nominal role as vice president. What his actual duties were, no one seemed to know.

With his brown, curly hair and round blue eyes, Derek didn't look anything like Trent, but they'd had different fathers. Local gossip had it that Trent, once he'd achieved success, had rescued his young half brother from a squalid life, sending him to university and making a place for him in the company. How much was true she didn't know, but Derek was loyal to Trent.

Would that loyalty keep him from being honest with her? She wasn't sure. It should be simple to have a private conversation with Derek now that she was living in the house, but so far he'd evaded her.

As if he knew she was thinking of him, Derek met her gaze. He gave her an understanding look, and his eyelid drooped in a slight wink. Hope rose. She'd find some way of talking with him away from Trent's dampening presence.

Melissa was more animated than Sarah had yet seen her. She leaned over to touch Robert's sleeve.

"Please, Robert. Tell us a Gullah ghost story." She shivered in anticipation. "Everyone wants to hear one."

Robert glanced at Trent, as if to ask permission. Trent nodded with an indulgent glance at his daughter.

"Well, now, there is one story about two haints that frequent an old burying ground on the island. Mind now, Melissa—" he bent a serious glance on the girl "—I'm a good Christian, and I don't believe in ghosts, but I know folks like the old stories. Just so you understand it's not real."

She nodded, eyes sparkling. "It's fun to hear a scary story when you know you're safe."

"Well, then," Robert said, "there once were two young people who lived on the island." His voice took on a singsong quality, deepening to a rich baritone rumble. "They loved each other, but their folks had been feuding for more years than anyone could remember."

It was a classic Romeo and Juliet tale, Sarah realized, transported to a Gullah setting by a skilled storyteller. Maybe it was the setting that made the tale so effective, with the candle flames flickering and the dark salt marsh pressing against the windows. Or maybe it was the quality of Robert's voice. He held his audience spellbound.

Was she the only one who felt uneasy as the tale proceeded toward its inevitable tragic end? Surely Robert could have found a story that didn't so closely parallel that of Miles and Lynette. Melissa didn't seem to notice, wrapped up as she was in the tale.

A slight movement from across the table drew her gaze. Joanna's fingers clutched her silver dessert spoon with such strength, it seemed she'd bend it. So Joanna wasn't as impervious to the situation as Sarah would have thought.

Sarah glanced at Trent to find his face impassive. The urge to shout at him, to blast his emotions free, startled her with its strength. She couldn't do anything for Trent. If he'd decided to deal with the tragedy by suppressing it, that was his choice.

In any event, Robert's tale took a slightly different turn, with the errant lovers killed by some unknown person, perhaps a jealous boyfriend or angry father, and destined to haunt the burying ground until their murderer was discovered.

Robert's voice dropped to a low, musical end, and everyone clapped. Trent rose.

"No one can top your storytelling, Robert. Let's take our coffee into the other room, shall we?"

She could take advantage of the movement to slip away. Joanna, apparently thinking the same, went quickly out the back door toward the patio. Because she preferred to be alone, or because she hadn't liked Robert's story, with its echoes of recent tragedy?

She'd find an opportunity to talk with Joanna, but if she hung around now, Derek's look had suggested he, at least, felt some friendship for her. She followed the others into the formal living room. Derek drifted to the grand piano and sat down, letting his fingers drift over the keys.

Before she could move in his direction, Robert appeared at her side, his face grave. "My little story upset you. I'm sorry."

Perhaps she should cultivate that mask Trent wore so well. "I thought perhaps the topic was a bit insensitive."

"Are you a Christian, Dr. Wainwright?" His dark gaze touched the gold cross she wore at her throat.

"Yes." She raised a startled gaze to his.

"Then you remember the approach the prophet Nathan had to take when God told him to confront King David with his sin. Sometimes the only way to tell the king an unpleasant truth is with a story."

Before she could ask any of the questions that jumbled together in her mind, he turned and walked away. She should talk to Derek, but all she wanted to do was be alone so she could sort this out.

SEVEN

Trent frowned, his head beginning to throb from his brother's endless tinkling on the piano. Or was it because he didn't want to let himself think about Robert's story?

The telling of it had been singularly tactless on Robert's part, and he was ordinarily not a tactless person. So what was behind that?

He watched Sarah and Robert in conversation. Robert moved away, leaving a distressed look on her face.

Poor Sarah—she probably considered herself a tough, no-nonsense professional who had her feelings under control. Unfortunately she couldn't do anything about that sensitive, vulnerable face of hers. As he watched she straightened her shoulders, assumed a smile and headed toward him.

Sarah stopped a few feet away. "If you'll excuse me, I'll say good night."

"I'll walk you to your room."

"That's not necessary." Her face revealed her reluctance to be alone with him. "It's just a step."

He took her arm. "I could use some air." He piloted her out through the French doors to the quiet patio.

She went with him willingly enough, but once the door had

closed behind them, she pulled her arm free of his hand. "Thank you, but I'm perfectly capable of walking to the room alone."

"You mean you don't want to be alone with me."

"That's ridiculous."

"Liar."

Sarah's lips quirked. "Didn't your mother teach you that it's impolite to call a lady a liar?"

His mother had been too drunk to teach him anything except how to avoid her fist. "Actually it was my grandmother who taught me manners." He took her arm again. "And she said a gentleman always escorts a lady to her door."

This time she did smile. "All right, I give up. Escort me the all of twenty steps to my door."

He matched his stride to hers as they crossed the pebbled patio. The lights of the pool glowed turquoise, but he hadn't bothered to turn the other patio lights on. The nearly full moon was bright enough, and the stars clustered more thickly without the competition.

As if she followed his thoughts, Sarah tilted her head back to look up. "I'd forgotten how bright the stars are here."

"They prefer shining on the island. Hadn't you noticed?"

"You may be right."

They reached the door to the guest suite. Sarah still looked up, the moonlight silvering her face. Strange, that the face he'd never considered beautiful should be so lovely now. Moonlight suited her, bringing out her delicate bone structure.

"Good night." She shifted her gaze to his. "And thank you again for your hospitality."

"You're welcome here."

They'd stood like this in the moonlight once before. Did she remember that? How they'd looked at each other, recognizing that in another moment they could have been in each other's arms? His hand still held her arm, and her skin seemed to warm under his touch.

Back away. Looking into Sarah's eyes is a dangerous thing.

He'd be better off to pick a fight with her. Fortunately that was always an easy thing to do.

"Are you ready to leave yet?"

For a moment his words didn't seem to register. Then she lifted her eyebrows. "I thought you said I was welcome here."

"You are, if you insist on staying. But you must realize by now that your being here, opening the past, can only bring pain to all of us. Especially to my daughter."

She winced at that, making an involuntary movement as if to push his words away. "I don't want to hurt anyone, particularly not Melissa. She's already had enough pain to last a lifetime."

He had to harden his heart. He could not let himself be touched by her caring for his child. "Then go."

For a moment she looked at him as if she stared through him, seeing something he couldn't see. She shook her head slightly.

"The first time I saw you since my return, you accused me of coming here to satisfy my Puritan conscience."

He remembered those bitter words, thrown at her from his own pain. "I didn't mean—" But he had.

"Maybe you were right." She seemed to drag in a breath, and he thought she wouldn't say more. "Maybe it is that." She went doggedly on. "I just know that if Miles betrayed me, that means I failed him somehow."

He didn't want to think that, because the corollary was that he had failed Lynette. "What they did isn't our fault." He had to keep telling himself. Maybe eventually he'd believe it.

She shook her head. "I have to know. I have to understand,

if I'm ever going to move on." Anguish laced her words. "Don't you see that?" She grabbed his hand, her fingers digging into his skin. "You of all people should see that."

He did. Her grief went right through all his barriers and pierced his heart, twisting it until he didn't know where her pain ended and his began. He wanted to help her, wanted to protect her—

He couldn't. He couldn't protect both her and Melissa, no matter how much he wanted to. And his first duty had to be to his child, even if that meant hurting Sarah.

It cost something to push her hand away. He had to drag in a breath of moist marsh air before he could speak.

"You're wrong, Sarah. I've accepted what they did. I think it's time you did, too."

He turned and walked away before he could drown in the hurt in her eyes.

Sarah stared at her reflection in the bathroom mirror the next morning. She'd like to say she was doing fine, but her image showed the lie to that. That difficult exchange with Trent had left her sleepless for most of the night.

Was she doing the right thing? If her search for the truth hurt a helpless child, how could she possibly justify that?

And what about that odd story of Robert's? He'd implied that he was trying to tell Trent an unwelcome truth, but the characters in his story had been lovers. Trent already believed that about Lynette and Miles. She was the one who doubted.

Robert's innocent lovers had been killed by someone unknown. If he intended to say that Lynette and Miles had met a similar fate, then her task was far more complicated and dangerous than simply proving to her own satisfaction that they had not been lovers.

She'd wrestled with the questions for hours, turning again and again to prayer until she'd finally realized she didn't have a choice. God had set her on this path, and she couldn't turn back. She could only push toward a resolution, trusting that He had some good in store for all of them.

She patted a little loose powder over the dark circles and pulled her hair back into a ponytail. That would have to do.

She went out, locking the door behind her, and crossed the patio toward the breakfast room. She couldn't prevent her steps from slowing as she approached the door. The last thing she needed was another private talk with Trent. Steeling herself, she went inside.

A quick glance assured her that Trent was nowhere in sight. Unfortunately, neither was Derek, and she'd hoped to manage a private word with him this morning. The only person in the room was Joanna Larson.

Joanna had always been pleasant enough to her in the past, but detached, efficient and wrapped up in her work. Miles, as she recalled, had admired the woman's loyalty and efficiency. If Joanna had outside interests, Sarah had never heard of them. She'd always seemed detached, but she hadn't been detached in her reaction to Robert Butler's story.

Sarah smiled and nodded when the woman looked up for a moment, her mind busy. She poured a cup of coffee, hesitated a moment and then moved to Joanna's table. Surely it would be natural to talk with the woman, wouldn't it?

"Joanna, I'm sorry we didn't have a chance to talk last night. How are you?"

The woman looked up, and all Sarah could think was that Joanna looked almost as bad as she did. Her pale blue eyes also bore dark circles underneath. Her cup clattered as she set it in the saucer, as if her hand trembled.

"I'm fine." Her face gave the lie to the words. "I couldn't believe you'd come back. Why are you here?"

Apparently she felt free to say this morning the words she'd suppressed the previous night. She shouldn't be surprised. Joanna's loyalty to Trent was notorious—she'd devoted her life to him. If Trent didn't want her here, then Joanna didn't, either.

"I came to take care of some things I left unresolved. I hoped you might understand that."

The words she considered soothing seemed to have the opposite effect. Joanna shot to her feet. "Understand? Why would I understand? It's nothing to do with me."

"I just meant—"

"You should leave." Joanna shoved her chair so hard it nearly tipped over. "There's nothing for you here." She brushed by Sarah and scurried out the door.

Sarah sank into a seat. She hadn't imagined the woman's reaction the previous night. She had strong feelings beneath that neutral exterior, but it didn't look as if she'd easily share those feelings with Sarah.

And if the others react the same way? Where will you turn then? Or will you just give up?

She glanced at the buffet, but her stomach protested at the thought of food. She'd saunter through the main part of the house to see if she could run into Derek. Maybe he didn't share the opinion that her absence was preferable to her presence.

She walked through the formal dining room, empty save for the disturbing memories of last night's dinner. Robert Butler and his story—what had he meant by telling it? And that odd reference to the prophet and King David. She'd looked up the story sometime in the wee hours of the morning. Nathan had told his story to convict David of his guilt. Surely

Robert wasn't implying any guilt on Trent's part, although Trent was definitely the king of his small island.

Music filtered from the formal living room—the piano, and a tune she vaguely recognized as a Mozart piece her hapless piano teacher had once optimistically thought she'd learn to play. She moved toward the door. She'd be able to catch Derek.

But it wasn't Derek at the piano this time. It was Melissa. Sarah stopped at the entrance to the room, unwilling to intrude. Melissa played with a skill that certainly would have astounded Sarah's teacher. Her hands moved over the keys with an enviable sureness, and her eyes were closed.

Sarah's throat tightened. Lynette had been a concert pianist before she'd given up her career to marry Trent. Obviously her daughter had inherited her gift. The music seemed to be a solace to the child, and she was glad. She stepped back softly. She wouldn't interrupt.

A door clattered above them, in the loft that housed a small sitting room and Trent's private study. "Melissa, can't you do that later? I'm trying to work up here."

Melissa froze, hands still on the keys. Then, without a word, she slid off the piano bench and ran out of the room by the opposite door.

Sarah took a step forward, propelled by anger. Didn't he see what the music meant to his child?

She looked up at Trent, and the words died on her tongue. He stood with his hands planted on the railing of the loft, looking after Melissa with an expression of pain and regret twisting his face.

"Go after her," she said before she could think too much about it.

He looked at her, face tightening. He would tell her to mind her own business. Tell her to leave.

"I can't. I'd only make things worse." He turned and slammed his way back into the study.

It was hopeless. She couldn't correct what was wrong between Trent and his daughter. But even so, she couldn't keep from going after Melissa.

The front door stood open, and she stepped outside. Melissa was in a corner of the wide front veranda, curled up in a porch swing padded with bright cushions. She was turned away, face buried in her arms, and she didn't move at Sarah's approach, though she must have heard her. Unsure what to do or say, Sarah sat down in one of the wooden rockers that lined the veranda.

The rocker squeaked slightly, and a breeze off the ocean lifted her hair and bent the golden sea oats on the dunes. Bougainvillea rioted over the latticework that marked the end of the veranda, and sunlight danced on the water. Only the humans were miserable.

"I'm sorry," she said finally. "Maybe your dad is working on something that needs a lot of concentration."

Melissa straightened, revealing a tear-stained face. "He hates my playing."

"You play beautifully. I'm sure your father is proud of that."

She shook her head, dark hair flying, and her lips trembled. "He hates my playing because I'll never be as good as my mother."

Her heart hurt so much for the child that she could scarcely speak, but somehow she had to find the words to reassure her. She leaned forward, reaching out to touch the knee of Melissa's jeans.

"I can see how you might feel that way, but I don't think it's true, not really. He loves you."

Hostility flashed in Melissa's eyes. "What would you know

about it? You—you've got something to give. You're a doctor. Everybody respects you."

Not lately, but she wouldn't tell Melissa that. "Maybe so, but my mother is the head of pediatrics at a university hospital. And my father is chief of surgery at that same hospital. They're both the very best in their fields. When I was growing up, I felt as if I could never live up to what they were. Sometimes I still feel that way."

And that was more than she'd told anyone about her relationship with her loving, overpowering parents in a long time.

Melissa just stared at her, her face as masked, in its own way, as her father's was. Then she slid off the swing. "You don't understand," she said, with the irrefutable logic of a twelve-year-old. "You're not like me at all. You're a grown-up."

She spun and walked away. Sarah watched. Was Melissa's step a bit lighter? She couldn't be sure. But at least the child wasn't crying any longer.

You're a doctor, she'd said. You've got something to give.

She leaned back, feeling somehow better than she had. Maybe she hadn't helped Melissa, but Melissa had helped her. She'd reminded her of something she'd been in danger of forgetting. She was a doctor. She was a grown-up. She'd better start acting like one, and get on with what she'd come here to do.

"There it is. Number 340." The man who ran the storage facility pointed out the obvious, his gaze avidly curious. Obviously he knew who she was. "Nothing's been touched in a year. You need any help?"

"No. Thank you." She fitted the key into the lock of the wide door of the storage locker. "I'll take it from here."

He lingered, probably hoping for more of a reaction. "You'd best prop that door open. It'll be awful hot in there."

"I will." She stood, staring at him, until he took the hint. He shrugged, turning back toward the air-conditioned cubbyhole where she'd found him.

"I'm off in an hour. You want any help before that, you call me."

She glanced at her watch. Nearly three. The day had slipped away while she'd tried to track down a few of Miles's coworkers and stopped at the clinic. She waited until he'd disappeared before grasping the handle of the garage-style door and yanking it up. She didn't need an audience while she went through the remnants of her life with Miles.

The door creaked open, letting out a blast of air as hot as an oven. Furniture, boxes, packing crates had been crammed into the storage compartment willy-nilly—everything that had been in the small cottage she and Miles had rented on the island. She wasn't even sure who'd done it. She'd just received a note and the key from their landlord, along with a bill for the storage.

She stared, eyes stinging. There was Miles's desk—an elegant old rolltop she'd found in an antique shop in Savannah. She'd paid the earth for it, but it had been an anniversary present. And the rocking chair her grandmother had given her— she should have taken that with her, but she'd been too shocked to think things through.

No longer. Thanks to Melissa's reminder, she was back on track. She'd already stopped by the clinic, faced down Esther and insisted on being put on the physician's rotation for the coming week. Now she would go through the remnants of her marriage, looking for any clue, however faint, to what had happened to them.

She stepped inside, letting go of the door. It slid down, and she grabbed it just in time. Holding the door with one hand, she groped for something to prop it. Obviously she'd have to keep the door open—she'd pass out from the heat if she didn't. Her fingers touched a broom that leaned against the wall, and she shoved it into place.

She wiggled the handle, but the broom held firm, wedged into the track of the door. The outside air was warm and moist, but at least it moved. She could tolerate this.

After fifteen minutes of work she wasn't so sure. She was already drenched with sweat. Maybe she'd better pack up any papers to take with her, then come back later to sort out what she wanted shipped back to Boston and what could be sold.

Grabbing a couple of boxes, she began emptying the contents of the desk drawers and file cabinet. Miles had been meticulous about keeping records—he'd saved every scrap of paper that might possibly be needed at tax time.

She hauled two boxes of papers to the door, pausing long enough to drink from her water bottle, and began going through the stacked boxes in search of anything else that might be personal.

Boxes of dishes. She dug in her pocket for the pen she'd brought and marked them. No point in doing this all over again. She yanked open another box, expecting to see pots and pans, and found instead items that had once been on Miles's dresser.

Her heart lurched. There was the paperweight they'd brought back from their honeymoon in Venice. And the small pewter tray he'd dropped change into each night. Her heart twisted at the image of him talking over his day as he went through the nighttime routine. That had been a comfortable part of the day—a time of conversation, laughter, intimacy. How could that have been a lie? She'd known him so well, first as a teenager in Boston, then connecting with him when they'd both been working in Atlanta. She'd known him as well as anyone could.

Trying to swallow the lump in her throat, she closed the box. Maybe she was being a coward, but she'd deal with those things later.

A hot and trying twenty minutes later, she had all the papers she could find packed into two more boxes. She carted one to the door, inhaled a breath of fresh air and started back for the other one. As she bent to pick it up, she heard an ominous rattling sound. She swung around, scrambling frantically toward the door, even as she saw that she'd never make it in time. The door slid inexorably closed.

For a moment she just stood, staring at it in disbelief. How could it possibly be closed? She grabbed the bar at the bottom and yanked, and the truth settled in. The door wasn't just closed. It was locked.

She pulled again, feeling panic rise. She searched the door with eyes and fingers, trying to find a latch to open it from the inside. Nothing. She was trapped. She didn't even have her cell phone with her—it lay on the front seat of the car. Just a few yards away from the door, but it might as well be on the moon for all the good it would do her.

She banged on the door with her fist, shouting. Surely the attendant would hear her. Or he'd come and check on her, wouldn't he? She glanced at her watch, heart sinking. Twenty after four. He'd said he was leaving at four. The chance that anyone else would come by the storage facility at this hour was slim.

She sank into the rocking chair, fighting down panic. At least she wasn't in the dark. Sunlight seeped through the translucent panels under the roof. Think—she had to think, but her mind seemed oddly fogged. She pressed her hand against her forehead, professional instincts clicking into gear. She couldn't sit here hoping to be rescued, like Rapunzel in her tower. If she didn't get out soon, heat exhaustion would take over and she wouldn't be able to think rationally at all.

Her fingers tightened on the arms of the chair. *Please, Father. Help me.*

Maybe it was the effect of the rocking chair, with its reminder of her grandmother. That formidable lady would not have sat around. Pray as if it all depends on God, she'd always said. Work as if it all depends on you.

Work. The word launched a train of thought. Miles's workbench stood against the wall, his tools packed into the red tool box he'd always kept in such meticulous order. She scrambled over intervening boxes to reach the work bench and grabbed the toolbox. *Thank You. Thank You.*

Back over the boxes—they seemed to have gotten higher. It was more of a struggle just to get to the door, to fumble the box open.

She dragged in a breath. Stop. Think. Don't go at it aimlessly. She forced herself to study the door. The mechanism that moved it was powered by a spring. She'd never be able to dislodge the heavy metal of the spring, but she might be able to release the bolt that held it. She scrabbled through the tools, her fingers closing on a wrench. That should do it.

Any hope that it would be a moment's work vanished when she applied the wrench to the nut that held the bolt. It was wedged into the panel in such a way that she could only move it half a turn at a time.

Easy, she reminded herself. Don't panic. Just keep working steadily.

Turn the nut, release the wrench, reattach it, turn again. The movement became rote, freeing her mind. She would not let herself think of Miles using the tools, Miles with his pride in fixing anything that happened to go wrong at the cottage.

Concentrate. Why had the door slammed shut anyway? She must have dislodged the broom when she'd put down that last box, though she'd been sure she wasn't that close to it. She frowned. The broom wasn't here. It must have fallen outside.

Turn, turn, stop for a swallow of water. Rub the bottle against your forehead. Try to keep your mind focused. Don't close your eyes, or you might not open them again.

Panic shot through her. She couldn't tolerate this much longer. She had to get out. Now.

She yanked on the spring frantically. It creaked, groaned and pulled free. She dragged at the door. With a moan that sounded almost human, it rolled slowly up, the spring dangling uselessly. She stumbled out into the air.

For a long moment she could only lean against the car, gasping in air. Her head cleared slowly, and she opened the door to grab another bottle of water and drain half of it, then dumped the rest unceremoniously over her head. She couldn't have been trapped for more than half an hour, but it had felt like an eternity.

She pushed wet strands of hair back from her face. She was okay. A cool shower, several long cold drinks and she'd be fine, but she didn't like to think what would have happened if Miles's toolbox hadn't been there. She shouldn't have been so careless with that last box.

She forced herself away from the car. Get the boxes, go back to Land's End. She thought longingly of the air-conditioned comfort of the guest suite. She would—

She stopped dead, staring. The broom lay outside the locker, as she'd assumed. But not near the door. It was a full ten feet away. It couldn't have gotten there on its own. Someone must have thrown it.

EIGHT

Sarah arrived back at Land's End fueled by a fierce need to confront Trent. If he hadn't personally trapped her in the storage locker, someone working for him must have. Surely he was the only one who wanted to be rid of her enough to do that.

It was anticlimactic to arrive at the house and learn he wasn't there. He'd gone out, Joanna Larson had said when Sarah stormed toward his office. Joanna had eyed Sarah's sweaty and disheveled appearance with a certain disdain. She declined to say when he would return, showing a flare of protectiveness toward her boss that made Sarah wonder about her feelings for him.

By the time Sarah had showered, dressed and taken a couple of aspirin for the headache that was the only aftereffect, she'd begun to question her assumptions. Trent might be the logical person to blame, but he wasn't the only possibility.

Farrell could still be on the island, ready to get even with her for having him fired. Or someone else, someone she hadn't even guessed at, might harbor ill will toward her. She thought again of Robert Butler's story, with its unknown killer, and pictured a knife slashing at her sweater, just where her heart would have been if she'd been wearing it. A faintly queasy feeling touched her stomach.

Enough. She'd have it out with Trent when he returned. That would either clear the air or make it murkier, but she had to do it.

Maybe Geneva could give her something light for supper. It was nearly six, but she definitely didn't want a big meal.

When she entered the main part of the house, she found Geneva and Melissa engaged in a lively argument. Melissa held a small cooler bag in one hand and a kayak paddle in the other.

"But my dad said we'd go today. I've got the sandwiches and drinks all ready. We were going to have a picnic supper." She waved the cooler. "If he's too busy, I'll go by myself."

Obviously Trent had forgotten a commitment to his daughter. She tried not to judge his actions.

"You know you can't go by yourself." Geneva sounded as if she'd said the same thing several times.

"Then you go with me."

Geneva's warm, rich laugh sounded. "Child, I'll no more put myself into that kayak than launch myself into space. Why don't you ask Dr. Wainwright? Maybe she'd like to go."

Melissa sliced a sideways glance at Sarah. "Would you?"

"That's no way to ask somebody," Geneva said. "Mind your manners."

Melissa gave an elaborate sigh, but the look she gave the older woman was affectionate. Geneva was probably as close to a mother as the child had.

"Sarah, would you like to take a kayak into the salt marsh with me? The tide is perfect, and if we don't go soon, it'll be too late."

It was the first time Melissa had referred to her by name. That, combined with the tentative peace offering, was too much to resist.

"Sure, I'd like to, if Geneva says it's all right."

"Go, go." Geneva made shooing motions with her hands.

"You've got a good hour and a half before sunset. And put some repellent on. Those mosquitoes will eat you alive if you're not careful."

"I've got some. Let's just go." Melissa scurried impatiently to the back door Sarah had just entered.

Sarah followed, wondering what Trent would make of this excursion when he found out. On second thought, she didn't need to wonder. She could figure that out with no trouble at all.

Melissa skirted the pool and strode down a wooden walkway behind the house, toward the creek that ran through the salt marsh. Downstream, toward the sound, lay Cat Isle and the cottage. To their right, the salt marsh stretched—waving fields of spartina grass, its roots in the water, cut by the winding creek.

Several kayaks were pulled up on the dock where the walkway ended. Melissa grabbed a two-person one, lowering it easily to the water, and then took life jackets from a metal locker on the dock, tossing one to Sarah.

"You could stand up anywhere in the marsh, but Dad insists on life jackets anyway. You'd think I was a baby."

"He loves you." Sarah thrust her arms into the lightweight jacket and fastened it. "He wants to keep you safe."

Melissa, climbing into the kayak, didn't answer. She steadied the craft while Sarah climbed in. The kayak scraped bottom as she settled herself, but Melissa quickly pushed them into deeper water, wielding the paddle as if she'd been doing it all her life.

Obviously she didn't intend to let Sarah paddle, although she could have. She'd been out with Miles several times. She seemed to see him, blond hair glinting in the sunlight, smiling at her, and her heart clenched.

"If I were a boy, it would be different," Melissa said over her shoulder, picking up the conversation again. "My dad wishes I were a boy."

Careful, careful. Father, give me the right words.

"Lots of men would like to have a son," she said. "Probably my dad would have, too, but it wasn't to be. That doesn't mean they love their daughters any the less." At least, she hoped that was true.

Melissa's only response was a grunt that might have meant anything. For a few minutes she paddled in silence. Sarah leaned back, ready to let the child take the lead. She wouldn't try to force her opinions.

Melissa raised her paddle, water sheeting from it in a glistening spray. "That's a night heron."

"He's beautiful." The elegant dark bird lifted its head to stare at them, unafraid.

"Sometimes we see dolphins. They come into the marsh to feed." She smiled suddenly. "Maybe we should, too. Feed, I mean. You want a sandwich?"

That was the first genuine smile she'd seen from Melissa. It lit the heart-shaped, too-solemn face with life and grace, reminding her suddenly of Lynette. Lynette had had that grace, too, but it had been brittle, always on the verge of snapping. In Melissa, it seemed tempered by a strain of her father's solidity, which was probably a good thing.

They ate in silence, but it was a companionable silence. Perhaps one of the reasons she'd been drawn back to the island was to be a friend to Melissa. The girl certainly seemed to need one. Did Trent realize how lonely his daughter was? Or was he too caught up in his own troubles to see?

When they'd finished, Melissa scattered the crumbs, watching as a flock of gulls arrived to scoop them up as if they'd heard a dinner bell.

Sarah laughed. "You've made their day. Chicken salad sandwiches and cookie crumbs."

"Greedy things." Melissa threw a last handful and studied the gulls as if they were the most interesting things she'd ever seen. "I wanted to say I'm sorry. For how I acted this morning. Geneva says it's stupid to be mean to somebody who wants to be your friend."

Her throat tightened. "Geneva's a wise woman." She tried to say it lightly. "I'd like to be your friend."

The girl shrugged, her shoulders thin and vulnerable under the striped T-shirt she wore. "Some of the kids at school act like they want to be friends, but they just want to find out about when my mother died."

Poor child. "I would never ask you to talk about that. I'd just like to be your friend, no strings attached."

Melissa seemed to assess that for a moment. Then she picked up the paddle. "We'd better start back. Looks like rain coming."

Sarah glanced behind her. Dark clouds massed, low in the sky. She'd been on the island long enough to know how fast a rainstorm could blow up. She should have been more alert.

Melissa paddled along smoothly. Apparently the conversation was over, as far as she was concerned. Then she shot a look over her shoulder at Sarah.

"People think if you're a kid you don't know anything. I know lots of things Dad doesn't think I do."

That sounded like a challenge. "Kids usually do know more than their parents think."

Melissa dug the paddle in so deeply that the kayak veered sharply. "I know lots," she repeated. "Like, my mother was sad. One time I heard her crying."

Her heart twisted. Children often felt they were to blame for their parents' problems. If Trent would take her advice about taking Melissa to a qualified counselor—but she suspected he wouldn't.

"Grown-ups need to cry sometimes. That doesn't mean anything serious."

Melissa's shoulders moved defensively. Sarah couldn't see her face, and she was afraid the child was crying, too.

The dock came into view, and Melissa drove the kayak toward it with swift strokes, as if she couldn't wait to be rid of Sarah. The child was like quicksilver, unable to grasp for more than an instant at a time.

Someone waited on the dock. As they neared, it didn't take any special insight to see that anger tightened every line of Trent's body. She felt herself stiffening in turn. Maybe he had reason to be angry, but she did, too.

Melissa skipped a stroke, resting the paddle across the boat and turning to look at Sarah. "She was sad," she said again, and Sarah knew she was talking about her mother. "She was sad, but that doesn't mean she'd do anything wrong. I don't care what anyone says. I don't believe it."

Trent was naive to think he could keep his daughter from hearing the rumors. And she was probably assuring his permanent enmity, but she couldn't help responding.

"I don't believe it either, Melissa. I just don't."

Trent watched the kayak come closer, and it seemed to him that it raced the dark clouds. Ridiculous, to be so keyed up now that they were in sight and he knew they were safe, but anger and fear still drove him.

When he'd come home and found that Melissa and Sarah had gone kayaking, apprehension had gripped his heart in a vise. Lynette's daughter. Miles's wife. Out on the water together. It was superstitious, but the idea filled him with dread. When they weren't back by the time he'd exchanged his suit for jeans and a T-shirt, he'd come down to the dock to wait.

They were close enough now that he could read their expressions—Melissa's defiant, ready for a fight. Sarah's apprehensive, no doubt knowing that a fight was coming. His stomach churned. What had they been saying to each other, out there in the quiet marsh?

The kayak's prow bumped the dock, and he reached down to grab it. Melissa hopped onto the dock lightly.

"You don't need to be mad. I didn't go out by myself, and we wore life jackets, see?"

He took a breath, trying for calm. "I'm glad you remembered that. But didn't you realize a storm's coming up?"

"Sure I did." She slid out of the life jacket and let it drop to the dock. "That's why we came back." Her voice lilted with a sassiness he hadn't heard from her in a while. "I timed it perfectly, didn't I?"

The first fat drops hit the weathered boards as she spoke. He could hardly argue. "Go on up to the house before you get soaked. Sarah will help me put the boat away."

He didn't need Sarah's help with the boat. He did need a few private moments with her.

Melissa's gaze darted toward Sarah. Then she nodded and ran toward the house, leaping up the steps like a deer.

Sarah grasped the pylon as she started to get out, and the kayak rocked. He grabbed her and lifted her bodily to the dock. She seemed to weigh barely more than Melissa. She clutched his arm for an instant, getting her balance, and then stepped quickly away. She probably wanted to run after Melissa to the house, but he pinned her to the spot with a glare.

"I thought we agreed you'd stay away from my daughter."

"I wouldn't have gone, if you'd kept your promise to her." A gust of rain-wet wind tore the words away, and she shivered.

He gritted his teeth. Unfortunately she was right. He not

only hadn't kept his word, he'd forgotten about it. He bent to grasp the kayak and heft it, dripping, to the dock.

"I'll make it up to Melissa," he said evenly. "But what about your promise not to talk to Melissa about her mother?"

"I didn't." She slid the life jacket off. "I didn't say anything to her about Lynette."

But he saw the struggle behind the words. Those clear green eyes had to be a hindrance when she wanted to evade the truth. He waited.

"Melissa brought it up." Her eyes seemed to cloud with concern. "Trent, please. I know she shouldn't talk to me. But she should talk to someone."

He knew what she was saying. She thought Melissa needed a counselor. He wanted to shove the idea away. It would be an admission that he was a failure as a father. But didn't he already know that?

"Maybe." He hated the grudging sound of the word. "But you were still wrong—"

The rain hit, coming down in a deluge, as if heaven had dumped a bucketful right on them. Sarah gasped, and in an instant her shirt clung to her like a second skin.

"Come on." He grabbed her hand. "Run for it."

Half helping, half dragging, he led her up the steps. By the time they reached the top she was running beside him. He could let go of her wet hand, but he didn't want to.

Rain pounded against them, drumming on the wooden walkway. The green of shrubs and trees turned iridescent in the deluge. The pool sparkled and danced as they hit the patio and turned toward the house. His spirits lifted. It was exhilarating to race the storm, making him feel like a kid again.

"We might as well stop running," Sarah gasped. "I can't get any wetter."

He stopped short, and she bumped into him. He steadied her with a firm grasp of her arm. Her skin was cool from the rain, but it warmed to his touch.

"Is this better?" He looked down at her, laughter in his voice.

Her hair, darkened by the rain, hung wetly around her face. Her cheeks were flushed from the run, and her eyes sparkled with laughter that matched his.

His grip tightened. He wanted to pull her close, hold her against the rain—

Sarah's pupils dilated, making her green eyes dark. She seemed to sway toward him. Then her breath caught in an audible gasp, she stepped back.

"I—I'll go dry off."

"Wait." Stupid, but he didn't want her to go.

"I'll come to the house once I'm dry. We have to talk."

Something about her tone alerted him. He wasn't going to like what they had to talk about. "What is it? What did Melissa say to you?"

She hesitated for a moment, as if she wouldn't speak. Then she turned back, the rain pelting down her face like tears.

"She knows what people are saying about Miles and Lynette. She doesn't believe it. She doesn't believe her mother would do anything wrong."

Sarah paused at the door to the family room. She was no longer shivering, but that didn't really improve her feelings any. The need to confront Trent about the storage locker had combined with the pressure she felt to help Melissa, tying her stomach in knots.

Well, she couldn't let that deter her. With a silent plea for guidance, she opened the door.

Trent turned from the dark fireplace, which he was facing.

He looked younger, less formidable, wearing jeans and a T-shirt, his hair still wet from a shower. The knots tightened. She'd forgotten to add that uncomfortable surge of attraction to her litany of problems.

"Feel better now?" His brows lifted.

"Drier, at least." She forced herself to move forward.

The family room was more casual than the rest of the house, its rattan furniture covered with bright sailcloth pillows and its bookshelves filled with an assortment of children's books and popular fiction. A coffee service was set out on the glass-topped table, adding a welcoming touch.

But she wasn't welcome, and she had to keep that firmly in mind. She'd let herself forget it during those moments when she and Trent had run through the rain together, and look what had happened. She had to keep her guard up with Trent for more reasons than that unpredictable spurt of attraction.

Like the incident at the storage locker, for instance.

Trent was looking at her, frowning a little. "What is it? You look as if you're ready to do battle."

"Maybe I am." She stopped a few feet from him. That was close enough. "I went to the storage facility this afternoon to check out the things I left here."

Wariness flickered in his gray eyes. "That must have been difficult."

"It had to be done." In the first flush of anger it would have been easy to accuse him. Now it was harder to get the words out. "I had the door propped open. When my back was turned, someone took the prop away. They locked me in. The attendant had already left. If I hadn't been able to free myself—" The memory robbed her of breath.

For a moment Trent didn't move. His expression didn't change, and it was impossible to read guilt or innocence in his face. Then he crossed the space between them in two swift strides. He grasped her hands, his grip hard and compelling.

"Are you all right?" His fingers moved against her skin, as if to assure himself she was there and safe.

Relief swept through her, its depth surprising her. Unless Trent was a far better actor than she gave him credit for, he hadn't had anything to do with it.

"I'm fine. Fortunately Miles's toolbox was inside the locker, and I was able to get the door open."

"In this heat, you could have died before anyone found you." Anger and passion colored his voice. "What were you thinking to go there alone? You should have let someone know where you'd be, at least."

She jerked her hands free. "Right. Blame the victim. Of course I should have guessed someone might lock me in."

He stared at her and then shook his head slightly. "Sorry. I didn't mean to act as if you're to blame." His frown deepened, engraving three deep lines between his brows. "Look, are you sure it wasn't just an accident?"

"The broom I'd used to wedge the door was lying ten feet away. It didn't get there on its own. Someone threw it."

He lifted his eyebrows. "So of course you thought of me."

She shrugged, uncomfortable. "It seemed the logical choice. You didn't, did you?"

"No. But it's hardly a compliment that you have to ask."

Trent hadn't done it. That left very few possibilities. "Are you sure Farrell left the island?"

"Farrell?" Clearly the thought hadn't occurred to him. She could almost see his mind ticking over that.

"I was responsible for his getting fired."

His lips tightened. "I suppose he might see it that way. If he's still on the island, I can find out easily enough."

Of course he could. The police chief would be happy to help him. That resolution was oddly anticlimactic. She'd been geared for a few more fireworks.

"That's really all I wanted to say." She made a slight movement toward the door, but he stopped her with a light touch.

"But not all I want to say." He shook his head. "I don't know why we're standing here. Come and sit down. The least we can do is to drink the coffee Geneva fixed for us."

He wanted to talk about Melissa. Her heart sank. She'd already said more than she should. She sat down on the rattan sofa. The cushions cradled her body and urged her to relax, and she sank into them. She must be more tired than she'd thought.

She leaned back, watching Trent's face as he went about the small business of pouring out coffee, adding sugar, stirring it. He wore his control like a shield, but she'd seen behind that barrier more than most people had, probably. He was hurting. Pain had driven those harsh lines into his face, not bitterness, as she'd first thought. He'd deny it, of course, but he needed to know the truth about Lynette and Miles as much as she did.

She barely sipped the coffee, knowing she didn't need any caffeine to ensure another restless night. Trent took a long swallow and then set his cup down firmly. She tightened. Here they came—the questions she didn't want to answer.

"Why did Melissa confide in you?"

The question, when it came, wasn't the one she expected, and for an instant it threw her.

"I'm not sure." She watched his hands, finding it easier than looking at his face. His long fingers were linked in what should have been a casual pose, but she read the strain he carried in every muscle. "Maybe she felt that we shared a common grief. I didn't ask any questions, Trent. Really."

He nodded. "I believe you. But—" He hesitated, then shook his head. "Did she say anything more?"

There were all sorts of reasons why she shouldn't tell him what his daughter had said, and only one reason to tell him. She cared about what he and Melissa were going through.

"She said that she knew her mother was unhappy." Her throat tightened, and she had to force the words out. "She said that she had heard Lynette crying."

His hands twisted against each other, the knuckles going white. It was no good thinking she could guard herself from his pain. She couldn't.

"Lynette—" His voice seemed to choke. He paused a moment, clearly fighting for control. When he went on, his voice had roughened. "She was always restless, always dissatisfied. I thought when she had Melissa it would make a difference, but it didn't. She seemed to need something I couldn't give her."

The raw honesty of the confession cut her already bruised heart. "I'm sorry," she whispered, the words inadequate.

His face was bleak. "If I'd realized what that was leading her to, maybe I could have found a way to stop it."

What it was leading her to—the isolated cottage and a rendezvous with a lover—that was what he meant. She tried not to picture the cottage, but she couldn't stop. She'd never get the image out of her mind—the softly padded furniture, the air of seclusion, the fire laid ready to be lit—it had been such an unusually cold, wet spring last year.

"It doesn't make sense." The words were out before she'd fully formed the thought.

He sighed. "I know you don't want to believe Miles could have betrayed you, but what else are we to think?"

She shook her head stubbornly. "No. I don't believe he would, but that's not what I meant." She sat up straight, suddenly energized. "If Lynette was there to meet her lover, why didn't she light the fire? It was ready. I saw it. Surely that would have been more romantic than a smelly space heater on a wet, rainy day."

"Sarah, that doesn't mean anything." He rubbed the back of his neck, as if her persistence gave him a headache.

The more she thought, the more convinced she became. "It's something that doesn't fit. It has to mean something."

"No."

A wave of anger swept over her at his stubborn refusal to consider any other verdict. "There could have been another reason why they were at the cottage. Why are you so ready to believe that she betrayed you?" She caught his arm, and it was like iron under her fingers.

"Because." He turned toward her, his face harsh and forbidding. He had the look of a man goaded beyond all bearing. "Because two weeks before she died, Lynette confessed to me that she'd been having an affair."

NINE

Trent moved blindly, driven by the need to get away from Sarah. She'd made him reveal something he hadn't breathed to another soul, and for a moment he hated her for it.

His stride took him to the fireplace. He stopped, pressing his palms against the smooth pine mantel as if he'd push it right through the wall. He glared down at the fireplace. If they hadn't been near it, maybe Sarah would never have come up with this absurd theory.

Her soft steps sounded on the heart pine floor. She stopped a foot away from him, but he was so intensely aware of her presence that they might as well have been touching.

"I'm sorry."

"So am I." He spit out the words. Sorry you came here, Sarah. Sorry you brought it all back to life again.

"You have to tell me." Fear laced her words. "Did she say it was Miles?"

For a moment he wanted to say yes. To hurt her as she'd hurt him. To bring an end to this.

"No." He swallowed, his throat cramping at the effort it took. "No, she didn't. She refused to say who the man was."

"You asked her."

"Of course I asked her." He'd stormed at her. Shouted out his hurt. All the control he was so proud of had deserted him completely. "She wouldn't tell me. She said it was over. She wanted me to forgive her." He kicked at a log.

Sarah's face was white. She had herself under such rigid control that it was too painful for him to watch. "I see. Did you forgive her?"

She didn't have the right to ask that question. He didn't have to answer her.

"No." It shamed him, remembering that. "Maybe I would have, given enough time, but we didn't have time."

Sarah stared down as if looking for an answer there. "That still doesn't mean it was Miles."

He swung toward her, half-afraid of the anger that raced along his veins. "Why won't you leave it alone?"

"Because I can't." Her head came up, eyes defiant. "You have no proof the man was Miles."

The anger went out of him as suddenly as it had come. Sarah was groping like a hurt child for any other explanation. There wasn't one.

"Lynette had been having an affair." He tried to gentle his tone. "She and Miles died together at the cottage. What else are we to believe?"

Sarah's eyes were bright with tears she seemed determined not to shed. "I know. It's very convincing. The only thing I have to put against it is my instinct. Miles wouldn't."

"Sarah—" He wanted to help her, but he didn't know how. "Don't you think I felt the same way? You don't want to believe that his love for you wasn't strong enough—"

"That's not it." Her mouth twisted. "It's not what I think he felt. It's who I knew Miles to be. He'd have told me. He'd have done the honorable thing. That's who he was."

Miles had been a lucky man, to inspire that kind of trust. "People don't always live up to our image of them."

She shook her head stubbornly. Maybe that determined stubbornness was all that kept her going now.

"Look." He blew out an exasperated breath. "You tell me. What do you want? What can I do to convince you?"

"Give me the freedom to learn the truth." She said it so quickly that it was obviously the only thing on her mind. "You're the man with the power here. No one will talk to me as long as they think you don't want them to."

"You're giving me too much credit. People always talk."

"Not here." Her smile flickered. "You're the king of St. James, don't you know that?"

"Even if that's true—" He wanted to protect her, but she kept rejecting that protection. "You'll end up hurting more."

Her chin came up at that. "I'll take that risk."

She had courage—he had to say that for her.

"All right," he said finally. "I'll arrange for you to talk to anyone you want. But at the end of it—"

"I'll go away." She held out her hand, as if to seal the bargain. "I know that's what you want."

His hand closed over hers, and he felt the by-now-familiar surge of emotion. She was wrong. He didn't want her to go away. But he knew she would. She had to.

They had no choice. No matter what they might feel, tragedy and betrayal would always stand between them. It bound them together, and it set an impenetrable barrier between them. There was nothing they could do about that.

When you don't know what else to do, do the thing that's in front of you. That had been one of her grandmother's favorite maxims, speaking as it did to duty. Do the next thing.

In this case, the next thing was working a shift at the clinic. Sarah fastened the braid in her hair in and picked up her bag. She hadn't seen Trent since that painful conversation the previous evening, and that was probably for the best.

She'd get away from Land's End for a few hours. A little distance and time might help her view things with more detachment. Now she simply felt sore, as if her body as well as her spirit had been bruised.

She closed the door to the guest suite and started across the patio toward the garage. The sun was already hot, the air already humid. Summer could come early to the Low Country—it was already late May.

She heard the door to the house open and turned to see Geneva waving at her.

"Ms. Sarah, Mr. Donner wants to speak to you for a moment, if it's convenient."

She doubted very much that Trent had put it that politely. She resisted the urge to keep on walking. Apparently the next thing to do was another difficult conversation with Trent.

Cool air rushed to meet her as she stepped inside. Geneva closed the door quickly, as if to keep the humidity at bay.

"He's up in his study." Geneva gestured toward the staircase that rose toward the loft. "Please go up."

The staircase curved like a bird soaring in flight—a tribute to the skill of the builder. Like everything in Trent's house, it was perfectly designed for the space. No doubt he'd secured the best architect to prepare his sanctuary.

She went up slowly, running her hand along the smooth banister. She wasn't eager for another meeting with Trent.

Please, Lord, help us not to hurt each other again.

The door at the top of the stairs opened as she approached. Joanna Larson came out, her face tightening at the sight of Sarah.

"Go in. Please." She bit off the words. "He's expecting you." She turned and went quickly down the stairs, as if disassociating herself from this meeting.

Sarah pushed the door open. Trent sat behind a massive cherry desk. In the chair opposite, looking ill at ease, was the patrolman she'd seen at police headquarters. Bobby Whiting—one of the men who'd found Miles and Lynette.

"Come in." Trent's voice grated, and she could hear how much he hated this. "This shouldn't take long."

Whiting, galvanized at the sight of her, stumbled to his feet. He was lanky in a crumpled-looking uniform shirt and pants, and he ran one hand around his collar when he nodded to her, as if it had suddenly tightened.

"Miz Wainwright," he mumbled, then flushed to his prominent ears. "I mean, Dr. Wainwright."

She nodded to him and sent a questioning look at Trent. He frowned back at her.

"I didn't want you chasing around the island and getting into trouble looking for Whiting. He's here to answer any questions you have." He turned the frown on Whiting. "You understand. Answer truthfully."

Whiting nodded. "Yes, sir."

Apparently satisfied, Trent stalked across the office to the long window that overlooked the salt marsh. He stood staring out, hands clasped behind his back. But his hands gripped each other too tightly and his shoulders were too stiff to make the pose anything but pretense.

She took a breath, realizing she hadn't spoken since she'd entered the office. A chair had been placed a few feet from Whiting's, facing his, obviously for her. She crossed to it and sat down, stomach churning. She had what she'd wanted. Now what was she going to do with it?

She'd have to plunge in and hope Whiting could make things clearer. "Will you tell me what happened that day?"

He cleared his throat. "Yes, ma'am. Mr. Donner, he called to say his wife had taken a boat out and hadn't come back. We notified the Coast Guard and started the search." He darted a look at her. "You see, we have a reg'lar way we do that."

She nodded. Trent must have been frantic. Because she'd been in Savannah at the hospital, no one had even realized Miles was missing, too.

"Go on."

"Well, I took the chief in my boat, going along the marsh. It was raining off and on, chilly that day. Tide was going out, so it was chancy handling, but when we saw the dock, with the two boats tied up, we knew we'd done right."

She knew about the boat Miles had rented. He'd never done that before, but he could handle it. He'd summered at Cape Cod every year when he was growing up.

"We figured it was gonna be awkward." Whiting stared at his shoes. "We had to go in, though. And we found them."

She swallowed. "How did they look?" Had he seen anything the chief, in his hurry to whitewash the situation, hadn't?

"Miz Donner, she was toppled over on the sofa, like she'd been sitting there when the fumes got her. Mr. Wainwright lay on that hooked rug between the sofa and the fireplace. There was a mark on his forehead, like he'd hit the coffee table when he fell. They looked—" He stumbled over the word. "Well, we could tell it was carbon monoxide right away."

She knew how that looked. "What did you do first?"

"The chief told me to get the windows open. He was holding a handkerchief to his face whilst he looked at them. So I did."

"What else did you notice, in those first couple of minutes?"

He frowned, eyes becoming distant as if he pictured it again. "Miz Donner's bag lay on the floor. She had a notebook laying on the coffee table in front of her, with a pen next to it. The cap was off the pen."

Trent swung around abruptly. "I was never told that."

Whiting's eyes widened. "Sorry. I mean, the chief, he does all the talking for the department. Guess he figured it wasn't important." He stopped, obviously not knowing what to do when he was caught between the two authority figures in his life.

Sarah leaned forward, heart thumping. "Was anything written in the notebook?" The man had a good visual memory. If anything had been written—

He squeezed his eyes shut. "No, nothing. Seems like as if—" His eyes popped open again. "The notebook was one of them spiral-bound ones. There was some little bits of paper laying on the table, like somethin' had been tore out."

"Before you opened the windows or after?" Trent's question cracked like a whip.

Whiting looked confused.

"Did you notice the notebook and the bits of paper before the chief sent you to open the windows, or after?"

But there Whiting's memory failed him. He shook his head. "I don't know. I was pretty shook up—I never seen anything like that before."

No, he wouldn't have. Things like that didn't happen here.

"Did you find out what was wrong with the space heater?"

"Yes'm." He looked relieved to switch to a more technical subject. "There was a leak in the pipe. The gas would build up, and they probably didn't even know what was happening 'til they were too sleepy to do anything about it." He moved his shoulders restlessly. "Was something like that on the mainland, four, five years ago. Three young guys at a hunting cabin—all of them gone before they could get out."

Perhaps Miles had realized, in those final moments when Lynette toppled over. He'd tried to get up, falling against the coffee table as the fumes took him. She swallowed hard. The image would be there forever now.

"You're sure there wasn't anyone else around the island?"

"Anybody come by boat, they'd have tied up at the dock, wouldn't they?" He shrugged. "Well, anybody but ole Lizbet."

Something in her snapped to attention. "Who is Lizbet?"

"Lizbet Jackson." Trent supplied the name. "She's an elderly Gullah woman with the reputation of being a healer. She's all over the marshes in a dugout, looking for herbs."

"She could pull that boat of hers up on the bank most anyplace," Whiting said. "She likes Cat Isle, says some special kind of moss grows there. But I didn't see her that day."

It was someone to talk to, anyway. "Where can I find her?"

He shrugged. "She's got a little house, but often as not she sleeps out rough, or bunks in with some of her kin. She's probably related to half the islanders."

Esther might know her, if Esther felt cooperative.

"Anything else?" Trent's voice grated.

"Just one thing." She looked at him evenly. "Did Mr. Donner's influence close down the investigation?"

Trent's gaze locked with hers, but he growled at Whiting. "Answer her."

Whiting straightened. "No, ma'am. I guess I can see how you might think that, but we did our job. Only thing the chief did different was close out the reporters." His lips twitched slightly. "The chief, he don't mind seeing his picture in the papers. But not that time, he didn't. He knew Mr. Donner didn't want any more publicity than could be helped."

"That's all, Whiting." Trent sounded as if he'd had all he could take. "You can go now. I'll square it with the chief if he gives you any trouble over this."

"Yessir. Ma'am." Whiting retreated rapidly, thumping down the steps as if escaping.

Trent looked at her, his expression unreadable. "You're thinking suicide. What put that in your mind?"

She didn't want to hurt him, but the paper and pen had to mean something. "She was unhappy," she said quietly. "You and Melissa both agree on that."

"You think I pushed her to suicide."

"No, that's not what I meant." But was it so hard to believe? She'd confessed her sin to Trent, and he hadn't forgiven her.

"Where does Miles fit in, then?" His voice was hard with anger. "Aren't you forgetting him?"

"No, I'm not forgetting." She stood, facing him. They were hurting each other again, and they couldn't seem to stop. "I don't have the answers yet. I suppose he might, somehow, have learned what she intended and tried to stop her."

"That would be a nice out for you, wouldn't it?"

"I'm not looking for an out, Trent. Just for the truth."

"Believe me, if Lynette intended to kill herself, she'd have wanted me to know I was to blame. She'd have left a note."

"Maybe she did." She strode to the door. "Maybe you ought to ask your police chief about that."

She went out quickly, feeling the salt taste of tears on her face.

By the time Sarah arrived at the clinic, she had herself more or less under control. At least on the outside she did. Inside she felt bruised and battered. Each step she took seemed to hurt someone.

Hopefully she couldn't do too much damage at the

clinic. And if she could get some help in finding Lizbet Jackson, she'd be satisfied that she'd made one bit of progress today.

Signing in on the board, donning a lab coat, greeting the receptionist—all the normal, routine activities helped to stabilize her. In this setting, she knew who she was and what to do. Elsewhere on the island she might be the outsider, blundering from one morass to another, but here she was at home.

"I see you made it." Esther's greeting was short.

"As you see." She smiled, determined to be pleasant to the woman if it killed her. "Seems pretty quiet so far."

"You can leave if you like. Dr. Sam can handle things."

Her smile felt frozen. "I'll stay. Since we have a moment, I wanted to ask you something."

Esther waited, unresponsive.

"I'm looking for Lizbet Jackson. Do you know her?"

"Lizbet." Her brows lifted. "Why do you want to see her?"

She could hardly say it was none of Esther's business. "I'd like to talk with her."

"'Fraid I can't help you." She turned away, picking up a chart with an air of dismissal. "You'll have to play Lady Bountiful to someone else."

She walked away, leaving Sarah staring after her.

"You look as if someone just hit you, Sarah."

Dr. Sam stood behind her. It was a relief to see his welcoming smile.

"You're pretty close. All I did was ask Esther to help me find someone, and she bit my head off."

He propped an elbow on the counter. "Who are you looking for? Maybe I can help."

"Lizbet Jackson. Do you know her?"

"Everybody knows her." He grinned. "She's our competition, treating everything from rashes to broken hearts with her herbals."

"You know where she lives, then."

"She's got a little house behind the Old Ebenezer Church graveyard. You have to walk right through the cemetery to reach it. Trouble is, she claims she doesn't like sleeping under a roof. Drives her relatives crazy by disappearing into the woods for days at a time."

That didn't sound promising. "Maybe I could find the house and leave her a note."

He shook his head. "You know what the Gullah community is like—closed to outsiders unless you're brought in by someone. Esther wouldn't help?"

"No." Esther definitely wouldn't.

"Let me think. Maybe I can find someone who knows her."

"Thanks, Sam. I appreciate it. It seems everyone I want to talk to is elusive—Lizbet, Guy O'Hara—"

"Guy O'Hara?" He blinked. "I might not be much help with Lizbet, but I know where Guy O'Hara is."

She blinked, startled. "You do?"

"He's back in Exam Room 3, sleeping off a roaring drunk."

Guy, here. The reason startled her. "Does he do that often? He was a friend of Miles, and I never saw him drinking."

Sam shrugged. "He's gotten a lot worse in the past year. Donner fired him, shortly after—well, after you left the island. He's not sober much of the time, I can tell you that."

She glanced down the hallway. "Do you think he's sobered up enough that I can talk to him?"

"Let's find out." Sam shoved away from the counter and led the way down the hall. "Can't hurt to try."

But when he opened the exam room door, they were

greeted by noisy snores. Sam advanced on the figure curled up on the cot and shook his shoulder.

"O'Hara, wake up. Somebody's here to see you."

Guy opened one eye to peer blearily at them. He didn't show any sign of knowing her, and she wouldn't have recognized him if she'd run into him. The trim, cheerful man she'd known was lost in unhealthy blubber and unshaved cheeks.

"Guy." She raised her voice. "I'm Sarah Wainwright. Miles's wife. Remember me?"

He pushed himself up on one elbow. "Miles? Sure, I know Miles. My best buddy." He slumped back down again.

Sam shook his head. "Give him another hour or two to get the worst of the alcohol out of his system." He grimaced. "He'll just go out and get tanked up again as soon as he can."

Pity twisted her heart. "Has anyone tried to help him?"

"We sober him up, try to talk him into rehab or AA. He makes all the promises, but he never keeps them." Sam shrugged. "I'm not giving up on him, Sarah. You know AA saved my life, and I'm at a meeting every day. But like the old saying goes, nobody can help him if he doesn't want to be helped."

"I know." She patted Sam's hand. "It's good of you to keep trying." As a veteran of that particular war, Sam could reach Guy if anyone could.

"Miles." Guy turned over, mumbling something she couldn't hear. "Always wanted to be a hero," he said, voice slurring. "Find out who was doing Donner wrong."

"What do you mean?" Sarah shook him, but Guy just began to snore again.

"You won't get any sense out of him now." Sam gave her a curious look. "Give it a try at the end of your shift."

"I guess you're right." With a last look at the snoring figure, she followed Sam back out into the hallway.

The clinic's doors had opened for the day, and she was suddenly booked solid with one patient after another. It was good to be back in harness, forgetting everything that haunted her. She barely had time to take a breath until her shift was up. She finally went to Exam Room 3 to check on Guy.

The room was empty. Guy was gone and no one, it seemed, had any idea when he'd left or where he'd gone.

TEN

Sarah was still struggling with frustration after dinner that night. Fortunately there had been enough people around the table to let her to pursue her troubled thoughts in private.

She'd had Guy in her clinic, and he'd slipped through her fingers. The clinic didn't have an address for him—he'd been evicted from his apartment. His rapid deterioration in just one year was hard to accept. She'd checked at the bar, but the friendly bartender claimed Guy didn't come in anymore.

Now the meal was over. People began to scatter. She lingered in the hallway, longing to retire to her room, but not wanting to be impolite. The few things Guy had said weren't helpful—just references to Miles's friendship and to the actions that had brought Miles to Trent's attention.

The implication, both from Guy and from Dr. Sam, had been that Trent fired Guy because he'd been Miles's friend. Given the depth of Trent's bitterness, that seemed entirely possible.

Tinkling notes from the piano intruded on her thoughts. A big-band tune from the forties, played with a light touch. Not Melissa, certainly, so it must be Derek. Trent had gone off to his study with Robert Butler, and Melissa had wandered outside. Maybe this was her chance to talk with Derek privately.

He sat at the grand piano that still bore Lynette's stamp. A multicolored silk scarf was draped across its polished surface, and a crystal bowl filled with pink roses sat on the scarf. Everyone knew pink roses had been her favorite. Did Trent keep them there as a tribute to his wife? A separate small pain pierced her heart.

"Hi." The soft notes broke off when Derek spotted her. "How's it going?"

"Don't stop playing." She leaned against the piano, her back to the flowers. Still, their aroma taunted her. "I love those sentimental songs."

His fingers moved over the keys. "That means you're a romantic at heart."

She didn't reply to that, and after a moment Derek seemed to lose himself in the music. The casual observer would have said that he and Trent didn't look alike. Derek's hair was light brown where Trent's was dark—Derek's expression had a light touch of charm that was totally lacking in Trent's. Only a faint resemblance around the eyes identified their relationship.

Derek glanced up, smiling. "What are you worrying about, sweet Sarah?" he said.

Derek had a compliment for every woman he met. Still, the friendly tone encouraged her.

"Not worrying. *Frustrated* might be a better term."

"You're not finding what you're looking for, then."

"I suppose Trent told you all about it."

He shrugged. "Trent doesn't tell anyone everything, but I do know you're here to find out about Miles and Lynette."

The casual way he coupled the names pricked her. "Do you believe it was true that they were having an affair?"

The soft notes segued almost imperceptibly into a love song. "Not before it happened, no. Afterward—" He shrugged eloquently "—what else could I think, given the way Trent acted?"

She leaned forward, her palm pressing against the smooth lacquer. "But you were around them a lot. You didn't ever notice any attraction between them?"

"No. But they'd have been careful."

It was all so amorphous. How did one prove a negative?

He hit a dissonant chord. "I did see that Lynette was unhappy. Still, she was like that—on top of the world one day, down in the depths the next. Artistic temperament."

She glanced at his fingers on the keys. "You're a musician. Do you claim that, too?"

"I'm not a musician the way Lynette was." For the first time, emotion sounded in Derek's light voice. "She could have been at the top, if she hadn't thrown it away to marry Trent."

She considered that. Could anyone, however talented, ever get to the top of any field without total commitment? She doubted it, but it didn't seem wise to say so to Derek.

"Did she wish she'd made another choice?"

He shrugged. "She was unhappy sometimes. That's all I know. Now her daughter is the unhappy one."

"And Trent?"

He tilted his head, considering. "I'd have said his feeling is more anger. Bitterness. Well, you've seen him."

"Yes." Pain clutched her heart.

"Poor Sarah." His fingers touched sad chords. "You want to heal the whole world, don't you? You can't heal Trent."

"Nor anyone else, it seems." Her mind flickered to Guy, lost in an alcoholic fog. "I saw Guy O'Hara today."

He played a few notes of a drinking song. "Was he sober?"

"No." Her fingers clenched, brushing the silk fringe.

"He seldom is, they say."

"I wanted to ask him some questions, but he walked out of the clinic. Have you talked to him lately?"

He shook his head. "He wouldn't talk to me. He's still angry at Trent for firing him."

She thought again of what Dr. Sam had said—that shortly after Miles's death, Trent had fired Guy. "Did Trent fire Guy because he was Miles's friend?"

"You said it, I didn't." He gave her a serious look. "I'd help you if I could, Sarah, but my loyalty has to be to Trent."

There it was again. Everyone's loyalty was to Trent, it seemed. "I know he's your brother—"

"Half brother. Same mother, different fathers."

"Half brother. It's surely not disloyal to him if you talk to me. You knew Lynette, you knew Miles, you know all about the business."

"Where does the business come into it?"

"Nowhere, I suppose. But Guy was rambling something about Miles wanting to be a hero in Trent's eyes."

"Oh, that. He used to tease Miles that Trent thought he was a hero because he uncovered that trouble at the Atlanta office. Miles was valuable to Trent, but I never understood exactly what he did." Derek gave her that charming smile. "Everyone knows that my title at Donner Enterprises is just an excuse for Trent to support me. That's all I can tell you."

That was all he was willing to tell her, and it led exactly nowhere, like everything else she'd tried.

Trent came down the stairs from the loft and paused, letting Robert go ahead of him. Derek and Sarah were at the piano, heads together like a pair of conspirators.

He wasn't worried about anything Derek might say. His brother might not always have good judgment, but he was loyal.

Frowning, he went the rest of the way down, noting the faint alteration in Sarah's expression when she saw him. Wariness.

Fair enough. That was what he felt for her. They both had reason to know how much they could hurt each other.

As if aware of his gaze on her, Sarah moved away from the piano. She drifted toward Robert Butler, engaging him in a low-voiced conversation.

Trent had some faint hope that letting her talk with Bobby Whiting would satisfy her need to know. Clearly it hadn't. He approached them.

"…if you could put me in touch with Lizbet Jackson."

Robert, caught off guard, clearly didn't know how to answer. He glanced at Trent, raising an eyebrow.

"You may as well help her, Robert. She'll only get into trouble trying to find the woman on her own if you don't."

Sarah shot him an annoyed glance, but she didn't speak, probably because she didn't want him to withdraw the permission.

Robert nodded. "I'll try to set up a meeting for you with Lizbet, but I'm not sure how much good it will do."

"Because she'd have come forward by this time if she knew anything?" Sarah asked.

"Actually, I was thinking that she might not cooperate. Lizbet lives by rules of her own that other people don't always understand. Still, I'll do my best."

"Thank you." Sarah clasped his hand.

He glanced at Trent. "If you don't need me, I'll drive out to the north end and see if I can locate her."

"Fine." He hoped he didn't sound as abrupt as he felt. There seemed no end to the paths Sarah wanted to follow, but none of them would lead to happiness.

Robert walked away.

Sarah swung toward him, her expression antagonistic. He'd cooperated, hadn't he? What else did she want?

"Did you fire Guy O'Hara because he was Miles's friend?" The condemnation in her green eyes told him she'd already decided that was true.

He glanced over her shoulder at Derek, tinkering with a tune on the piano but obviously listening with all his might. He took Sarah firmly by the elbow.

"Let's get some air."

She didn't make any protest as he led her out the French doors and onto the veranda. Once they'd moved a safe distance from the open doors, he turned to face her.

The moonlight touched her face, exposing the impatient frown that creased her forehead. "Well?"

"I fired O'Hara because he was an unreliable alcoholic who wouldn't get the help he needed. The only reason I kept him as long as I did was because Miles covered for him."

Her expression turned uncertain. "He did?"

"Yes. You didn't know that?"

"No. I didn't." Something lost showed in her eyes, wringing his heart unexpectedly. "I thought I knew all about Miles's friends, but he didn't tell me that."

He shifted, unsure what to say. "Maybe he didn't think it was important. Or he didn't think you'd approve."

She winced. "I suppose so."

"Have you talked to O'Hara?"

"Briefly." She seemed to censor her words. "He didn't have anything helpful to say."

"I don't suppose he would."

Sarah turned, leaning against the railing to look out over the strip of pale, glistening sand to the ocean beyond. "I thought he might remember something."

"What could he remember?" He stood next to her. Moonlight traced a silvery path along the water, but like so many things, it wasn't real. On either side of that illusory path, dark water moved restlessly, hiding what lay beneath.

"I don't know." The sleeve of her soft sweater brushed his arm. "Something. Surely if Lynette and Miles were involved, someone saw something. Knew something."

"They were discreet. They'd have to be." He heard the grimness in his tone.

"Even so—" She let that drop and looked up at him, her hair falling away from her face and exposing the vulnerable line of her throat. "Did you talk to Gifford?"

"Yes." He bit off the word. But she deserved more than that, didn't she? "He swears there was no note. The notebook had nothing written in it, just a few pages torn out."

"You believe him."

"I don't have any reason not to. He wouldn't lie to me."

"I suppose not." She still didn't sound convinced.

"Sarah, you're twisting everything to suit your own theory. Don't you suppose if there was any evidence of something other than an affair, I'd jump at it?"

"I don't know." Pain twisted her words. "I just know I have to look at every possibility. And you won't."

Her pain caught at him sharply. He clasped her hands in his, feeling that instant connection and knowing that she felt it, too.

"Sarah—" Almost without thought he drew her closer.

Her eyes wide and dark, she swayed toward him.

"No!"

The sharp cry had them both spinning toward the steps. Melissa stood there, staring at them, her face an angry, accusing mask.

"Melissa—" He took a step toward her.

"I saw you. I saw you standing like that before—at Adriana's party last year. You thought no one saw you, but I did."

"It didn't mean anything." Strain tightened Sarah's voice.

"You're the reason my mother was unhappy." She flung the words at Sarah like a missile. "I hate you."

She whirled and ran into the house.

Sarah's breath caught on a sob. "I should go after her."

"No." He came to his senses then and knew it was the worst thing they could do. "Leave it alone, Sarah. We've done enough damage already. Just leave my daughter alone."

If she wasn't lost, she soon would be. Sarah drove down a narrow road the next night, trying to follow the directions Robert Butler had given her. He'd said Lizbet's house would be difficult to find, and he was right.

Robert had set up a meeting for nine o'clock, when Lizbet had promised to be at her house waiting. Sarah had left Land's End early, knowing nothing on the island was easy to find at night. Houses and shops hid in the darkness behind the lush vegetation that always seemed about to overwhelm them.

She'd turned off the main road onto one of the many narrow lanes that wound through the maritime forest. No big houses or swimming pools at this end of the island. Once in a while the trees grudgingly gave way to a clearing with a small house or a barn and a few cultivated acres. Otherwise all she could see was the thick growth of pines and the live oaks draped with Spanish moss, reflecting silvery green and ghostlike from her headlights.

Depression blossomed in a place like this, in the gathering dusk, and it had come all too easily after Miles's death. What was she doing on such a fruitless quest? Just because Bobby Whiting had said Lizbet went to Cat Isle to gather her moss, that didn't mean she'd seen anything.

She forced herself to repel the gloomy thoughts. They'd debilitate her if she let them, sapping her strength and her determination. She had to go on. She'd caused so much trouble already that anything was better than not knowing.

Trouble for herself, for Trent, for Melissa. The thought of the girl's sensitive face, twisted with grief and anger, tore at her heart. If Trent had let her talk to Melissa—

But what could she have said? Melissa had seen them and had recognized instinctively the attraction that surged between them. They hadn't acted on the attraction, but they'd felt it, and Melissa had known.

It's all so tangled, Lord. I hope Melissa was mistaken, that I didn't cause her mother's sorrow, but how can I know? If Lynette sensed something, too…

And that was yet another burden of grief and guilt. Rationally she might know that she hadn't done anything wrong, but somehow that didn't ease the weight.

The road narrowed yet again, so that the forest pressed menacingly, ready to swallow the slight strip of sand and gravel with a single gulp. Spanish moss slapped against her windshield, fragments breaking off and clinging as if they'd attach to the car as they did to the oaks.

She had to be lost. Somewhere, at one of the many small turnings that she'd thought were driveways, she'd missed the main road and driven herself deep into the forest.

Father, I'm lost. I don't know what to do. Let me see Your path before me.

The road, always erratic, seemed to peter out entirely. A small deer bounded in front of her, and she slammed on the brakes, heart pounding. The deer leapt on without a backward glance. She clutched the wheel, letting her pulse slow. If she had an accident here, would anyone find her?

At least people knew where she'd gone—or where she'd

been attempting to go. After the anger Trent had shown when she'd gone to the storage locker without telling anyone, she'd taken the precaution of making sure Geneva knew about tonight's excursion.

Now there was nothing in her headlight beams but tall grass. No road. She'd have to turn around and go back, hoping to find someone who could tell her where she'd gone wrong. She drew forward into the grass, turning the wheel.

Something reflected whitely when the headlight hit it. A gravestone. She wasn't lost after all. She'd found the cemetery.

She parked and got out slowly, gripping the flashlight Robert had advised her to bring. How right he'd been. And luckily she'd worn sturdy shoes and long pants for the trek through the cemetery. But where was the house?

She'd only taken a few steps when she spotted it—a black rectangle against a darkening sky. One window showed a feeble yellow gleam, but that was the only sign of life.

Shining her flashlight on the tall grass, she started cautiously forward. It was really a pity that she was such a city girl at heart.

Evening hadn't brought much coolness to the air once she'd gotten away from the shore. It clung to her, heavy and oppressive, as if she wore a wet wool blanket. Her hair stuck to her neck, and she swatted at a mosquito that attempted to dive-bomb her arm.

A tall monument reared itself skyward on her right, topped with a weeping angel. Her light picked out the lettering, worn shallow by years of weathering. Rufus Allen, 1801–1889. Rufus had had a long life.

A sweep of the torch showed her a wife buried on either side of him, their tombstones suitably smaller. In front was a row of four small stones, each holding a stone lamb. Her heart clenched. Infant mortality rates had improved over the years, thank the Lord.

Rufus's tombstone would be a good marker to the car on her way back. She was half tempted to leave the headlights on, but it was senseless to risk a dead battery. Her eyes already grew accustomed to the dark.

She went on, the damp grass brushing her legs, swinging the torchlight ahead of her. She tried to cut in a straight line toward the house, but the tombstones were set in nothing that resembled straight rows. Her light touched one with a rounded top, moss-covered, the lettering worn to oblivion—one of the oldest ones, probably. The Ebenezer graveyard had been here since the earliest settlement on the island. In fact, it was probably the graveyard of Robert's folktale.

Like Robert, she was a good Christian who didn't believe ghost stories. Nevertheless, there was something a bit uncanny about walking through the deserted cemetery alone at night.

Not that the cemetery was entirely deserted. The night was alive with chirpings, whisperings, the cries of night creatures she couldn't possibly identify. *City girl*, she thought again.

Something sounded near her that was uncommonly like a human footfall. She spun around, her heart in her throat, holding the flashlight like a weapon.

A raccoon stared solemnly back at her, his masked eyes oddly menacing. She gave a shaky laugh.

"Am I trespassing on your territory? I'll soon be gone."

He turned his tail to her, apparently unimpressed.

Ridiculous, for her heart to be thumping this way. She was only yards from the house now. She should call out to let Lizbet Jackson know she was coming, so she wouldn't startle her.

Even as she formed the thought, the shrill yapping of dogs assaulted her ears. The barking accompanied a metallic sound, as if the dogs leaped against a fence or pen. She half expected to see a door open, hear a voice call out, but nothing happened except that the dogs' clamor grew even louder.

A shiver went down her spine. They sounded positively frantic, menacing, as if they'd burst through the fence and attack her for daring to come near.

I'm not afraid. Well, I am, but You are with me.

Another rustle sounded behind her. The raccoon was nothing if not persistent. He must think a human was a source of food. She turned. She'd yell at it, scare it away—

The darkness was cleft by movement. She barely saw a dark figure, the shape of a heavy branch coming at her, barely heard the hoarse intake of breath. Then the branch hit, pain exploding in her shoulder and arm, sending her staggering, stumbling, falling into darkness.

ELEVEN

Her mind couldn't comprehend what had happened, but her body worked on instinct, sending her rolling away from another blow that could have killed—but he was on her, so close, the branch swinging upward to plummet down again in its deadly arc.

Without thinking she struck out with the only weapon she had—the heavy flashlight. If she could intercept the blow… The branch struck the flashlight and she heard the cylinder shatter in the same instant that the lights went out, leaving her alone in the dark with someone who wanted to hurt her, maybe even kill her.

Her vivid imagination presented her with an image of the heavy branch crashing into her skull, shattering bone as readily as it had metal and glass. A wave of terror ricocheted through her, setting every nerve vibrating. No one who was intent on robbery or rape would stage so violent an attack.

Think. She had to stop acting on instinct. He was as trapped by the darkness as she was. Unless—a second ticked by, then another. No light came on. Either he didn't have a flashlight or he was unwilling to turn it on.

A separate thrill of fear went through her. She must not see her attacker, for fear she might recognize him.

Listen. The night sounds that had filled the cemetery as she walked had ceased, shut off by the murderous presence. Even the dogs had gone quiet, as if they didn't want to draw attention to themselves.

She held her breath. Swish. Swish. She knew what he did, as surely as if she could see him.

He swung the branch in a wide arc through the grass, searching for her. The sound increased. He was drawing nearer. If she didn't move quickly, he'd be on her.

She forced her legs to move, to creep backward through the grass, every movement a separate chance for him to hear her. *Please.* Her mind sobbed a prayer. *Be with me now. Hide me.*

The tall grass closed around her. Before it had been a danger; now it was a sanctuary. The human menace terrified her far more than any night creature could.

She flattened herself to the ground. When she looked up, the grass around her made a tunnel through which she saw the sky. Full dark now, thank the Lord. Dense clouds covered the moon. She hadn't even noticed when she'd had the flashlight on. Her ignorance could kill her if she weren't careful.

Freeze, listen. Pretend you're one of the marsh creatures— a rabbit hiding in the shadows from a hawk. The swish-swish sounded ever nearer, methodical as death's scythe. He searched for her, making ever-widening circles. If she screamed—

If she screamed, Lizbet would hear, but what could she do? She didn't have a phone, and Sarah's spirit cringed away from the thought of bringing the elderly woman out into danger.

She couldn't. But he was coming closer. He'd find her.

Her heart pounded so loud that he must hear it. She'd let panic take over, freezing her to the feeble shelter of the grass. The grass wouldn't protect her from the force of a blow. She couldn't wait for him to find her. Wait to die.

Die. The word galvanized her, sending adrenaline pounding. She had to move. This wasn't an attempt to frighten her, as shutting her in the storage locker might have been. If she hadn't turned when she did, thanks to the raccoon, that first blow would have landed on her skull. Even now her left shoulder throbbed from the glancing strike.

She moved her fingers cautiously, feeling pins and needles. At least they moved. Her arm—she realized she'd been holding it clamped against her side. She flexed it, sending pain radiating. Nothing broken, she didn't think, but useless in a fight.

Silently she crept backward, always keeping the sound of his approach in front of her—an atavistic impulse not to turn her back on the enemy. *Please, God, please, God.*

Her foot hit something. Hard. Stone. One of the gravestones. She crept into its denser shadow. She was suddenly a child of eight or nine, playing hide-and-seek on a summer night, searching out the deepest shadows, knowing her pale hair would give her away in the slightest glimmer of light.

And on the thought, the moon came from behind the cloud, etching the graveyard in silver and black, a living scene with all the color leached out of it. She could see the figure now, a black bulk, face masked with something dark, too shrouded to betray even its sex. He was closer than she'd hoped. She couldn't stay, but she couldn't move—

Her foot hit something that clattered, obscenely shattering the silence—a metal vase that clanked against the stone and sent the black figure whirling toward her.

No hiding now. Run.

She scrambled to her feet, running desperately in the direction she thought the car was. She could scream now, but she sobbed for breath. Save the breath for running. A step lost could mean he caught her.

She had a head start. If she could get to the car, get inside, lock it, she'd be safe. Had she locked the doors? She didn't remember. She glanced up, frantic to locate the car.

The moment's inattention cost her dearly. She stumbled, felt the ground rushing at her, caught herself, stumbled on, but he was closer. She could hear him, could practically feel his breath. She wasn't going to make it; he was going to catch her—

Someone turned off the lights.

The moon went behind a cloud, the darkness swept down to cover her. In that last instant of moonlight she'd seen it—the tall monument with the weeping angel atop. Without thinking, she dove for its shelter, clutching cold stone like a savior.

He hideth my soul in the cleft of the rock.

She caught her breath. She couldn't see him, but she could hear him. He'd gone back to swishing the branch through the grass, coming nearer. She mentally measured the distance to the car, clinging to the rock, reluctant to let go. To run, exposing herself again in a last perilous flight.

But already the blessed darkness thinned. The clouds moved on, driven by an impersonal wind. In another moment it would be bright again. She had to move now.

Please.

She plunged toward the car, seeing chrome gleam as the moon came out, hearing him behind her, praying the door was unlocked, stumbling, fingers connecting with metal, fumbling for the handle, feeling it swing open.

Thank You, Lord, that it wasn't locked.

Diving into the seat, slamming the door, locking it. The dark figure soared toward the car, raising the branch, ready to shatter windows to get at her.

Look at the ignition, not at him, force the key in, turn it.

The motor roared, the sweetest sound she'd ever heard. She stamped on the gas and saw the attacker lurch backward as she rocketed past.

Trent paced from one end of the formal living room to the other. If he wanted to walk, he could do it more effectively outside, but the advantage of the living room was that he'd see Sarah when she returned.

It wasn't that he believed her visit to Lizbet Jackson would resolve anything. If the woman had anything to tell, she'd long since have done so. Still, for his own sake, he had to keep tabs on Sarah's investigation.

That was all it was—the need to keep Sarah under control. He certainly wasn't motivated by personal interest. If he told himself that often enough, he might begin to believe it.

Headlights pierced the darkness, and he moved closer to the window to watch the car pull up. He frowned. Odd, that she was leaving her car in front. Normally she pulled around to the garage. A breath of apprehension touched his skin.

She stumbled out of the car, and apprehension vanished in a wave of panic that propelled him to the door. She was disheveled, dirty, limping. As he flew down the steps he saw that she held her left arm close against her side.

"What is it? What's happened?" He reached for her. She seemed to sag, as if her feet could carry her no farther.

"Sorry," she murmured, stumbling against him.

"You're hurt." He scooped her into his arms. Time enough for questions later—right now he had to take care of her.

In a few steps they were inside, and he kicked the door closed behind him. "Geneva!"

His shout brought the housekeeper running from the kitchen. Not surprising. He didn't think he'd shouted in this house more than two or three times. That wasn't his style, but his fear for Sarah overwhelmed other considerations.

"Dear Lord, what's happened to the child?" Geneva's words were as much a prayer as a question. "Here, bring her into the family room where she can be comfortable."

"Call Dr. Sam. Tell him to get here now." He strode back toward the family room as Geneva rushed to the telephone.

Sarah stirred in protest at that. "You don't have to bring Dr. Sam rushing here at this time of night. I'm fine."

He lowered her gently to the sofa. "Of course you are," he agreed. "Just because you're white as a sheet and you seem to have broken your arm, that doesn't mean anything is wrong."

"It's not broken." She moved, searching for comfort, he supposed, and winced, cradling her arm against her.

"You're the doctor. I'll have to take your word for that." He slid a cushion under her arm, moving it slowly, alert for any sign that he caused her pain. "Is that better?"

She leaned back, sighing. "Better." Her eyes closed for a moment, the curve of her lashes dark against her pale skin. "I don't need Dr. Sam."

"You're getting him anyway," he snapped. If a more stubborn woman existed on the face of the earth, he had yet to meet her. "Tell me what we can do to make you comfortable. Do you want aspirin? An ice bag?"

He thought she'd argue, but she didn't. "Ice would help. Not the aspirin—Dr. Sam might have other ideas."

"Geneva—" He raised his voice, and she appeared in the doorway, clutching something wrapped in a kitchen towel.

"Dr. Sam's on his way. I brought an ice bag for Sarah's shoulder."

"You're way ahead of us." He put his arm around Sarah to lift her so Geneva could slip the ice bag into place. "What about some of that herbal tea you foist on people for everything from headaches to hives?"

"Coming right up." She bustled out.

"She doesn't have to go to any trouble."

He pulled the ottoman over so that he could sit next to Sarah. "There's nothing Geneva likes better than taking care of someone. Let her enjoy it."

She nodded, eyes closing again, as if even the slightest effort exhausted her. She turned her head against the pillow and he saw the bruise, extending from her neck to disappear under her shirt at her left shoulder.

The passion he felt to smash whoever had done this shocked him. "What happened?" It took an effort to keep his voice low.

"I was going through the cemetery toward Lizbet's house. Someone attacked me."

Fury pounded along his nerves. "Did he take your bag?" Sudden fear washed over him. "What did he do to you?"

"He wasn't trying to rob me. Or rape me." A shudder went through her. "He swung at my head with a heavy branch. If he'd connected, I wouldn't be here."

He grappled to get his mind around it. "You're saying someone tried to kill you."

"I don't know what he intended, but that's what would have happened. No warning. Just a blow coming out of nowhere. If I hadn't turned at that moment—"

The phone was on the end table. He grabbed it, hitting the button for Chief Gifford.

Gifford picked up almost immediately, and Trent cut through the man's pleasantries.

"Dr. Wainwright was attacked tonight out at the old Ebenezer cemetery. Get some men out there now. I want to know who did this." He turned away from the squawking phone to look at Sarah. "What about Lizbet? Was there any sign of her?"

Her green eyes darkened until they were almost black. "I never saw her. Do you think he'd attacked her first?" She started to move, and he pushed her gently back down.

"Have them check on Lizbet Jackson. She was supposed to meet Dr. Wainwright. Get back to me immediately." He clicked off while Gifford was still assuring him he'd take care of it.

He turned to Sarah, covering her hand with his. "Tell me the rest, before we have everyone here. Did he run away?"

She shook her head, pupils still dilated with what he realized was shock. "He chased me. Through the cemetery." She swallowed, the muscles in her neck working. "If it hadn't been so dark, I'd never have gotten back to the car—" She stopped.

He reached out to touch her face gently and realized that his hand was shaking. Now was not the moment to pour out his shock and horror. "It's all right. You're safe now."

She met his eyes, and he cradled her cheek in his hand. He wanted to do more—to draw her close against him and protect her from anything in the world that might harm her.

But Sarah, in spite of her current state, was no princess in a tower. She didn't want to be protected. She wanted to be part of the fight.

"Sarah—" But what could he say? He didn't have any rights where Sarah was concerned. He didn't want any, did he?

"Now, you just drink this." Geneva hurried in with a steaming mug. "It's hot, and it'll do you good."

He used her fussing over Sarah as an excuse to get a safe distance away. The doorbell rang.

"That'll be Dr. Sam. I'll let him in."

* * *

"She'll be fine." Dr. Sam rose from his position next to Sarah as Trent entered the family room a half hour later.

"You're sure she shouldn't have that shoulder X-rayed?" He couldn't quite get all the worry out of his voice.

Dr. Sam stretched and cocked an eyebrow at Sarah. "Permission to discuss your case, Doctor?"

Sarah's face relaxed for the first time since she'd stumbled out of the car. "Tell him I'm all right."

"I wouldn't go that far." Dr. Sam's face sobered as he turned to Trent. "It's just a good thing—well, never mind. Torn ligaments, bruising, scrapes. All of that will heal, but I want that left arm to stay in a sling for a few days, at least."

Sarah looked rebellious, but she nodded.

"I've given Sarah some medication for the pain and swelling. Make sure she takes it."

Trent nodded, relief moving through him. Sarah would be all right. "I'll sic Geneva on her if she doesn't behave."

Now the job was to catch the person who'd done this to her. The man would regret this night for a long time.

Sam picked up his jacket, and Trent clapped him on the shoulder. "Thanks, Dr. Sam. I'll walk you out."

When they reached the door, Gifford was strutting up the steps. Dr. Sam's face tightened. "I'll say good night." He skirted Gifford and headed for his car.

Trent focused on Gifford. "Well?" He held the door, ushering him into the hallway. "Did you find him?"

Gifford shrugged. "If anybody was there, he was long gone by the time my people got there."

"If?" He invested the word with the full force of his anger. "*If* you had seen Dr. Wainwright when she came in, you wouldn't doubt that."

The chief might not be the sharpest knife in the drawer, but he caught a whiff of the anger. "Sorry. Didn't mean I doubted the lady's word. Just a figger of speech, y'know."

Trent jerked a nod toward the family room. "In here. You'd better talk to her yourself."

He might think Sarah shouldn't be bothered with this tonight, but he knew she wouldn't agree. Any attempt to soften things for her just made her fighting mad.

She pushed herself up as they went in, and he understood. She didn't want to appear weak before Gifford.

"They didn't find the man," he said quickly.

"What about Mrs. Jackson?" Apprehension colored her eyes.

Gifford took off his hat belatedly and turned it in his beefy hands. "Well, Lizbet wasn't there. The dogs had been fed, everything looked okay, but there was no sign of her."

"You've started inquiries of the neighbors?" Trent said sharply, making it more an order than a question.

"Yessir. Trouble is, nobody's house overlooks hers, so there's no one to say she's come or gone 'cept the folks in the graveyard, and they're not talking."

When his attempt at humor didn't raise a smile, his look soured. "Anyhow, I've got my people trying to trace her down. She's got kin all over these islands, and if she wants to disappear, ain't nobody gonna find her."

"Did you find any trace of the man?" Sarah adjusted the sling as if it bothered her.

He tensed, waiting for Gifford to imply this had been a figment of Sarah's imagination, but Gifford just shook his head.

"Lots of grass trampled down in the cemetery—that was about it. We could see where your car had been parked, but no other trace. He'd be smart enough to leave it on the gravel."

"It had to be beyond the house, then. I'd have noticed a car if I'd passed one."

"We'll look in the morning. Could be we'll find something by daylight. You got a description of this fella, Doc?"

"I never saw his face. I'm not even sure it was a man."

"To do that much damage to your shoulder—" Trent began.

"Plenty of women wield a tennis racket hard enough to do that," she said. "My impression is that it was a man. Dark clothes, something dark over his head and face."

Gifford shook his head disapprovingly. "Not much to go on. That's not what we'd call the most salubrious part of the island." He produced the word with a humorless smile. "Seems like you'd have better sense than to go out there after dark."

Sarah's mouth tightened into a thin line. "I had an appointment. Are you saying it's my fault?"

"No, ma'am. I just figure—"

Trent caught Gifford by the arm, silencing him with a look. They didn't need to know what Gifford figured. "Thank you, Chief. Check in with me first thing in the morning, please."

Gifford nodded to Sarah and then lumbered to the door. "Will do. 'Night."

Trent waited until the door had closed behind him before he turned to Sarah. She was looking at him disapprovingly.

"I suppose you agree with your pet police chief. This is my fault for being in the wrong place at the wrong time."

Actually, he was relieved at the snappish tone in her voice. The encounter with Gifford had banished the shock from her eyes, and a little color had come back into her cheeks.

"Strange though it may seem to you, I'm on your side."

He sat down on the hassock. That was as close to her as he intended to get for the moment, or he might give in to the temptation to tell her how worried about her he'd been.

She shook her head and winced at the movement. "I don't understand why you don't see this situation the way I do. If Miles and Lynette were having an affair, why would someone be so eager to keep me from talking to Lizbet, they'd try to kill me?"

He couldn't let himself agree with her, even though the same questions were ricocheting around his brain. "I know how serious this was, but it's possible the attacker didn't intend to hurt you so badly. He may have miscalculated the damage the branch could do."

"If he just wanted to frighten me, he didn't need to keep coming after me." The fear was back in her eyes again, and he wanted to kick himself.

"I don't have the answers." He wrapped his hands warmly over hers. "But we'll get to the bottom of it. We'll find Lizbet, we'll get answers. I promise you."

That brought the faintest suggestion of relief to her face. "Thank you."

He wanted to tell Sarah this couldn't be what she thought, that her suppositions were ridiculous. But somehow he couldn't. Because what if she were right?

TWELVE

Sarah knew what she'd prescribe for a patient in this condition, but she wouldn't spend the day in bed. She frowned in the mirror and adjusted the silk scarf she'd arranged over Dr. Sam's canvas sling. Not beautiful, but it would have to do.

When she'd first looked in the mirror this morning, she'd been appalled at the gaunt, shadowed face that stared back at her. Just the sight had been enough to start her shaking, reliving that terrible race through the cemetery.

The discreet application of makeup had improved matters, and she could face the world without frightening little children. She had a shift at the hospital, and she intended to do it, even if she did look more like a victim than a doctor.

Slinging her bag awkwardly on her right shoulder, she managed to get the door locked and headed for the breakfast room. Geneva had made a valiant attempt to bring her breakfast in bed, but she'd managed to forestall that. It would only remind her of how helpless she'd felt the night before.

The only person in the room was Melissa. She checked on the doorstep, wondering if she were letting herself in for a repetition of Melissa's accusations. But the child stared at the sling, a shadow of fear in her eyes.

"Good morning." Sarah headed for the coffee. If Melissa didn't want to talk, she wouldn't press it.

Melissa slid off her chair, and she thought she was going to run out of the room. Instead, she came to Sarah and took the cup out of her hand.

"I'll get your coffee for you. And your breakfast. Do you want scrambled eggs?"

"Thanks—that would be great." And quite a turnaround.

Melissa deftly fixed a plate with eggs, toast and fresh fruit, then carried it and the coffee to the small round table where Sarah sat. Beyond the table, the French doors gave a view of the swimming pool, its water sparkling in the morning sun.

"There. Anything else you want?"

"That's fine, thanks."

Melissa hesitated for a moment and then slid onto the chair opposite hers. "Does your arm hurt much?"

"Not too much," she fibbed. She'd skipped the painkillers. She couldn't function at the clinic with them in her system.

"Geneva said you were really brave. She said you fought off the man who attacked you."

That trace of hero worship in Melissa's tone probably explained her changed attitude. "Mostly I hid and ran, but that's nice of Geneva to say."

"Were you awfully scared?" Her eyes were wide, and Sarah sensed something—she wasn't sure what—behind the questions.

"Yes." She didn't have to think twice about that. "I knew I had to keep running. And keep praying."

Melissa glanced at the display of photos on the wall opposite her—pictures of Melissa at various stages, a younger Trent proudly holding his baby daughter, a studio portrait of Lynette. That portrait was what held Melissa's gaze.

"My mother hated cemeteries," she said suddenly. "Dad wanted her to go to where his grandparents are buried, but she wouldn't. He goes by himself, every year on Memorial Day."

She censored a number of responses. "Some people feel that way about cemeteries. Now that you're old enough, you could go with your father. He'd probably like that."

Melissa looked startled at the idea. "I guess." She glanced at Sarah, then back at the picture of her mother. "My mother was really beautiful, wasn't she?"

"Yes. Very." She could say that without reservation, relieved that Melissa seemed to have eased up on blaming her for Lynette's unhappiness.

"I wish I looked more like her." She tugged at a lock of brown hair, as if wanting to turn it red.

What did she say to that? Melissa would see through insincere flattery.

"I think you look like your father. Sometimes girls do."

Melissa's gaze jerked back to hers. She stared at her for a long moment. Then she shoved her chair back.

"No! I don't!" She almost shouted the words, and she turned and ran out of the room.

Sarah stared after her blankly. That hadn't gone well. What on earth had she said to provoke an outburst?

She'd just been feeling relieved that her relationship with Melissa was improving. Obviously she'd been wrong.

She forked Geneva's perfect scrambled eggs into her mouth, trying to concentrate on the breakfast rather than Melissa. She'd be better off to avoid the Donner family.

But that plan proved destined to failure when she went out the front door and nearly ran into Trent coming up the steps. *Ran* was the operative word, since he wore shorts, T-shirt and sneakers, and had clearly been jogging on the beach.

He caught her good arm. "Whoa. Where are you going?"

Battle ahead, she decided. "To the clinic. I'm on duty."

"Dr. Sam said you were supposed to take it easy." He frowned, tightening his grip.

"Trust me, they won't let me do too much." She met his gaze. They stood so close that she could see the tiny fan of lines at the corners of his eyes, the slight beads of perspiration on his forehead. "I have to go. If I sit here and do nothing, I—I'll think too much."

That was probably the one thing she could have said that he'd understand. He nodded reluctantly.

"All right. But you're not driving with that shoulder. Give me five minutes to change, and I'll take you."

"That's not necessary."

He raised his eyebrows. "It's the only way you're getting out of here. I still have the keys to your car after putting it away last night. I won't give them back until Dr. Sam says so."

Pick your battles, she reminded herself, and much as she hated to admit it, he was probably right. She shouldn't drive in this condition.

"All right. Five minutes."

When he'd vanished into the house, she walked across to the railing. Ahead of her the low dunes rolled down to the beach. The tide was out, and pale sand stretched invitingly. No wonder Trent had wanted to jog this morning. She'd be tempted herself, if every inch of her body hadn't been in protest mode at the very thought of moving.

The breeze off the ocean lifted her hair, carrying the salty tang that would have told her she was at the ocean if she'd been blindfolded. This view was totally different from the rocky New England coast where she'd summered as a child, but familiar nonetheless. Gulls swooped and screamed, the waves murmured. Last night's dark terrors seemed an eternity away.

This is the day that the Lord has made. We will rejoice and be glad in it. It's Your day, Lord, and it's a beautiful one. Help me to follow the path You have for me this day.

A car pulled around the house from the garage area, with Trent at the wheel. He'd forsaken the Rolls for a mid-size sedan. He drew to a stop and got out to open the door for her.

"That was less than five minutes," she said, getting in, careful not to bump her arm.

He slid behind the wheel. "I didn't want you to get any ideas about stealing one of my cars and taking off."

"I might be tempted by the sports car," she admitted. "With the top down, on a day like this."

"It'll be hot later," he said, glancing at the clear sky.

True enough. "I'm glad I didn't need a cast. That would be miserable in the heat."

Her comment seemed to remind him of something unpleasant, because a frown settled between his brows. "I didn't want you driving because of that arm, but that's not all there is to it. I don't think you should go anywhere alone for the time being."

She studied his hands, strong and tanned on the steering wheel as he took the road along the shore. They were competent and sure, like everything else about him.

"I thought you might agree with Chief Gifford that the attack was nothing personal."

"The day I start taking Gifford's assessment for fact is the day someone else better take over running the company." Grim lines bracketed his mouth. "You'll be driven and picked up wherever you want to go."

She could argue, but she didn't want to. The terror of the previous night was too fresh in her mind. "All right."

He flashed a sideways glance at her. "It's going to be that easy?"

"Only for the moment," she said primly.

He laughed. "That's our Sarah." He turned onto the road that led to the clinic, reminding her of the back roads she'd traversed the night before.

"Any news on Lizbet Jackson?" She knew he'd have told her if he had any news, but she had to ask.

"Nothing. I have Gifford and his people going door to door. They'll come up with her sooner or later."

Judging by the determined set to Trent's jaw, Gifford better hope it was sooner.

"I'll try talking to Esther about Lizbet again, but she hasn't been very cooperative so far."

Trent pulled up to the clinic door, ignoring the No Parking sign. She started to get out, but he reached across to put his hand over hers.

"Just call the house when you're ready. Someone will come to pick you up." His grip tightened. "And be careful. I can guarantee your safety when you're inside Land's End. It's outside that you could be in danger."

She nodded, because if she tried to speak, she'd probably trip over the words. Trent was way too close—his hand over hers, his face scant inches from hers.

Trent was wrong. She was in danger inside Land's End as well as out—in danger from her own foolish heart.

The clinic was quiet and apparently deserted when she walked inside, but the door had been unlocked, so someone must be in. "Hello? Anyone here?"

Someone straightened from behind the counter. Esther. She always had been the first person here.

"Morning." Esther studied the sling, her face giving nothing away. "We didn't expect you'd be here today."

Welcoming as ever, obviously. Sarah pinned on a smile. Regardless of what had caused Esther's antagonism, Sarah wouldn't contribute to it by taking offense.

"I'm on the schedule. I can manage."

"No need." Esther rounded the counter. "Dr. Sam said he'd fill in this morning. We'll get along fine without you."

Maybe because she was already edgy, maybe because of the pain, the careful control she kept on her temper suddenly shattered into a million pieces. She slammed her bag down on the counter with her good hand.

"What is it with you, Esther? You act like I'm a raw intern who can't be trusted with live patients. Haven't I proved my worth to the clinic?"

She should be ashamed of herself, yelling at the nurse that way. Esther was staring at her as if she were a total stranger.

She shook her head. "Look, I didn't mean to yell. I suppose you feel I deserted the clinic when it needed me, but—"

"You've got it backward," Esther snapped. "You deserted the clinic when *you* needed *us.*"

She blinked. "What on earth are you talking about?"

"You were in trouble. Bad trouble." Esther planted her hands on her hips. "We wanted to help you, but you couldn't turn to us."

"But I—"

Esther swept on, obviously letting out what she'd thought for a long time. "You always had to be Lady Bountiful. You could give, but you couldn't accept help. That would have meant you were a real human being like the rest of us."

"That's the most ridiculous thing I've ever heard!" To her horror, she was shouting at the woman, and she couldn't seem to stop. "I don't think I'm superior to anyone."

"Ha!" Esther waggled her finger under Sarah's nose. "Miz 'I'm the fancy lady doc from Boston, here to help the poor folk' not think she's better than us! 'Course you do."

"I do not think any such thing." She grabbed Esther's finger. "And if you dare call me Lady Bountiful again, I'll throw the nearest chair at you!"

For a moment they stood toe-to-toe, glaring at each other. Suddenly Esther threw her head back and laughed—that rich, hearty, belly-shaking laugh that made everyone within earshot want to laugh with her.

Sarah let go of Esther's finger, shocked. She never acted that way. She'd always hated doctors who took advantage of their position to yell at nurses, and she never—

"Okay." Esther pulled her into a quick, warm hug. "Now you're treating me like an equal. Like a friend."

Still chuckling, she headed for the door to put out the Open sign.

Sarah sagged against the counter. What had just happened here? Had Esther meant what she'd said?

More importantly, had she been right? Had Sarah been coming across that way to the very people she wanted to help? She'd always thought she was treating the people at the clinic with respect, but apparently she'd been wrong.

Lord, this is a tough pill to swallow. If I needed a lesson in humility, You've certainly given it to me.

For some reason, that idea cheered her up. And the reckless freedom she'd felt yelling at Esther had wiped away the lingering remnants of nightmare. She felt as if she could tackle anything.

"Esther?"

The woman paused, lifting an eyebrow.

"Thanks."

"For yelling or for calling you names?" Esther asked.

"Maybe both." Her smile finally felt natural.

"Anytime." Esther vanished into her office, and Sarah headed for the staff lounge to get ready for the day.

By the time a couple of busy hours had passed at the clinic, she was no longer sure about what she could handle. Her shoulder ached so badly that the whisper of a chart page being turned felt like a battering ram.

Dr. Sam, who'd been on her case from the moment he arrived, finally sent her into Esther's office with orders to call for her ride and rest until it arrived. Exhausted, she sank down at the desk and called Land's End, telling Geneva she was ready to come home.

When she hung up, she sat staring idly at the computer, an idea slowing forming in her fogged brain. Sooner or later, probably sooner, she'd leave the clinic again, on good terms, she hoped. Maybe she could find a way of showing them all how much they meant to her.

A few clicks of the keys brought up the clinic's annual report. If she couldn't do anything else, maybe she could get some foundation funding. Her mother was always working on committees for grants—she might have some suggestions.

Energized, she began paging through the report. She could get a copy from Esther, probably, to take with her.

A few minutes later she leaned back in the chair, frowning at the screen. By the looks of it, the clinic didn't need her aid. How on earth were they managing to make ends meet without funding?

She flipped through a few more screens and had the answer. They weren't. The clinic was already funded, generously, by a grant from Donner Enterprises.

She could hardly take it in. She vividly remembered all the battles she'd had with Trent over supporting the clinic. He'd declared he was only donating the building to shut her up. She'd have expected, after what happened, that he wouldn't want anything to remind him of Sarah and her husband.

She scrolled back through the records, looking for the initial gift. There it was. A month after Lynette Donner died, Trent had begun funding the clinic.

She didn't understand. She was grateful, but she didn't understand.

"Sarah?" Esther poked her head in. "Your ride's here."

"Okay, thanks." She stood, feeling as if she needed a crane to pull her out of the chair. "Coming."

Esther put her arm around her and walked with her. "Quit trying to be a superwoman. Take it easy for a couple of days."

"I'll try." Impulsively she threw her good arm around Esther in a hug. "Thanks, Esther."

"That's okay." Those might have been tears brightening Esther's dark eyes. "Listen, Dr. Sam told me about Lizbet Jackson disappearing. I'll see if I can find her for you."

"Thanks." She managed a smile. "Better watch out. I might start leaning on you too much."

"That'd be the day. Get on with you."

She turned to look for her ride and discovered she didn't have to look far. Trent had come himself, instead of sending someone, and he held the door open for her.

"I'd have brought the sports car, but I thought this might be an easier ride if you've been overdoing it."

She sank into the passenger seat of the comfortable sedan

and turned to watch him as he slid behind the wheel again. "How did you know I'd overdo it?"

"Because I know you, Miz Sarah. You always have to do everything the hard way. Must be that Puritan streak in you."

"You'd better be careful. I threatened to throw a chair at Esther if she called me Lady Bountiful again. I could do worse if you keep using the P word."

His face crinkled into a grin. "My, you're really loosening up, aren't you?"

"I guess so." Relaxed, she watched him as he drove. They'd undoubtedly battle again, but for the moment she felt oddly at peace with Trent. "Will you tell me something?"

"If I can." His answer was cautious.

"Why are you supporting the clinic?"

He frowned at the road ahead of them as if the curving sweep of sand and gravel fascinated him. "Who told you I was?"

"Nobody. I saw it in the annual report. So tell me."

He shrugged. "No big deal. I needed a tax write-off."

"I don't believe you."

His brows lifted. "Did anyone ever suggest tact and diplomacy to you as a way of finding things out?"

She shrugged that off. "I don't understand. I fought you every step of the way to get you to donate the building. A month after I left, you started funding the whole clinic."

"It's a worthwhile project. I can afford to do it."

"Then why did you give me such a hard time?" She couldn't help the exasperation in her tone.

"Oh, that." His smile had a faintly mocking edge. "Maybe because it was so much fun to fight with you. What's wrong? Can't you believe that a business-obsessed ogre like me could want to do some good with his money?"

"No—I mean yes, I believe you want to do good, I guess."

Well, that hadn't come out very intelligently. "I never called you a business-obsessed ogre, if that's what you're implying."

He lifted an eyebrow. "I seem to recall something like that being said in the heat of battle."

"You do not. I was always perfectly polite to you. After all, you were Miles's boss."

The moment she said it, she wanted the words back. Now was not the time to remind him of Miles.

"Maybe you were just thinking it." The bantering tone had gone out of his voice. "What difference does it make? The clinic is funded, you got what you want, everyone's happy."

"Is everyone happy?"

His lips formed a thin, straight line. "As happy as we're going to be." He turned toward the Land's End gate, clicked the remote and waited for the gate to slide open. "Or as happy as we deserve to be."

THIRTEEN

Trent frowned at the stack of mail on his desk. The morning sun streamed through the window, and outside the breeze ruffled the sea oats and called to him. But duty kept him here. Sarah probably wouldn't believe that he had a sense of duty to match her own, but he did.

Speaking of Sarah—he glanced toward the door. That was her voice, raised in battle. Joanna guarded that door like a lioness. For a moment he was tempted to let her turn Sarah away, hoping that with her would go the problems and doubts she'd brought into his life. But he couldn't.

He flicked the intercom. "Let Dr. Wainwright come in."

"But you don't like to be disturbed in the morning."

True enough, but Joanna seemed on the verge of arguing with him about his own schedule. "Send her in," he said shortly.

The door opened, and one glance at Sarah's face had him out of his chair and around the desk to meet her.

"What is it? What's happened?" He closed the door in Joanna's annoyed face.

She blinked. "How do you know?"

"The fact that you're white as a sheet is a giveaway." He led her to a chair and sat opposite her, relieved that his sharp question had brought the color back to her face. When she'd walked in, he'd been afraid she was going to pass out.

"Sorry." She cradled the sling she still wore. "It's nothing—I mean, I need to go to Beaufort today. I'm probably not safe on the road, and I hoped you'd have someone drive me."

"I will." He studied her face, noting that her shadowed eyes evaded his. "But only if you tell me why."

She shot him an exasperated look. "I'm not sure that's any of your business."

"I'm sure it is. You wouldn't be running off to Beaufort unless you'd learned something. What is it?"

"Fine." She took a breath, and he realized that whatever it was, it was something that hurt her. "I finally went through the boxes of papers I'd brought back from the storage locker."

Papers—things from the house she and Miles had shared on the island, she meant. His fists clenched involuntarily, and he forced them to relax. "You found something."

"Yes." She stared at the intricate pattern of the Kirman carpet beneath their feet. Its colors glowed like jewels against the pale pine floor. "I found something. A receipt from a hotel in Beaufort, last spring."

He tried to remember a time he might have sent Miles to Beaufort on business. Atlanta, New York, yes—but not a sleepy tourist town up the coast. "You think it means something."

Sarah rubbed her forehead. "Beaufort was one of the places we'd planned to visit. I wouldn't have forgotten if he'd told me he was going there."

"Anyone can forget things, Sarah." But his instinct told him she was right.

"Not that." She seemed to force her eyes to meet his. "The receipt was for a double room."

Lynette—that's what she was thinking. Miles had gone to Beaufort with Lynette. The image set his stomach burning.

He took a deep breath, trying to quench the anger. Stupid, to be angry with two people who'd been dead a year.

"Let it go, Sarah." He reached out to clasp her hand in his. "Just let it go. It won't do any good to pursue it."

"I can't." She shot out of the chair, walked to the window and stood staring out. "I have to know." Her shoulders tensed. "If it's true, I'll deal with it, but I have to know."

"You propose to go to Beaufort and play private detective."

She turned, outlined against the pristine seascape beyond the window. "I'm going," she said. "I can at least ask at the inn where they stayed. Maybe someone will remember something."

He stood, longing to stop her. He might prevent her from going to Beaufort today, but sooner or later she'd go. And find what? Evidence that Miles and Lynette had been lovers?

"A year later? Sarah, make sense."

"I have to try." She frowned at him. "Maybe you can ignore it. I can't."

"Ignore it?" That almost made him laugh. "How can I possibly ignore it? I see reminders every day." He shuffled through the stack of papers on his desk, found what he sought and tossed it at her. "Like that."

Sarah's face whitened as she read the ugly anonymous letter, vilifying Lynette, that had come in the day's mail. He was suddenly ashamed that he had given in to the impulse. She didn't deserve that from him.

"I'm sorry." He snatched the paper, ripped it in two, and threw it in the wastebasket. His fingers still felt dirty.

She took a step toward him, her eyes dark with concern. "Do you get those often?"

He shrugged. "They used to come in droves. Now once in a while, when something stirs up the anonymous letter writers."

She winced. "Like my being here, you mean."

"Don't blame yourself. I'm used to it."

"Nobody gets used to that." The passion was back in her voice. "You're just lying to yourself."

He turned away from that passion. He didn't want to see it, didn't want it to touch him. "It's how I cope."

"You're not coping at all." She grasped his arm, tugging at him as if she'd force him to face her. "Melissa's not coping. I'm not coping. We're just going through the motions."

"That's enough for me." Why wouldn't she leave him alone?

"No. It's not." The sorrow in her voice made him look at her. Her green eyes swam with tears. "The past isn't buried, Trent. It can't be, until we know the truth."

He wanted to rail at her—wanted to deny her, ignore her, do anything but agree with her. But he couldn't. She was right.

He turned away, staring down at the desk, cluttered with the work he should be doing. It was yet another thing he used to armor himself against the past.

Why, Lord? Why can't Sarah leave it alone? Why can't I?

"All right," he said heavily. "All right. Let's go."

She blinked. "What do you mean?"

"I'll take you to Beaufort. If there's something to be found there, we'll find it together."

It had taken an hour to get the car, drive across to the mainland and take the back roads to Beaufort. That was plenty of time to think twice about this expedition of Sarah's.

Still, no matter how much he might argue with himself, the bottom line was that Sarah was right. The past wouldn't stay buried, no matter how hard he tried.

Beaufort's quaint, narrow main street was choked with camera-laden tourists. Sunshine sparkled on the waters of the sound. But Sarah's face was drawn, her eyes shadowed with questions to which she probably dreaded hearing the answers.

"Horse-and-carriage tours," he pointed. "The drivers have a line of patter about Beaufort's checkered past."

She nodded, obviously not interested in the tourist attractions she'd once wanted to see.

He and Lynette had taken Melissa on a carriage ride, long ago. The charming old town had seen plenty of grief and tragedy and had come through it with grace intact. What was his and Sarah's tragedy but another drop of blood in its history?

He spotted the sign and turned onto a narrow street lined with live oaks and magnolias. Bayberry Inn was about half-way down the block, a typical Low Country building with its long, white-columned second-floor porch. Twin stairways curved up to it, black wrought-iron railings glistening.

He stopped in the shade of a live oak whose heavy branches, draped with gray-green moss, almost touched the ground. Romantic, he thought sourly. A lovely spot for a rendezvous.

"Why don't you let me go in and ask the questions?" He knew when he said it Sarah wouldn't agree, but he had to try.

"I'll be fine." The tension in her face belied the words, but she opened the door. "Let's go."

He walked beside her up the stairs. Ironic, that he was here with Sarah where, presumably, Miles and Lynette had been.

Maybe it wasn't true. Maybe Miles was here with someone else. Maybe— But none of that seemed to lead anywhere.

Sarah's hand trailed along the black railing, as if she dreaded this as much as he did. It was probably harder for her.

After all, he'd already known that Lynette had had an affair. He'd gotten through it.

Or had he? Did you ever get through that bone-deep betrayal?

He paused at the top of the stairs, facing the shiny black door. He touched her arm, stopping her. "You were right, you know. The past won't stay buried."

Her gaze met his evenly. "So we have to do this."

"Right." He took a breath, trying to calm his churning stomach. "Let's do it." He opened the door and stepped inside.

The entry hall was cool and quiet, with no one other than the desk clerk to hear their inquiries. Sarah marched forward like a soldier, shoulders stiff, but Trent knew only her indomitable will kept her moving.

She didn't wait for him to broach the subject, but plunged right in with the desk clerk, a sandy-haired kid who looked as if he should be sitting in an algebra class instead of manning the desk.

"I'd like to ask you about someone who stayed here last spring." She planted the receipt on the counter.

The kid took a step back, skittish, staring at the receipt as if it were a snake. "I—I don't think I can do that."

"Why not?" There was an edge to Sarah's voice that told Trent she couldn't take much more.

"We'll see the manager." Trent slid his card across the counter. "Give him that."

The boy snatched the card and fled through the office door.

"You scared him," he said.

"Me?" She looked ready to argue, but a man emerged, his sandy, thinning hair an older version of the boy's.

"Mr. Donner." He extended his hand eagerly, eyes alight at the thought of gaining Trent's business. "It's a pleasure to meet you, sir. What can we do for you at the Bayberry Inn?"

Sarah probably didn't care to be ignored, but being who he was would get answers. It would also open him to some nasty gossip, but that couldn't be helped.

"You have a charming place here, Mr.—?"

"Milton, sir. James Milton."

"Well, Mr. Milton, you can help me with some inquiries. I'm looking for anything you can tell me about this."

He slid the receipt to the man, watched him assess it, recall the year-old scandal and add up two and two to make sixteen, at least.

"Of course, of course." Milton turned to the computer, keying in the information quickly. "Ah, here we are. Mr. and Mrs. Wainwright checked in at around eight that evening."

Sarah jerked as if she'd been shot at the casual words. She yanked a photo from her bag. "Is this the man?"

He nodded. "Yes, I remember him. An associate of yours, I think, Mr. Donner."

He nodded. It was true, then. But they'd already known there couldn't be another answer. "When did they leave?"

The man frowned at the screen. "That I can't tell you." He sounded apologetic. "Guests can just leave their keys in the box on the desk. We had a group tour coming in that next day, and I'd have been run off my feet."

"Do you remember the woman?" He had to ask.

Milton flushed, obviously torn between his deserve to help a wealthy potential client and his discretion. "I can't say I ever got a good look at her. She stayed just outside the door." He obviously considered that suspicious now, if he hadn't then.

An anonymous woman—but it must have been Lynette.

"You remember anything else?" He slid the receipt back in his pocket.

He shook his head regretfully.

Sarah seemed to sag, as if she couldn't go on standing there much longer. He tightened his grasp.

"Thank you. I appreciate your help." He turned Sarah toward the door, and she moved like a puppet in his grasp.

It wasn't that easy, of course. Milton walked them to the door, voluble in his eagerness. Trent cut him off with a vague suggestion that Donner Enterprises might be interested in holding a meeting at the Bayberry Inn and hurried Sarah out of the door.

By the time they reached the walk, he was practically supporting her. "Easy," he muttered. "At least we know."

She looked up at him, her eyes darkened with shock. "Maybe he was just telling you what he thought you wanted to hear."

The control he thought he had snapped. "We know that Miles came here with another woman, don't we? What else do we need?"

She stared at him, face twisting with grief and pain. He had enough time to call himself a few names before her tears spilled over.

"It's okay. It's going to be all right," he said. Stupid. Nothing was all right. "I'm sorry, Sarah. I'm sorry."

By the time Sarah emerged enough from a haze of misery to think straight, she was seated across from Trent in a padded booth. The small restaurant, perched on pilings over the water, was empty in midafternoon. Trent had guided her inside, ordered for them, nagged her into eating a bowl of she crab soup, saying she needed it. He'd been right. The warmth seeped into her, and she no longer felt like bursting into tears.

"Better now?" He studied her, concern deepening the lines around his eyes.

"Much, thank you." She put down the spoon. "I'm sorry I fell apart on you. I just—" Her voice began to choke.

"You were entitled." He frowned. "Look, we won't talk about it until you're ready, okay?"

She nodded, relieved. Of course they'd have to talk, but not until she'd come to grips with one ugly fact. She'd have staked her life on Miles's integrity, and she'd been wrong.

Trent pushed a plate toward her. "Taste the sweet-potato fries. Genuine Gullah cooking. Tastes like home."

That surprised her. "I thought you were from Chicago."

"Everyone thinks that. My mother lived in Chicago, but my grandparents lived here, on an island too small for you to have heard of. When I was lucky enough, I got to stay with them."

Something in his voice told her that had meant more to him than a casual vacation. "You loved being with them."

"They kept me sane." He gave a wry smile at her startled look. "Sound like an overstatement? I'll tell you something that never appears in the business magazine articles about Trent Donner. They always repeat the line that I came from a working-class background in Chicago. They don't mention that my mother really deserved the term, 'working girl.'"

"Your mother—" She stopped. She'd imagined, whenever she'd read a bio of Trent, that his parents had been factory workers, proud of their brilliant son.

He shrugged. "She was an alcoholic and an addict. The wonder is that neither Derek nor I inherited the tendency."

"I'm sorry." That was inadequate, but she didn't know what else to say. "Your father?"

"I have a couple of pictures of him—proud in his marine uniform. He married my mother right before he shipped out to Vietnam. I never saw him."

It didn't make sense to repeat that she was sorry, but she

was. Maybe that background explained something about Trent's toughness. He'd had to be tough to survive.

"Derek had a different father, then."

He nodded. "He never knew who his father was. I don't know what saved Derek from the hell on earth she created. What saved me was getting sent down here, to my father's parents."

The bitterness he felt toward his mother showed so clearly. She'd betrayed him in the most fundamental way. "Alcoholism is a disease. That doesn't excuse bad behavior, but—"

"What a nice, professional way of putting it, Sarah." His tone was faintly mocking. "You're right, but that didn't help when we were her victims. All I could do was try to protect Derek when she was drunk or high."

That explained the strong bond between them. No wonder Derek would do anything for his older brother.

"You've come a long way. How did you manage?" She thought of the advantages she'd taken for granted and was ashamed.

"My grandparents." A faint smile touched his lips. "They didn't have much, but what they had they gave with open hands. I was their only son's only son. When I was with them, I felt like the most important person in the world. That was a good antidote to being treated like unwelcome trash."

"They must have been wonderful people."

He nodded. He paused in the act of sliding money from his wallet and pulled out a faded photograph. "There we are, the summer I was twelve. She let me stay with them the whole summer, and I was in heaven. I didn't ask anything more than to go out fishing every day with Grandpa and come home to the smell of my gramma's Low Country boil."

She held the photo. A skinny kid in faded shorts and a

T-shirt stood with his arms around two people. The man had Trent's height and a lean, weathered face. The woman, short, softly rounded, looked at the boy with an expression of such love that it put a lump in Sarah's throat.

"Melissa looks like her—your grandmother, I mean."

He nodded. "She was a lovely woman all the way through. Strong, determined, a woman of faith. Never let me get away with a thing, though. If I tried any street language on her, she washed my mouth out with a bar of laundry soap. Whatever good I have in me, I owe to them."

"That's a beautiful tribute." She wanted to put her hand over his, but touching him would be dangerous with her emotions already high. "They must have been proud of your success."

"Not the money." He smiled ruefully. "I remember their reaction when I tried to give them money. 'Use that money to do good for someone who needs it,' Gramma said. 'We just need to see you turning into a fine man like your daddy was.'"

It was hard to speak when her throat seemed to be closing. "And did you use it for someone else?"

"Derek." His fingers tightened on the pen he held. "We'd been out of touch for a while by then. I managed to find them. Got Derek away, made sure he had an education. He was bright enough to make the best of it."

"And your mother?" She said it softly, wondering if that was one question too many.

"She died in a treatment facility."

She didn't need to ask who had provided that treatment for his mother. He might think he hated her for what she'd been, but he'd still tried to take care of her, because that's the kind of man he was.

He pushed his empty soup bowl back, dropped the restaurant bill on the table, and rose, seeming to signal that the confidences were over. She wasn't surprised. A private man like Trent didn't let down his guard often.

They reached the wooden walkway outside the restaurant and he paused, as if not ready to go back to Land's End and all that waited for them there. She stopped, too, hands on the railing, looking out at the gulls that swooped and soared, probably hoping for handouts from the restaurant.

"So then you became rich and famous," she said lightly.

He planted his hands next to hers on the wooden railing. "I worked hard, made some lucky guesses, surrounded myself with the right people—and here I am. Successful." The mocking undertone wasn't for her. Now it was for himself.

"I've always believed—" She stopped, unsure.

"What?" He focused on her, his fingers closing over hers.

Her heart stumbled over a beat. "I've always believed that God had a path marked out for me." She nodded toward the smooth beach. Sandpipers darted through wet sand of the ebbing tide. "Sometimes it's a walk on a pleasant beach. Other times—"

"Other times it's being in a small boat in a big storm." He finished the thought for her. "The waves over us seem pretty high right now."

"We'll get through." That probably sounded as if she bracketed herself with him, but she couldn't help that. They were tied together in this particular storm, at least.

"Will we? I wish I had your optimism, Sarah. It doesn't seem to me that we're much closer to a safe harbor after what we found out today."

She took a breath, hoping her voice wouldn't shake. "If we don't learn anything else about them, if we never understand why the affair happened, at least we know this much. I hope—". Her voice petered out.

"What do you hope?" His tone was intense, as if he wanted more from her.

"I guess I hope they loved each other." Her throat was thick with tears she was determined not to shed. "If they had to die together, I hope at least they had that."

His hand froze. He swung to face her, grasping her arms and pulling her closer. "How can you say that?" Anger pulsed in his words. "How can you find a way to forgive them?"

His face was dark with fury. Then, quite suddenly, something else flared in his eyes. With a sharp movement he pulled her against him, and his mouth covered hers.

The boardwalk rocked under her feet, and then all she could think or feel was Trent, his arms hard around her, his heart pounding. Or was that hers? She wasn't sure.

The kiss ended as suddenly as it had begun. He drew back, looking at her with a kind of baffled anger.

"I guess that's why," she managed to say. "I guess that's how I can begin to understand them."

His face closed, rejecting her words. Rejecting her. "I can't." He turned and stalked toward the car.

FOURTEEN

Any rational person would accept what they'd learned the previous day as the final answer. Sarah brooded over her second cup of coffee in the breakfast room, wondering if rationality had escaped her entirely. She couldn't quite vanquish the little voice of doubt in the back of her mind.

That anonymous woman who'd stood outside the door at the hotel—every grain of common sense said it was Lynette. Trent certainly believed that.

She winced, because if she thought of him, she had to think of that kiss. And remembering that made her feel as bruised and battered as if she'd been in a fight.

She cared for him, too much, and there was no possible future in that. Her heart ached. That was yet another reason why it was time to accept what she'd learned and go.

Her struggle had lasted most of the night as she'd prayed for guidance. *Show me what to do, Father. Give me a sign.*

Melissa came quickly around the corner into the breakfast room, checked for an instant and then walked straight to Sarah.

"I have something for you. Something I found in my mother's room." She held out her hand. From it dangled a necklace—a thin gold chain with a shell pendant.

Sarah blinked, startled. The girl's small face, which seemed to change so abruptly from the child she'd been to the woman she was becoming, was very serious.

Sarah took the necklace, turning it to examine the shell. The pale, translucent ivory bore an image, painted in fine brushstrokes—a night heron lifting from the marsh grass.

"It's beautiful. But you should keep it."

Melissa clasped her hands behind her as if to refuse. "It was hidden," she said abruptly. "In with her clothes. I never saw her wear it." Her voice trembled just a little. "I thought maybe Miles gave it to her. So you should have it."

That struck right at her heart. "Melissa—" She reached toward the girl, necklace dangling from her fingers.

Melissa shook her head, whirled, and ran out of the room.

Sarah stared at the shell for a moment, trying to push away the image it brought to mind—Miles fastening it around Lynette's neck, Lynette lifting her beautiful face, smiling, for his kiss.

She started after Melissa. She didn't want it, and— She rounded the corner and ran straight into Robert Butler.

"Careful." He steadied her courteously. "Are you—" He stopped, his gaze focused on the necklace and drew in an audible breath. "Where did you get that?"

"From Melissa. Why? You seem startled to see it."

He shook his head. "Not startled, exactly. I'd thought about buying it myself. Amos Stark's work is increasing in value, and I decided it was worth the price he was asking."

"Amos Stark?" The fineness of the painting had already told her this was no cheap tourist bauble.

"A local Gullah artist who specializes in shell painting." He smiled. "Well, you have a fine piece of his work there."

"It's not really mine," she said slowly. "Melissa thought that Miles had bought it." No need to tell him why.

"Miles?" His eyebrows lifted. "Miles didn't buy this."

Her breath cut off. "What do you mean?"

"Amos told me who bought it. Not Miles. Jonathan Lee."

For a moment she couldn't speak. "Are you sure?"

Robert shrugged, his dark eyes curious. "Positive. Jonathan has bought a number of pieces from him. Amos wouldn't make a mistake about that. Why did you think Miles bought it?"

"It—it was a misunderstanding, that's all. Excuse me. I have to find Melissa." She hurried away, leaving him staring.

She'd nearly reached the stairs when she stopped. She couldn't tell Melissa. If the necklace was a gift from an admirer—

Jonathan Lee. She pressed her hand to her temple, trying to shake her thoughts into some sort of order. How did Jonathan fit into this? She took a breath. She should tell Trent.

She went quickly toward the office wing, intent on doing this before she gave in to the cowardly urge to throw the necklace away and pretend she'd never seen it. But when she reached Trent's office, Joanna rose from her desk.

"I'd like to see Trent, please. I'll only take a moment."

"I'm sorry, but that's impossible." The secretary's smile said she wasn't sorry at all. "He's out."

The momentum that had carried her this far collapsed. "When will he be back?"

"He has an extremely busy schedule today." Joanna smoothed back sleek hair. "Your visit to the Bayberry Inn yesterday put him behind in several important matters."

The Bayberry Inn. The words repeated in her mind. She couldn't imagine a scenario in which Trent would discuss with his secretary where they'd gone and what they'd found out.

"How do you know that's where we went?" She flung the question at Joanna.

Joanna drew back as if she'd seen a snake. "I don't—I mean, I'm sure Mr. Donner must have mentioned it."

"I'm just as sure he didn't." She planted her palms on the desk, leaning toward the woman. "What did you do? Eavesdrop?"

"No! I didn't. I just knew, I mean—" She stumbled to a halt, face turning crimson.

Sarah, staring at her, read the truth with incredulous shock. "It was you. You were the woman at the inn with Miles." She didn't even feel anything, not yet.

"Yes!" Joanna shot to her feet, the flush ebbing, leaving her face white. "All right, now you know. I loved Miles, and he loved me." There was a triumphant ring to the words. "You never even appreciated him. I gave him more love than you ever imagined, and he loved me."

Reeling, Sarah struggled to make sense of it. "You had an affair with my husband."

Joanna glared at her. "Not some sleazy little affair. Oh, we went to the inn, but once we were there, Miles wouldn't go through with it. He said it wouldn't be honorable."

It was what she'd said herself. *Miles would do the honorable thing.* She felt numb. "You—he loved you."

"Why not? You were always pushing him. 'Do the right thing, Miles.' I just loved him. He was going to ask you for a divorce, so we could be together." Her voice broke, her face crumpling. "But he died."

Sarah forced herself to breathe. This didn't make any sense. "You and Miles. But what about Lynette?"

The mention of Lynette's name seemed to galvanize Joanna, and she glared at Sarah as if she'd insulted her. "Lynette! There was never anything between them. He loved me. Don't you understand? I don't know why he was with her that day, but it had to be some kind of freak accident. He loved me."

She broke down completely, collapsing in her chair, sobbing.

Someone should comfort the woman, but it couldn't be her. Her stomach churned, and her head was spinning. She had to get out. She hurried out of the office, back to the main house and on out the door. She had to get away from Land's End. She couldn't face anyone until she'd made sense of this.

She felt as if she'd walked for miles. No, not walked—run away. She'd been running from Land's End and everything it represented, but she couldn't run from herself.

Sarah sank down on a sea-battered tree trunk, bleached white and left high on the shore. Warm and smooth beneath her, it was oddly comforting in a world composed, just now, of sea, sand and the merciless blaze of the sun. If not for the ocean breeze, it would be unbearable.

About as unbearable as her thoughts. *Why, Lord? How could Miles fall in love with someone else when we promised ourselves to each other before You? And how could I not see that something was fundamentally wrong with our marriage? Was I that blind? Or did I just not care enough?*

She swallowed the tears she was determined not to shed. Not now. She could collapse all she wanted once she was safely back in Boston, but for now she had to find answers.

She leaned back against sun-warmed wood. The only sounds that broke the stillness were the incessant murmur of the waves and the screech of a solitary gull. They had no answers for her. Those had to come from within.

Miles and Joanna. Put aside the pain that causes, and think it through. Joanna had been the woman at the inn with Miles. It was ludicrous to think that he could have been involved with both Joanna and Lynette at the same time.

Jonathan. She drew the necklace from her pocket. Jonathan had bought the necklace. He must have given it to Lynette. And what Melissa sensed had been true—that Lynette would not have hidden so valuable a gift unless she'd had to.

She stood. Perhaps God had guided her aimless flight down the beach. Beyond the dunes was the Lee house. She fastened the necklace around her neck, the pendant cool against her skin. She had some questions for Jonathan.

By the time she reached the house, her impulse had begun to falter. How did a well-brought-up Bostonian walk into a house and accuse her host of adultery? She sent up a silent prayer. If God was guiding her quest, she had to believe she was intended to be here now.

Jonathan could have been out, of course, but she saw him immediately, relaxing with a newspaper at a tile-topped table on the patio. He put the paper aside and rose at the sight of her.

"Sarah, how nice. Did you walk all this way? Let me get you a cold drink."

"No, thanks." She didn't want anything to distract from the questions she had to ask, and once she'd asked them, he wouldn't offer her anything. "I have to talk with you."

"Of course." Wariness showed in his glance as he pulled out a chair for her. She sat, relieved to be out of the glare.

Just get it out. "I have to know. What was your relationship with Lynette Donner?"

His movement arrested at her words for a fraction of a second, and then he was sitting down, smiling across the table at her. "How fierce you sound, my dear. We were friends."

"Close friends, I suppose." She drew the necklace out from beneath her shirt. "Very close friends, for you to give her such an expensive gift—one she felt she had to keep hidden."

Jonathan's expression didn't change, but she could almost

see the frantic thoughts tumbling behind his dark eyes. How much did she know? What could he tell her?

She was suddenly tired of the whole thing, tired and sick from thinking about it. "Don't bother to make up a story for me. Two weeks before her death, Lynette confessed to Trent that she'd been having an affair. It was you, wasn't it?"

He held out against her for a moment longer. Then, with a small sigh, he nodded.

"Yes. It's almost a relief to say it." He looked away from her, out toward the dunes. "I'm not even sure how it happened. I was infatuated. It was a few weeks of insanity."

He was letting himself off easily, but it wasn't her job to confront him with his sin. "Did you break it off, or did she?"

He flushed slightly. "She did. But if you're thinking that gave me a reason to want her dead, you're wrong. I was relieved. I didn't want to destroy my marriage. I love Adriana." He focused on her, eyes pleading. "Don't tell her, Sarah. I don't deserve her, but I can't bear losing her."

She wouldn't willingly put another woman through her pain. "I don't intend to tell her, but Trent has a right to know."

His face tightened. "Why? So he can look for revenge?"

"Trent wouldn't do that." But she could hear the lack of conviction in her voice. Given the depth of his sense of betrayal, she wasn't sure what Trent might do.

Probably he sensed her hesitation. He leaned forward. "Listen to me before you say something you can't take back. I don't think what happened to Miles and Lynette was an accident."

Ironic, that the person who agreed with her was Lynette's lover. "Why?"

"I saw Trent that day, a couple of hours before the call came that Lynette was missing. He was out in his boat, and he was headed toward Cat Isle."

"No." Her rejection was pure reflex. "If you're saying Trent found them and killed them, I don't believe it."

He shrugged. "You're under his spell, I suppose. Women fall for him. But you should ask him why the police hushed up everything up so quickly."

"I've already been through that with him and the chief. He didn't deny that he wanted the investigation closed quickly, but the chief insists they didn't cover anything up."

"He owes Trent. Everyone on the island does. He'd say whatever Trent wanted."

Little though she liked him, she couldn't swallow the idea that the police chief was corrupt enough to hide murder, and that's what Jonathan was suggesting. "I don't believe it."

He shrugged, standing. "That's your choice. I'll have someone drive you back to Land's End. But be careful, Sarah. Trent Donner can be a dangerous man."

She didn't believe what Jonathan so obviously did. Sarah returned to Land's End without a thought for danger. Trent wouldn't hurt her, and he certainly wasn't a murderer.

But how much should she tell him? *All of it*, her heart insisted, but her mind was more cautious. If she told him about Jonathan, she couldn't be sure what his reaction would be. Would it be better never to know?

No. That answer, at least, she knew. She hadn't been able to rest until she knew the truth about Miles. Trent wouldn't, either. She had to find the words to tell him.

She walked through the quiet house to the patio. Melissa sat on the edge of the pool, kicking her feet in the water. Sarah waved, not eager to talk to anyone, and unlocked the door to her room, leaving it ajar to let the breeze flow through.

She'd tell Trent, but first she needed to pray about it. She took the necklace off, laying it on the dresser. In the mirror's reflection, she caught sight of something white on the blue pillow sham of the bed.

A note, folded over. The room was very still, the only sound the murmur of pool water circulating. A gull cried sharply, and her hand jerked.

Idiot, she scolded herself, and picked up the paper, unfolding it.

Leave Land's End now, unless you want to wind up as dead as Lynette.

Her impulse was to shred it into tiny pieces. She had to force herself to assess it as calmly as she would a conflicting lab report. Computer generated and printed—unlikely there'd be any way to trace which computer or printer, and there were probably a dozen in the office wing. Anyone could have access.

Anyone in Land's End. The thought chilled her. She'd come here for safety, but it wasn't safe even here. She ought to—

"You got one, too." Melissa stood in the doorway, shoving her hair back from her face. She stared at the paper in Sarah's hand. "You did."

Sarah started to thrust the paper behind her in an automatic need to protect the child. Then her words registered. *Too.* "What do you mean, Melissa? Did you get a note like this?"

"Not just one." She clamped her hand over her mouth, clearly regretting her words.

Sarah caught her arm when she'd have turned and fled. "Don't, Melissa. You can trust me." She gave a shaky laugh. "Looks like we have a common enemy. What did yours say?"

Melissa's gaze was wary. "You first."

She held the paper out silently. There was little point in

trying to protect Melissa when she'd already been a victim of someone's sick mind.

Melissa took a breath that caught on a sob. "Mine always say it's my fault that my mother died." She pressed her lips together for an instant. "And that my father isn't—my father."

The depth of her anger at the anonymous letter writer shocked her. If she had him here, she might give in to the atavistic impulse to attack for what he'd done to a child.

Melissa didn't need her hysterics right now. And one part of that she knew how to deal with. She caught Melissa's hand.

"Come on. I'm going to prove to you that isn't true." Tugging the protesting child by the hand, she surged through the house and straight to Trent's office. She braced herself to confront Joanna, but the woman wasn't there.

Trent turned from the computer, eyebrows lifting at their tempestuous entrance.

She came to a halt at the desk. "Show Melissa the picture of your grandmother."

Something of the urgency in her voice must have convinced him not to argue. He pulled out his wallet, withdrew the photo and handed it to Melissa.

"That's your great-grandmother. I thought I'd shown you a picture of her before, but I guess it was a long time ago."

Melissa studied the photo for a long moment, her hair hanging down to hide her face, while Sarah held her breath and prayed. Finally she looked up, frowning.

"But I—I look like her."

"Of course you do." *Let her believe it, Lord. Let her understand*.

"You look very much like her," Trent said, his voice cautious. He obviously knew something was going on, but how could he begin to guess what?

Sarah touched her arm gently. "Genetics is a funny business. Once in a while someone has that kind of resemblance." She hesitated. Should she spell it out?

The wonder that broke through on the girl's face gave her the answer. "I look like her because I'm related through my dad." She spun and threw her arms around Sarah.

Sarah held her, knowing the girl wavered between laughter and tears, just as she did.

Trent came around the desk and touched his daughter's shoulder. "Can I know what this is about now?"

"Tell him." Sarah squeezed her. "I'll start." She handed Trent the note. "I found this on my bed just now."

He looked at it, his face darkening with rage. She shook her head slightly. It wouldn't help Melissa if he exploded.

"Melissa happened to see me. She told me she's been getting notes, too."

"You've been getting nasty letters like this, here in our house? Why didn't you tell me?"

The child straightened, and Sarah felt the moment at which she decided to tell her father everything.

"The first one came the week after Mama's funeral. It said—" She stumbled a little, and Sarah nudged her.

"It's okay. Tell your dad."

"It said what happened was my fault."

"Melissa, that's nonsense. You should know that." Trent was probably hanging on to his temper by a thread. "You should have told me right away."

"Wait." Her fingers brushed his. "There's more."

"It said I wasn't your daughter." Melissa looked up at her father, her eyes huge. "But that's not true, is it? It can't be, if I look like your gramma."

"Of course it's not true." Trent's voice went deep with a

mix of grief and love, and he pulled his daughter into his arms. "You're my daughter, and I love you."

He held her tightly, their two dark heads very close. Melissa had found her way back to the heart where she belonged.

Sarah discovered that her throat was tight with tears. She lifted an unsteady hand to brush away the few that spilled over onto her cheeks. If she didn't do another good thing while she was here, this would be enough.

She should leave them alone. She took a step back and Trent glanced up at the movement.

"We need to talk," he said quietly.

"Yes." He didn't begin to know all that they needed to talk about, and when he did— Well, she'd deal with that hurdle when she came to it. "But not now. Right now you need to concentrate on Melissa."

He nodded, turning away quickly, absorbed in his daughter. That was good. That was the way it should be.

But she couldn't banish a sense of emptiness as she walked out of the room.

FIFTEEN

There was so much to discuss with Sarah, Trent didn't know how he'd begin. He waited in his car at the clinic early the next afternoon, tapping his fingers on the wheel. She should be out soon, and they'd get things clear between them.

After the bombshell with Melissa that Sarah had somehow engineered, he'd been in shock. He'd resented—still did resent—the fact that Sarah had interfered, but he couldn't argue with the results. He knew now what had come between him and Melissa.

Fury still burned inside him to think of his child's anguish. He should have seen that more was going on than pre-adolescent moodiness. He should have made her tell him.

The clinic door opened. Sarah paused, shading her eyes against the brilliant sunshine, spotted him and started toward the car. The moment she slid inside, he knew something had happened. She positively sparked with impatience and energy.

"Esther told me where Lizbet is." She snapped her seat belt with a decided click. "She found out for me." She said that as if it meant something special.

He turned the ignition. "Where? I'll drive you." His own patience strained at the leash.

She handed him a slip of paper. "Esther wrote out the directions. Do you know the place?"

He spun out of the parking lot. "We'll find it. What did she tell you? Where has Lizbet been?"

"Apparently she's been staying with this distant cousin since the night I tried to see her." She glanced across at him. "She was attacked that night, too, but a neighbor found her before the police arrived. They've been hiding her ever since."

That surprised him less than it obviously did Sarah. Lizbet's community took care of their own, and if they could avoid contact with the police, they did. "That washes out the chief's theory that you were attacked by a random thief."

"I never believed that, in any event." She frowned, leaning forward as if to make the car go faster.

"What does Lizbet say about what happened?"

"Nothing, according to Esther. She hasn't talked, and no one's pushed her. But Esther says she wants to see me."

"Maybe she'll level with you." No point in ranting about why it had taken the woman this long to decide to talk. "You may as well relax. This is as fast as I can go on these roads."

"Sorry." She leaned back, her green eyes darkening with concern when she looked at him. "How is Melissa doing?"

"Much better. I'm sorry we didn't get a chance to talk last night, but—" He shook his head, still surprised by what happened. "Melissa wanted to go to the cemetery where my grandparents are buried." His throat thickened at the memory of his daughter's straight, slim figure kneeling at his grandmother's grave, flowers in her hands. "Afterward we stopped at a restaurant and talked for hours."

"That's the best thing you could have done." Her voice was warm. "I didn't intend to interfere. Melissa walked in on me when I'd found that note and just blurted it out."

He nodded. He shouldn't be angry with Sarah because she'd found out what he couldn't.

"About the notes—" she began.

"I took them to a lab in Savannah—the one you received and a few that Melissa hadn't destroyed. They have better facilities than the local police. We'll see what they make of them."

"Computer printouts will be hard to trace."

"This lab is the best. If there's anything to find, they'll find it." He smacked his hand against the steering wheel. "I want to know how the notes got into Melissa's room, and your room, for that matter. Only someone with access to Land's End could do that."

"There is someone." She hesitated. "Joanna Larson."

He read the strain in her voice when she said the name. "You don't have to tell me. She spilled the whole thing after she'd talked to you."

"I haven't seen her since." There was an unspoken question in the words.

"She's gone," he said shortly. He hated messy scenes, and the scene with Joanna had been well over the top. "We both agreed she'd do better elsewhere. I gave her a generous severance and a glowing reference and sent her on her way."

Sarah nodded, but her brow wrinkled. "She could have been the one to leave the notes. She certainly had access."

"But no reason to torment Melissa that way." His jaw clenched painfully. "Why? That's what I want to know. Why?"

Sarah pushed her hair back from her face with both hands, gripping her head as if she'd force an answer from her mind. "It doesn't make any sense."

"Frankly, I'd like to believe Miles was involved with both Joanna and Lynette, but I can't. It's plain absurd."

She winced at his words, and he regretted them. Was there nothing they could say to each other that wouldn't cause pain?

"Why was Miles at the cottage that day?" she said. "We keep coming back to that."

"Maybe we're about to get answers. This is the house." He pulled into an overgrown driveway next to a tobacco shed, cut the engine and opened the door. Hot, humid air rushed at them, carrying with it the fecund scents of the marsh. "Let's go."

As they approached the sagging porch, he let her go ahead. The woman had asked for Sarah, not him. He'd have to contain the fierce impatience that drove him if he wanted answers.

Sarah rapped at the door. For a long moment nothing happened. Then he heard the shuffle of footsteps, saw a curtain twitch as someone satisfied herself as to who was there. The door creaked open.

He'd seen Lizbet Jackson before, so he was prepared. He suspected Sarah held back a gasp at first sight.

Lizbet stood nearly six feet tall, and her erect posture belied her seventy or so years. The colorful head scarf she wore hid her hair and may have been what allowed her to escape the attack with a mild concussion instead of something more serious. The equally colorful long robe glowed against the dim interior of the cabin.

"You've come at last." She reached a hand toward Sarah, gold bracelets jingling a tune. "I be waitin' and waitin' for you, and you never come."

Sarah blinked, obviously not expecting that. "I tried to visit you at your house. The man who attacked you attacked me, too. I'm sorry. I'm afraid I led him to you."

That was Sarah, taking responsibility on herself, he thought. It wasn't her fault that some maniac—

No. He stopped himself. There was no random maniac,

however comforting that theory might be. There was logic behind everything that had happened, if only they could see it.

"You don't carry the burden for the evil that lives in that soul, chile. You here now. That's all that counts. Come in." She drew Sarah across her doorstep.

Trent waited, letting her look at him. He wouldn't attempt to enter without her invitation.

"All right." She inclined her head regally. "Come'yuh, too. Guess you got the right to hear what I got to say."

She crossed to a rocking chair next to the room's fireplace. She sat, and Sarah jerked involuntarily when a black cat jumped into the woman's lap.

"Set. Set." She gestured toward two straight chairs opposite her.

Staged, he thought. She'd known they'd both come.

Lizbet rocked once or twice, taking her time. She stroked the cat with a strong, long-fingered hand. "I knew you'd come one day." Her black eyes focused on Sarah. "I knew you'd come to learn the trute o' what happened that day on Cat Isle."

Sarah's heart seemed to stop at the woman's words. *She knew.* Lizbet knew something about Miles's death. She felt Trent's tension, strung as tightly as her own.

"You were there that day, weren't you?" That had to be it.

Lizbet's black eyes lost focus, as if she looked back in time. She fingered the gold cross that hung at her throat.

"Done took my little boat over to gather the moss for poultices. S'pose you know I be a granny, a healer, you'd say."

Sarah nodded, her nails biting into her palms. "Did you know someone was at the cottage?"

Lizbet nodded. "Thought it was funny, but none of my business. I heard a boat leave, and I thought they was gone."

Her breath caught. A boat had left?

A shiver broke Lizbet's calm. "I went closer, saw they was still two boats at the dock, but no sound from the house. Seemed the good Lord was telling me I had to go look, so I did."

"The fumes—" she began, but Lizbet shook her head.

"I left the door open. Didn't take a minute to see they was both dead." Her eyes focused on them. "You got to believe, if there was any chance, I'd a done more. But I seen plenty of dead folk in my time, and they was gone."

"Where were they?" Trent's voice was so harsh she barely recognized it.

"Woman lay on the sofa, man on the floor. There was a little pad of paper on the table, and a pen. And a note."

Trent jerked as if he'd been shot. "My wife left a note? What did it say? What happened to it?"

"I took it," Lizbet said calmly. "It wasn't true, was it? Note say she and the man kill themselves for love, but I know better, don't I? I hear t'other boat leave. Someone with evil in his heart wanted folks to think they killed themselves when they didn't."

"You should have turned it over to the police. Told them what you heard." Trent's voice was ragged.

Sarah gave him a warning touch. He glanced toward her, took a deep breath and nodded.

The woman watched that byplay with wise old eyes. "I don't hold much with police. Thought about coming to you, but how did I know t'wasn't you in the other boat?"

"It wasn't," he said shortly.

Lizbet rocked, as if the movement soothed her. "I had to think on it." Her eyes met Sarah's, and it felt as if the wisdom of generations was held in that dark gaze. "It come to me that you were the one to have the note. When I heard you were back, I knew you'd come. Trouble was, I put it in the cash box I use when I sells my herbs. Couple weeks ago, some no-count took the box and the note with it. If'n the man who attacked us wanted it, he was too late." She spread her hands out, palms up, empty. "So I got nothing to give you but my story."

"If I get a police officer to come to you, will you tell the story again? Sign your name to it?" Trent leaned forward.

She assessed him for a moment and then nodded. "I will." She rocked again, closing her eyes. Their audience was over.

Sarah got up, feeling as if she'd aged twenty years in the twenty minutes they'd sat there. "Thank you."

Lizbet opened her eyes. "You be careful now, y'heah? You on a dangerous path."

"It's the one God set me on." She hadn't said that to anyone else, but it seemed right to say it to Lizbet.

She nodded. "You got to stay on it then, come what may."

"I'll be in touch about the statement." Trent frowned. "Maybe you'd be safer if you came back to Land's End with us."

"No." A shiver seemed to go through her. "I got my own kin around me now. I be safe."

There was clearly no use in pressing the subject, and the woman was probably right. Safety was in short supply on St. James just now. Even at Land's End, malice moved unchecked.

She let Trent lead her to the car, her mind moving a thousand miles an hour. How? Who? The avalanche of discoveries was threatening to bury her.

One of those discoveries, at least, she hadn't shared with Trent yet, and she had to. He had a right to know, especially if— Her mind stopped there. Could she possibly picture Jonathan, urbane, detached Jonathan who seemed to care little about anything, killing two people?

Trent started the car, sending a welcome rush of cool air from the vents. He pulled back onto the narrow road.

She swallowed. "At least now we know."

His frown deepened. "Do we?"

"You heard what Lizbet said. You surely don't believe she was lying." The woman's story had had the undeniable ring of truth. Sarah had been so caught up that she'd almost seemed to see what Lizbet had that terrible day.

"I believe she told the truth, as far as it went. But her interpretation isn't necessarily correct." His detached tone didn't fool Sarah. He was clamping down on fierce emotion, and if he clamped down too hard he just might explode.

She suppressed the impulse to argue. "I suppose. If you believe strongly in coincidence, you might accept that someone else came to the cottage, found them dead and ran away without ever speaking of it. And the attacks on Lizbet and me, the notes Melissa and I received—"

"All right." His hand sliced through the air, cutting off whatever else she might have said. "Granted. Someone has guilty knowledge, whether he committed a double murder or not. And he's willing to attack anyone who gets in his way."

He jerked the wheel savagely as he turned onto the main road, and she grasped the armrest.

"Sorry." He glanced at her, his tone moderating. "Do you know why I came here, built Land's End?"

The question startled her. "I suppose this felt like home to you, because of your grandparents."

"That's true, but not all of it." His thoughts engraved lines around his mouth. "A man in my position makes enemies. When Lynette was pregnant with Melissa, we lived in Atlanta. A man broke into the house one night—a crackpot convinced I'd stolen one of his ideas. If I hadn't come home when I did—"

He stopped, but he didn't need to finish the thought. Her imagination was vivid enough to do that.

"I'm sorry. I had no idea."

"I built Land's End, moved my headquarters here, where I could protect them." His knuckles were white on the steering wheel, and his pain reached across the space between them to clutch at her heart. "It didn't do any good, did it? I couldn't protect them, even here."

"It's not your fault." The words were useless. Trent couldn't stop blaming himself any more than she could.

He didn't even bother to respond to that. "If Lizbet was right, someone killed them and tried to make it look like suicide. And I was so willing to believe the worst of my wife that I bought into it, even without the note he'd planted."

Her heart ached for him. "Anyone might think that, under the circumstances."

"You didn't."

No, she hadn't. "I came back to find the truth."

"Are we ever going to know the truth—all of it?"

She had to tell him, no matter what the cost. "Yesterday I found another piece of it. I've wanted to tell you, but life keeps interfering."

He gave a wry smile. "An understatement if ever I heard one. Well, we're alone now. What is it?"

"Melissa gave me a piece of jewelry she'd found hidden in her mother's room. She thought—she assumed—that Miles had given it to her, but of course he hadn't."

His lips tightened. "Obviously I was wrong to think I'd protected Melissa from the gossip."

"Robert Butler recognized the piece. He knows the artist. He knew that it was sold to Jonathan Lee."

For an instant his face didn't change. Then he abruptly pulled off the road, into the deserted parking lot of a shuttered restaurant. "Jonathan." He turned toward her. "You should have told me right away."

"You weren't there. Besides—" She shook her head. She wouldn't get into the dreadful scene with Joanna that had wiped everything else from her mind. "I'm telling you now."

"I can't believe it. There must be some other explanation. Jonathan wouldn't—"

She couldn't let him go on. "I confronted him. He admitted it. I'm sorry, Trent. He admitted that he and Lynette had an affair." She took a deep breath. "He also said he knew you were out in the boat that day. He implied that Gifford hushed up the investigation because of you."

He leaned toward her, very close in the confines of the car. "Is that what you believe, Sarah? That I'm a murderer?"

"If I believed that, I wouldn't be here with you, would I?" It took an effort to hold her voice steady.

His gray eyes bored into hers, as if he'd see into her soul. "But there's a shred of doubt there, isn't there?" He shook his head. "No, don't bother to answer. Anyone would doubt. You saw one of the anonymous letters that vilified Lynette. I didn't show you the ones that accuse me of murder."

She wanted answers, but she was absolutely no good at confrontations. Sarah had pushed her chair as far back as it would go in the corner of Trent's study, but it wasn't far enough. The emotions that filled the room assaulted her.

Jonathan sat opposite Trent. He'd abandoned his usual casual air, sitting bolt upright, looking with distaste at the occupant of the other chair.

Chief Gifford had planted himself firmly, feet apart, elbows on his knees. His attitude suggested a bulldoglike intensity as he glared at Jonathan.

"You saying my force didn't do its proper job?" His tone was just short of a bellow.

"I just repeated what I've heard." Jonathan drew a bit farther from him. "People talk."

"Yes. They do." Trent wore the expression he no doubt wore negotiating a business deal—contained, focused, sharp as a laser on Gifford. "And apparently, from what Mr. Lee says, they're saying the investigation was hushed up."

Jonathan sliced his gaze toward Sarah, and his expression said she wouldn't be invited back to the Lee house. "I repeated what I'd heard. There's even a rumor going around that the results of the autopsies were changed."

She felt bruised herself at this moment. The detachment she'd learned as a physician escaped her. They were talking about Miles and Lynette—two vibrant human beings who'd deserved to live, whatever their sins.

"Well, Chief?" Trent impaled the man with a look that didn't brook evasions. "Is that true?"

Gifford shifted under the impact of that gaze. "You can talk to the medical examiner yourself if you don't believe me. He found one bruise on the man's forehead, that's it. Seemed straightforward enough. The fumes overcame them before they realized what was happening."

"So you say." Jonathan's tone was malicious.

Sarah suddenly saw past the courtly Southern gentleman exterior to the truth. He was jealous of Trent, maybe even hated him. A shiver went through her. Did he hate enough to cast blame on Trent for something he'd done himself? Did he hate enough to kill? The sunny room seemed darker.

Gifford shoved himself to his feet, frowning at Trent. "Maybe we did rush matters a mite. But you wanted the investigation shut down, fast and quiet. You didn't want any bad press. I gave you what you wanted."

"You're saying you cut short the investigation because you thought I wanted you to?"

She almost felt sorry for Trent. He'd never really recognized the kind of power he wielded. Now he had to face it.

"It was what you wanted," Gifford muttered, but the way his gaze slewed from side to side suggested he was no longer sure.

"I want the truth, including a complete report from the medical examiner. Put together everything. Get it to me by tomorrow morning."

He didn't bother to say "Or else." People in Trent's position didn't need to threaten. Did he even realize that he was still using his power to bend the police to his will?

She leaned back, head throbbing. Trent wouldn't change. Probably he couldn't. At least now he seemed determined to get at the truth, no matter how much it hurt.

"If that's all this interesting little gathering has to offer," Jonathan said, "I think I'll be on my way."

"Not quite." Trent's voice was colorless, and he didn't look at her. "I understand you saw me out in my boat that day."

Jonathan raised an eyebrow. "That's right. I did."

"You didn't see me at Cat Isle."

"Perhaps not. But you were headed in that direction."

"I cut around by the old oyster beds and never went near Cat Isle."

The two men eyed each other like fencers looking for an opening. Then Jonathan shrugged. "So you say. I guess we'll never know, will we?"

"We know one thing now that we didn't before. We know that you were out on the water that day. And we don't know where you went, either."

For an instant Sarah thought Jonathan would spring on Trent. Then he spun and stalked out of the room.

SIXTEEN

Sarah sat with her Bible in her lap that evening, trying to sort out her prayers. The situation had become so complicated that she no longer knew how to pray for it.

Father, only the truth will do now, as far as I can see. No matter how it hurts.

And so far the truth certainly had done that. She smoothed her palm over the worn leather cover. Knowing about Miles and Joanna hurt, but she could come to grips with it. Worse was realizing that her marriage had been in trouble, and she hadn't known. A profound sadness swept through her.

Trent was smothering his sorrow in anger, but how long could that last? His mother had betrayed him first, in the most fundamental way. Now he faced the betrayal of both his wife and a man he'd considered a friend.

Neither Trent nor Melissa had appeared at dinnertime. When she'd asked Derek where they were, he'd shrugged. Trent had taken one of the boats out. It was what he did when he wanted to clear his head. And Melissa was closeted in her room, upset at the investigation being reopened. Derek had done his best to lighten the atmosphere, but it hadn't helped. The air had still seemed oppressive, as if a storm were about to break on them.

Someone tapped lightly on the door. Her nerves jumped, and she took the precaution of peeking out the window. Melissa, barefoot and in her pajamas. She opened the door quickly.

"Melissa, what is it? Is something wrong?"

"No. Yes." Melissa stumbled in. "I have to talk to you." She clutched Sarah's hands. "Please let me talk to you."

She could imagine Trent's response. "Maybe your dad—"

"No! I can't talk to him about this." Tears welled in her eyes. "I have to tell somebody. The police started investigating again. They might find out!"

Sarah recognized rising hysteria when she saw it. She led Melissa to the love seat and brought a quilt from the bed to wrap around her. She sat next to the child, putting her arm around her and drawing her close. Melissa's small, wiry body trembled, sparking an unexpectedly strong protective urge in Sarah.

"Okay. Just take a deep breath. You can tell me."

Melissa's eyes widened. "You have to promise not to tell my dad. Promise!" Her voice rose.

"All right, I promise." She smoothed her hand down Melissa's back. "It'll be okay."

Melissa sucked in a breath that choked on a sob. "I keep thinking about it. I can't make my mind stop."

She certainly knew how that felt. "It'll be better after you've told someone, Melissa. That's always better than carrying a trouble alone."

"It was that day." Melissa squeezed her eyes shut. "The day Mommy died. I didn't mean to do it."

She was obviously blaming herself for something to do with Lynette's death—probably some small fault or argument that she'd magnified in her own mind.

"Of course not," Sarah soothed.

"She told a lie." Her voice trembled. "I heard her. Dad

asked where she'd been one day, and she said she'd gone shopping with me. But she hadn't. And then, that day, she was taking the boat out and I wanted to go, but she wouldn't let me. I was mad at her, and I told Dad about the time she lied."

It took a moment to sort out. Lynette had lied about where she'd been, possibly at a time when she'd met Jonathan during their brief affair. The day Lynette and Miles died, Melissa, in a fit of childish pique, had told her father about it.

"It's okay, Melissa. I'm sure your mother understands. She wouldn't blame you for that."

"That's not—" Melissa stopped, her tears spilling over. "I told Dad, and I could tell he was mad. He went out in the boat. And that night they said Mommy was dead."

Sarah's heart clutched. She shouldn't touch this, but what could she do? Melissa had unloaded this secret on her, and she had to deal with it. *Please, Father, show me the way.*

Maybe the only way was to bring her fear into the open. "Did that make you think your father had done something?"

"No!" The very vehemence of Melissa's reply told her that it had. "He didn't. He wouldn't."

But she so clearly feared that her words had caused her mother's death.

"Melissa, think this through. Aren't you blaming yourself because of what those notes said?" Lizbet's words echoed in her mind—a man with evil in his heart. "They were written by someone who wanted to stir up trouble. You can't trust a person like that—someone who wouldn't even sign his name."

Melissa took a shaky breath, and she could almost feel the child begin to hope. "Do you think so?"

Sarah hugged her. "Of course I do. You've kept this to yourself, and it's preyed on your mind." Anger burned bright at the person who'd done that. "You feel better now that you've told me. You'd feel even better if you told your father."

"No!" Melissa went rigid. "And you can't. You promised."

"I'll keep my promise." And what would that cost her? "But I want you to promise me you'll think about telling him yourself. Pray about it. Will you do that?"

Melissa nodded. "Okay. I guess I can do that." She took a deep breath and got up slowly. "Guess I better go back before somebody sees me."

Sarah walked her to the door, then watched as she crossed the patio to the main house, trailing Sarah's quilt around her. She looked as if a weight was gone from her shoulders.

It had transferred to Sarah's. *I'm better equipped to carry this load than she is, Lord. But what am I to do with it? And how will Trent react when he learns I've kept this from him?*

"Dr. Wainwright, message for you." The clinic receptionist handed her a folded paper, and Sarah tensed as she took it. She'd been keyed up since the previous night, and not even her morning shift at the clinic had been enough to distract her.

Well, this, at least, couldn't be another of the anonymous notes, unless the perpetrator had changed his methods. She flipped it open and couldn't suppress the gasp that escaped her. She'd been wrong. It was anonymous.

But not, she'd guess, the same person. This paper was dirty and crumpled, and the words on it were printed in a nearly illegible hand. *I got that paper Lizbet had. It cost you a hunnerd bucks.*

"Where did this come from?" Her sharp tone brought the receptionist swiveling to face her.

"A boy brought it."

"What boy? When?"

She glanced at the clock. "Maybe an hour ago. I didn't know him—just a kid, running an errand, I thought."

An errand for the person who'd stolen Lizbet's cash box and the note as well? It looked that way, although it was possible that Lynette's suicide note had passed through several hands since then. Only it wasn't a suicide note, if Lizbet's story was true.

Still, it might tell the police something, if it could be found. She frowned at the note in her hand. It set up a meeting place—two o'clock at the Cat Isle dock. Come alone.

Alone. That had all the aspects of a classic black-and-white thriller. As if she'd be foolish enough to do that.

She told herself that all the way back to Land's End, driven by the taciturn security guard. Trent had gone off the island. Back to Savannah to check with the lab there? He hadn't confided in her.

If he were here, she could tell him about this. As it was— who else could she trust? Regretfully, there was no one. She glanced at her watch as she entered the house. Nearly one-thirty now. If she were going to do this—

She could. She'd take one of the little jet boats. It would get her away quickly if there was trouble. She'd have to go alone. Whoever he was, he'd be able to see from a distance across the water. He'd know if she had someone with her.

But that cut both ways. She could see and be seen. No one would dare attack her in broad daylight. She was taking a risk, of course, but she wouldn't go anywhere near him—she'd keep a safe stretch of water between them. She'd have her cell phone as well. And if she could get her hands on that phony suicide note, they might begin to see their way out of this maze. She'd begun to feel so desperate for the truth that any risk seemed worth it.

Fifteen minutes later she shoved off from the Land's End

dock, Geneva's cautions ringing in her ears. *I'll be careful*, she'd told her, but Geneva hadn't known she needed to be cautious of more than the tide. Still, according to Lizbet, this was nothing but a sneak thief, trying to cash in on the note, probably hearing the stories that were circulating again about the deaths.

The little craft skimmed across the water. She patted the pocket where she'd stowed the money, wrapped in plastic, weighted with a stone. If he showed, she'd toss the packet to him, and he could give her the note the same way. It wasn't a perfect plan, but it was the best she could come up with. She wouldn't go any closer, even if it meant losing the last chance of clearing this up.

Her sore shoulder had begun to ache by the time Cat Isle came into view. Obviously it hadn't healed quite enough for steering the jet boat, but she was almost there. She cut the motor. The dock was empty. He hadn't come.

The roar of a motor cut the still air. She turned, startled, rocking the jet boat. A speedboat, a big one, swung around the spit of land between the sound and the creek, coming fast.

For a moment she watched, bemused. Odd that he'd be heading up the creek with a boat that size when the tide was turning. He'd probably swing toward the channel. Then she saw he was turning, but not toward the channel. Toward her.

Hands fumbling on the ignition, she fought to start the motor again. The motor of the bigger boat roared, nearly deafening her. He was almost on her, he'd ram the jet boat, she couldn't get out of the way—

She dived clear just as the speed boat smashed into the little craft. The explosion of sound dazed her, and then she was under, swallowing a mouthful of saltwater, choking, struggling to find the surface.

She burst into the air, lungs burning, gasping. Where was

he? For an instant her eyes blurred with brackish water. The roar of the motor rent the sky. She was helpless, dead in the water, and he was bearing down on her again, the boat huge and white from water level, the person behind the windscreen nothing but a blur of dark clothes and dark glasses.

Help me, Father! Muscles burning, eardrums roaring, she dived away again. She couldn't keep this up long, already she was tiring, all he had to do was wait until she floundered enough to catch her.

She surfaced, choking. He'd turned sharply, coming at her in a tight circle. He'd get her this time. She was too tired, she couldn't evade him. One agonizing impact. Then she'd be safe in her Father's arms.

And leave Miles's killer free to kill again? No! She thrust out frantically, legs reaching. Her feet hit bottom. For an instant she was too shocked to respond. Then she threw herself toward the shallows. He couldn't pursue her there—he'd run aground if he tried. She had to get a few more feet.

She stumbled, choking again as her face went under, feeling the swell rush over her head as he swept close, too close, she could almost feel the impact—

And then he was rushing away, the roar of his engine fading, vanishing as he rounded the curve out into the sound. She stood blinking, chest-deep in water, trying to focus on the boat. Useless. It looked like dozens of other white boats.

And there was the reason he'd fled. A small fishing boat putt-putted toward her.

"You okay, ma'am?" The boy who leaned out couldn't be more than fourteen or fifteen, and his eyes were round with shock. "He prêt near hit you. What was he, crazy?"

"I guess so." She clasped his strong young arm, letting him pull her into the boat. She collapsed on a seat smelling strongly of fish. He'd gotten an odd catch today, she thought, and knew it for the beginning of hysteria. She took a long, gasping breath, then another, and lifted her face toward the sun's warmth. She was alive.

Thank You, Lord. Thank You.

A rough wool blanket surrounded her shoulders, and a worried dark face stared at her. "Sure you're okay?"

She managed a smile. "Fine, thanks to you." And the One who sent you. "Did you recognize the boat?"

The whites of his eyes showed. "No'm. Fancy. Belongs to one o' the big houses, that for sure."

She'd already figured that out, hadn't she? No random acts, no outsiders willing to sell a piece of evidence. Just a calculating killer who would kill again to keep his secret.

She forced herself to sit up straight. She wouldn't be tricked again. "Can you take me back to Land's End?"

"Yes'm." He nodded toward a bit of floating orange fiberglass. "You want I should get the pieces for you?"

She couldn't quite suppress a shudder. "No. Just take me to Land's End."

Trent stalked down to the dock. According to Geneva, Sarah had gone out alone in the jet boat over an hour ago. What on earth was she thinking? Hadn't he told her not to go anywhere alone?

As if he had a right to tell Sarah what to do. And as if she'd listen if he did. Couldn't she see that he was only trying to protect her?

He'd said that to Lynette, more than once, when she'd complained about living on the island, isolated from the urban pleasures she enjoyed. He'd been trying to protect her. He hadn't succeeded.

He stopped at the dock, shielding his eyes to scan the

waterway. No little orange jet boat bobbed along the surface. There was nothing in sight but some kid chugging along in an underpowered fishing boat. He'd take the motorboat out and try to find her. She might have tired out, further injured her shoulder—

He was already turning toward the sleek white boat when it registered. There were two people in the fishing boat, headed straight toward the Land's End dock.

Sarah sat up straight, as if she felt him watching her, but she couldn't disguise the way her hair hung wetly around her pale face or the smear of mud across her cheek. It was all he could do to stay on the dock until the fishing boat bumped gently against the fenders.

The kid steadied Sarah as she rose. Trent caught her under the arms and lifted her to the dock. His arms went around her solidly, and he didn't know whether he wanted to shake her or kiss her senseless.

"What happened? Where on earth were you? Are you hurt?"

She shook her head, looking too exhausted to speak. He turned toward the boy, eyebrows lifting.

"Down by Cat Isle. I come round from the sound. First thing I see is a big white speedboat ramming that little bitty jet boat." He shook his head. "If'n he didn't swing round and try 'n' hit the lady again. Never saw anything like it my whole life."

The shudder that ran through Sarah reverberated through him. "Is that true?" He tilted her chin up and read the answer in her eyes. "Did you see who it was?"

"No." Her voice was husky. "Dark glasses, dark clothing. That's all I saw."

"What about you?" He frowned at the boy.

"Fancy boat." The kid jerked his head toward the *Gypsy*. "Like that'un. Belong to one of the big houses, I reckon."

"Wait a second." Trent reached for his wallet, but the kid just shook his head and pushed off.

"Don't want nothin', no, sir. Just take care of the lady."

He hadn't done well so far. His stomach twisted at the thought of what might have happened to her. Sarah, gone in an instant, all because she was too stubborn to ask for help.

He snapped open his cell phone, punched in the number for the house and cut Geneva off before she could say anything. "Get down to the dock and bring a blanket." He didn't need to say more.

He brushed wet hair back from Sarah's cheek. "What were you thinking?" he muttered.

A ghost of a smile crossed her face. "I thought I had it under control. Guess I owe you a jet boat."

"No. Someone else does."

Someone who owned a fancy white boat, from one of the big houses. That limited it to a relative few, and only one of the island residents with fancy white boats had been having an affair with Lynette. Anger seared along his veins.

"What made you go out alone?" He tried to control the rage, but it seeped into his voice.

"You weren't here."

Her words stabbed at him. He hadn't been here.

She pushed wet hair back from her face. "I got a note at the clinic."

His fists clenched, and she shook her head.

"Not like those. This was printed, nearly illiterate, saying that he had Lynette's letter and would sell it to me."

"And you went? It was a trap!" Something was shaking inside him at the thought of the danger she'd wandered into. No, not wandered. Gone into deliberately.

"Well, now it's obvious it was a trap." The snap was back

in her voice, even though she still shivered. "I thought I'd be safe enough out on the water in broad daylight. I thought I was dealing with a sneak thief, not a murderer."

"Obviously Lizbet was wrong. The thief wanted the note, not her cash. And now he's desperate."

His arms tightened around her, and she turned her face into his shoulder. Somehow that simple gesture robbed him of the ability to speak. He could only hold her, pressing his face against her wet hair.

"What's happened to Sarah?" Geneva sounded as shaken as he was. She reached them, throwing a blanket around Sarah and gathering her into her arms. "Child, are you hurt?"

She spoke to Sarah as if she spoke to Melissa. Geneva, at least, thought Sarah belonged here.

"Take her up to the house and tend to her, Geneva. There's something I have to do." The need burned in him. Get to Jonathan now, before the motor of that fancy white boat of his had time to cool off. Confront him with what had happened to Sarah. His fists clenched. Get the truth this time.

He stepped lightly from the dock to the deck of the *Gypsy*. She was gassed up, of course. He paid someone well to see that the boat was ready at a moment's notice. He turned the ignition, and the motor roared to life.

Leaving it idling, he turned to cast off the lines and found Sarah charging toward him, leaving Geneva shaking her head. "Where are you going?" she demanded.

"To see Jonathan. See if he's had his boat out."

"Trent, no. Not now. Let Gifford handle it."

His mouth twisted. "You're advising me to depend on Gifford?"

She stood well back on the dock. "Will you at least come

up here and talk to me about it? I don't feel like being this close to the water right now."

The urgency still burned in him, but he could hardly say no to that. Grasping the upright, he pulled himself up onto the dock and took one step toward her.

"What—"

The *Gypsy* exploded behind him in a sheet of flame, the concussion throwing him toward Sarah. Somehow he registered her horrified face before everything went black.

SEVENTEEN

She couldn't see Trent. Sarah tried to peer around Gifford's bulk, barely hearing the questions he pounded at her. Trent sat on the rear of the EMS vehicle, bent over as an emergency worker tended his back. Gifford had pulled her away from him, onto the veranda.

"Can't this wait?" She interrupted Gifford in midspate. "I'm a physician. I should be taking care of Mr. Donner."

"You?" His goggling eyes reminded her unpleasantly of a frog's. "I'm not letting you anywhere near him. Nothing happened around here 'til you came back."

"You can't think I had anything to do with this." How many kinds of an idiot was the man? "Why would I?"

He shrugged beefy shoulders. "Revenge. Jealousy." He fingered the handcuffs that hung from his belt.

Queasiness snaked through her stomach. Gifford could arrest her on nothing more than his own suspicion.

"That's nonsense." She forced strength into her voice. "I came here to find out the truth about what happened to my husband. If you'd done your job, I wouldn't have to."

Gifford purpled, yanking the handcuffs free. "You're coming with me. We'll talk down at the station." He reached for her.

"What do you think you're doing?" Trent's harsh voice slammed between them like a barricade. "Get away from her."

She could breathe again. She swung, to find him striding toward them, face dark with anger. His shirt was in shreds and a bruise darkened the side of his face. But he was alive. Her knees didn't want to hold her up. He was alive.

"She knows something," Gifford said stubbornly.

"Trent, you should go to the clinic and let Dr. Sam check you out."

"I'm all right." He swung on Gifford. "Dr. Wainwright has told us everything she knows. You just don't want to hear it."

Gifford shook his head. "You're not thinkin' straight, sir. It's my job to protect you."

"Protect me from what?" Trent's voice took on a deadly tone. "Wake up and see what's in front of your face. Ask yourself why someone tried to kill Dr. Wainwright and me as soon as the investigation was reopened."

"We've only got her word for it somebody tried to kill her."

"That, and the shreds of a jet boat, and an eyewitness." He jerked a nod toward the dock. "You've also got the remains of my boat. Obviously someone knew that when she didn't come back, I'd take the *Gypsy* to look for her. Ending his problem nicely."

"She could'a set that bomb herself, then lured you down to the boat."

Trent's fists doubled. "If Dr. Wainwright hadn't called me back from the boat, you'd be picking up pieces of me. Now go do your job." He seized Sarah's arm and headed for the door.

They reached the hall, and Trent slammed the door behind them, cutting off the turmoil outside. The house was blessedly quiet.

She took a deep breath. Trent was all right. She was all

right. They'd both come too close to death in the past hour, but they'd come through. *Thank You, Father*.

"Turn around and let me look at your back." She tried to sound as if she talked to any patient.

He shook his head. "I'm fine. The paramedics took care of me."

"I'm sure they wanted to take you to the clinic, and you refused."

"I don't need the clinic. And there's too much to do here." He frowned at her. "Do you think I'm leaving you and my daughter alone at this point? Sarah, he's desperate. He's willing to do anything."

"You think it's Jonathan, don't you?"

His face tightened in pain. "Who else could it be?" He started to turn. "I should tell Gifford to get over there—"

Footsteps sounded on the stairs, and a slight figure hurtled toward him. He opened his arms, and Melissa flew into them. He held his child, rocking her back and forth. "It's okay, sweetheart. I'm all right."

His voice held a tenderness Sarah had never heard. Her throat choked, and a few hot tears splashed onto her cheeks.

This was how it should be between father and daughter.

"I'm sorry, Daddy." Melissa hugged him tightly, her eyes squeezed shut. "I'm sorry I thought—"

Tell him, Melissa. Tell him.

Trent stroked her head. "You thought what, sugar?"

She raised her face to his. "That day, you know. When I told you about Mommy telling a lie. And then you went out in the boat, and then I heard that Mommy was dead."

The progression was a child's inevitable logic, nurtured by another's evil intent. Now that it was out, perhaps Melissa could begin to heal.

"Oh, honey." Trent held her small face between his hands. "Is that what you've been thinking all this time?"

"I didn't believe it, not really." Melissa's lips trembled. "But I couldn't make it go away."

"Melissa, I promise you, I didn't go anywhere near Cat Isle. I took the boat out, like I always do when I need to cool off. That's all. I didn't hurt Mommy. I would never do that."

They looked into each other's eyes for a long moment. Then Melissa gave a sharp little nod. "I know, Daddy. I know."

Tears stung Sarah's eyes. It was going to be all right between them.

Trent held her close, dropping a kiss on the top of her head. "Thank you, sugar. You'll see. It'll be better now that you've told me."

Melissa nodded. "That's what Sarah said, too."

Trent stiffened. "You told Sarah about this?"

Melissa was happily unaware that she'd said anything to upset him. "She said I should tell you, and she was right."

"Will you run out to the kitchen and tell Geneva I sure could use some coffee? I want to talk to Sarah for a minute."

She nodded, practically skipping toward the door that led to the kitchen. "I'll tell her."

He waited until the door had swung shut behind her. Then he turned to Sarah, his face forbidding. "You knew about this. You didn't tell me."

"Just since last night. She had to tell somebody." She had known, and she'd kept it secret.

"You should have told me!" The words came out in a barely suppressed explosion. "She's my daughter, Sarah. Not yours. You didn't have the right."

Her temples throbbed, and her legs had turned to rubber. Apparently her body thought she'd had enough.

She swallowed. She wasn't going to apologize for this. "Melissa was nearly hysterical when she came to my room. She made me promise I wouldn't tell you."

He stared at her, and the distance between them widened in the iciness of that stare. "She's my child," he repeated.

Why couldn't he understand? "I did what I thought was best for Melissa at that moment. I urged her to tell you."

"You should have told me. I won't have you interfering between me and my daughter."

"I promised her. I couldn't break my word."

"I'm not interested in your ethics, Sarah. She's my daughter. Don't interfere again."

His implacable tone set the barriers firmly in place. He might hold her, confide in her, let her care about him. But this boundary she couldn't cross.

She understood what was driving him. He had to be the one to protect his daughter. He had to. Protecting his own drove his every action. He'd tried to protect Lynette, even after she was dead. He'd protect Melissa, with his life, if necessary.

And she was on the outside, looking in.

The lump in her throat would choke her if she tried to speak. She could only nod, turn away from him and blindly stumble to her room.

She'd expected to talk with Trent after he'd cooled off, but the chance never came. Land's End was more than usually full of people after the accident, between the police guards Gifford posted, the staff that rallied around and Dr. Sam, who showed up as soon as he heard.

Finally Sarah went to bed, exhausted enough to sleep without resorting to any of the white tablets Dr. Sam pressed on her. By morning, without consciously thinking it through, she'd come to a decision.

She'd move back to the inn. Her presence was only making the situation more difficult for Trent. He thought he had to protect her, even while he was furious with her for what he saw as her interference with Melissa.

She could hardly blame him, under the circumstances. And maybe that anger would make leaving easier to bear. But she didn't think so. She'd go, but she was leaving part of her heart at Land's End.

She'd packed up most of her belongings by the time she walked toward the breakfast room. If Trent was there, she'd tell him. He might make some token objection, but he'd probably be secretly relieved to have her out of the house.

Was the danger over? Possibly not, since the police hadn't charged anyone yet. But after the wholesale attempt to wipe out both her and Trent had been unsuccessful, surely he wouldn't try anything again. Not now that the police were investigating.

Jonathan. She still couldn't quite believe it, but who else had a motive? She understood Trent's reasoning.

The house was quiet—the breakfast room empty. Where was everyone?

She poured a cup of coffee and sat with it warming her fingers, staring out at the merciless sunshine beating on the flagstones. Unfortunately it was Trent's face she saw.

Was I wrong not to tell him? I took responsibility for Melissa by not telling him, I suppose, but that's what I do. I take responsibility when I see someone hurting. Isn't that what I should do?

She didn't seem to have any answer to that. Maybe she never would. She frowned at the coffee mug. The best thing would be to seek out Trent, try to clear matters between them so she could leave.

Rapid footsteps sounded on the hall tile. Her heart thudded and she rose. Trent—

But it was Derek who burst into the room, his hair disheveled, his face anxious. "Sarah, thank goodness. I need your help." He grasped her arm, pulling her toward the hall.

"What is it? What's wrong?" Her stomach churned. Trouble, more trouble.

"I saw them. Jonathan and Trent were in one of Jonathan's boats, headed for Cat Isle." He tugged her arm. "Hurry."

Fear clawed at her. "Did you call the police?"

"Yes, but we can get there faster from here. Come on. If something's happened, we might need a doctor." His voice tightened on the words.

His urgency infected her. Jonathan and Trent, going to Cat Isle together. That couldn't be good. If Jonathan was guilty, if Trent confronted him there—

She hurried alongside Derek, out the hallway, across the veranda, down to the path. She glanced back, seeing Melissa watching them from an upper window.

"There's Melissa—I should tell her what's happening." Melissa, waiting, wondering, as she had the day her mother died.

"We don't have time." Derek pulled her along the dock. "Nothing she can do, anyway." He helped her into one of the boats and jumped in lightly. The motor roared to life, and she winced.

"It's okay." He seemed to catch the slight movement. "They checked out all the boats two or three times. It's safe. Cast off that line, will you?"

She hurried to do it, her hands fumbling awkwardly with the heavy coil. *Trent. Please keep him safe, Lord.*

She stumbled to the bench seat, falling into it as Derek roared away from the dock. "Sorry." He flung the word back over his shoulder.

"I'm all right. Just get us there."

He accelerated, wake surging out behind them. The motor whined to a higher pitch, echoing the fear that ricocheted through her. Trent. Jonathan.

"He wouldn't dare hurt Trent now. The police—"

"He probably thinks the police are too stupid to add two and two." The glance he shot her almost seemed exhilarated as the wind tore his words away. "Aren't they?"

"I guess so." She gripped the side of the boat, wishing she'd taken a moment to put on a life jacket. Still, no matter how fast he was going, Derek handled the boat as if it were an extension of himself.

"We'll get there in time. I promise."

That was a promise he couldn't guarantee, but he was trying to ease her fear. He couldn't. Nothing but the sight of Trent, alive and well, could do that.

Cat Isle came into view. She strained toward the dock. "I don't see a boat. Are you sure they were headed here?"

"Positive." Derek eased back on the throttle, letting their forward momentum glide them to the dock. "It doesn't mean anything. There's a place on the other side of the island where you can take a boat in if the tide's right."

She stood before the boat stopped. "Hurry."

"Wait a second." Derek gestured toward the locker behind her. "My gun is in the locker. I was target-shooting over at Sandy Key the other day. We'd best take it with us."

She couldn't shoot anyone, but maybe she could threaten, if she had to. If Trent were in danger— She flipped the lid up.

The gun, stubby and mean looking, lay atop a folded tarp. She forced her fingers to close over it.

"Here." She handed it to Derek. "You take it."

He stuffed the weapon into his waistband. "Don't like guns, Sarah?" He climbed onto the dock, reaching out a hand to help her up.

"I've seen what they can do," she said shortly. She wouldn't let herself think of Trent lying in a pool of blood, life seeping out of him. She headed up the path, her sandals slipping on wet grass. "Hurry."

Derek's footsteps were soft behind her. Impossible to run up the path—the encroaching undergrowth had eaten away at it since the last time she was here. In a few more weeks it would be completely obliterated.

"It doesn't look as if anyone has been here recently." What if Derek was wrong? What if Jonathan had taken Trent somewhere else? Even now, he could—

"They're here." Derek's voice was in her ear. "Go on."

She burst through into the clearing in front of the cottage. Race across, heart pounding. Run up the steps. Fling the door open.

Her momentum carried her several feet into the room before her eyes adjusted to the dim light. It was empty. They weren't here. Her heart seemed to stop. Jonathan had taken Trent somewhere else. Even now, he could be dead.

No! The pain that arrowed through her heart told her the truth. She loved him. And he was in mortal danger.

"They're not here. We have to go. We have to find Trent."

"Don't worry." Derek's voice was soft. "He'll find us."

She swung around, staring at him. At the gun in his hand, pointed at her heart. At the expression that subtly distorted his face, letting malice show through the pleasant, ordinary facade of the man she'd considered a friend.

"What's wrong, Sarah?" His voice mocked.

"You." She could barely take it in. "It was you."

He smiled. "Are you going to say you can't believe it? You never suspected me, did you? All your investigating went for nothing. You never even looked at me."

"You—but you weren't having an affair with Lynette."

"No." Something flickered in his eyes and was gone. "Maybe I loved her once, but Trent took her away from me."

"He's your brother—"

"Half brother!" Anger reverberated through the word. "He deserted me. You think I owe him? I don't! This wasn't about love. It was about money. Lots and lots of money. Trent didn't think I was smart enough to have a real role in the company, but I was smart enough to steal from him for years, and he never suspected a thing."

She saw. Finally. Too late. *Please, Lord, help me.* "It was Miles you wanted to kill, wasn't it? He'd have found you out. Told Trent."

"I didn't give him a chance!" His anger spurted again, dangerously. "Too bad I had to use Lynette, but with her dead, too, everyone would think it was about love, not money."

She saw now that it was too late. He'd rigged the gas. And if it hadn't finished them, he'd have been ready to do something else.

"How did you get them here?"

"So easy. I told Lynette Trent wanted her to meet him here."

"And you told Miles the same." Easy, he'd said.

"Miles suspected something. I had to hit him, knock him out. But Lynette was already unconscious, so it didn't matter." He seemed to be congratulating himself.

She took a step backward, searching with her mind's eye for a weapon. She'd only been in the room once, but emotion had painted it clearly on her mind.

"You sent those notes to Melissa." Talk to him. It was her only defense, the only way to keep him from pulling the trigger.

He took a step toward her, the gun never wavering. "She saw me coming out of her mother's room the day I took a letter to fake the suicide note. I thought I'd keep her too upset to wonder about that."

Fury burned in her. He'd tormented a child he claimed to care for. Well, that was the answer, wasn't it? He didn't really care about anyone but himself. Sometime during those years with an abusive mother, he'd learned to disassociate himself from the rest of the human race.

"It didn't do you any good, did it? Lizbet took the letter." She edged a step toward the fireplace and the poker that leaned carelessly against its stone.

"Lizbet interfered. Like you."

Her mind on the poker, she didn't even see the blow coming. The backhanded sweep knocked her off her feet, her head colliding painfully with the floor. Before she could do more than blink at the rush of tears, he'd dragged her hands behind her.

Rough cord tightened. Something not as heavy as mooring line—she'd seen it, hadn't she, lying carelessly at his feet while he's steered the boat? He'd come prepared.

"Derek, don't do this." She struggled to keep a sob out of her voice. "You won't get away with it. Trent will—"

He nudged her with his foot. "Trent will come. He's already gotten the message I left, saying you're in danger." His face twisted in a parody of his pleasant smile. "He'll run to rescue you, just as you did to rescue him. Then there'll be another murder/suicide. Poetic, isn't it?"

"No one will believe that." She twisted her hands against the rope.

"They will." He sounded almost tranquil. "No one but you wanted to look into Lynette and Miles's deaths. They won't look too closely at your death, either." He took a step away from her. "Now, I really have to get outside. I think you'll shoot Trent coming up the path before shooting yourself. Your fingerprints will be on the gun. No one will think twice about it."

The door banged shut behind him. She choked on a sob. She had to act. She couldn't wait for Derek to kill them. Trent. Her heart contracted. He could be coming up the path even now.

Please, Father. Show me what to do. We can't die like this. Help me. Help us. She strained against the ropes. Panic rushed through her, rising in her throat like a scream.

If she screamed, would Trent hear and be warned? Or would that make him rush faster to his fate?

We can't be destined to die here, Father. Enough injustice has been done here. Lynette. Miles. Trent coming here to grieve for what had happened, his anger when she'd intruded—

The glass. He'd smashed a glass vase against the wood stacked in the fireplace. Surely no one would have cleaned it up.

She rolled across the hooked rug to the fireplace. Yes, there it was—a large, jagged chunk of the glass sparkled where a shaft of sunlight hit it. *Thank You, Father.*

She wiggled closer, groping blindly with her hands behind her back. Where? Where? Her fingertips fumbled against stone, embers, kindling. And then, finally, glass.

A moment's effort, the cost of a few drops of blood, and she had it positioned against the rope. She sawed, fighting for the angle that would cut through the rope. *Please, Lord, please, Lord.*

She felt a strand break through. One down, how many to

go? Too many? Panic rose again, and she sought for something to calm it. Focus, focus.

The Lord is my shepherd, I shall not want. The beautiful old words echoed in her mind like the ringing of crystal. She sawed in time with them, and they held back the terror.

Before she reached the end of the Psalm, the rope parted. *Thank You, Lord.* She scrambled to her feet and heard the roar of a boat motor. Trent, rushing to the rescue. Rushing to death.

Think, think. You'll only have one chance. Her fingers closed over the cool, hard poker. One chance would have to do.

She crept to the door, a prayer running like a silent litany behind her active thoughts. Careful, careful. Ease the door open, hope he doesn't hear. Heart pounding, she peered through the crack.

"Sarah!" Trent's voice shouted her name, and she heard his footsteps, pounding up the path.

She didn't dare shout back, give away her position to Derek. Where was he? Clutching the poker, she eased the door open a little more and nearly choked on a gasp. Derek stood only a few feet away, his back to her, gun held steady in his right hand, aimed at the opening of the path.

Even as she raised the poker, Trent burst through the bushes. She imagined the poker connecting with fragile skull, killing. She swung at the gun arm instead, connecting just as he fired, the explosion of the gun echoing with Derek's shrill scream. He staggered, falling from the porch, the gun flying.

Trent stood, clutching his chest, looking at her with an expression of surprise. Then his knees buckled and he went down.

EIGHTEEN

Terror choked her as she shot like a bullet off the porch, racing toward him. Trent. *Dear Lord, let him be alive.*

Sarah sent a frantic glance over her shoulder. Where was Derek? He stumbled to his feet, glaring after her, mouthing something she was glad she couldn't hear. If he came after her— But no, he was searching for the gun, sweeping his hand through the weeds, giving her precious seconds to reach Trent.

He stirred as she dropped to his knees beside him, trying to swing his body up. She grabbed him, hands groping for the source of the blood that stained his shirt. *Shoulder, thank You, Father, not the chest, not the lung.*

But bad enough if she didn't get the bleeding stopped. She pressed the heel of her hand against it, and he grunted, the pain shooting his eyes open.

"Sarah. What—"

"He's found the gun." She grabbed Trent's good arm, saw Derek's smile of triumph, saw him raise the gun, aim at them—

They dove for the dense undergrowth. She didn't know whether she pulled Trent or he'd pulled her. Branches closed around them like a shield, but they wouldn't stop a bullet.

Quickly, quietly, work through the tall grass, hear Derek's frustrated shout behind them. Hurry, stumbling, brambles tearing at clothes and skin. A wiry vine snared her foot, pitching her off balance.

Trent caught her, falling, and they both went down behind the thick, gnarled trunk of a cypress. His body pressed her against it, and he put his mouth against her ear.

"Wait," he whispered. "Listen. See where he is."

She nodded. Let Trent listen. She had to stop that bleeding, or he wouldn't be able to move at all. She tugged the shirt from his shoulder, automatically assessing the wound. Not life threatening, she'd have said in the emergency room, but they weren't in an emergency room.

She wadded a piece of the shirt against the wound, pressing hard.

Trent's breath caught. "Nice going, Doctor," he whispered. "You trying to make me pass out?"

"You'll pass out anyway if I don't slow the bleeding." But his words encouraged her. Trent was strong. He'd be all right, if he was treated properly.

But first they had to escape a maniac with a gun.

Trent put his cheek against hers. "I don't hear him. We'd better try to circle around, get to the boat."

Derek would think that's what they'd do. But what choice did they have? Trent couldn't play hide-and-seek out here for long. Once he collapsed, she'd never get him to safety.

She nodded. *Please, Lord.* She put her arm around Trent's waist, bearing as much of his weight as he'd allow. One step, then another, and they were in the water up to their knees.

Luckily Trent seemed to know the way. She was totally disoriented. Her mind shuddered away from the thought of the other creatures that might occupy the swampy water with them.

Trent stumbled, dragging her down with him, on their knees in the water. His face was gray under the tan, his pulse ragged under her fingers. His chances were going down with every moment that passed.

He jerked his head toward the clump of thick growth ahead of them. "There. Beyond that, water. Few yards to boats."

She hitched her arm around him, feeling him sag against her. A few yards, but he might not have a few yards in him.

Give me strength, Father. I don't have enough of my own.

Somehow her legs worked, her arms held. They stumbled forward. Too late to worry about the noise they were making. Just get there, that's all she could do. They broke through the tangled brush. The dock slept peacefully in the sun, off to their left.

"In the water," Trent murmured. "Keep low. Get to my boat."

He was right, of course. They'd make less of a target in the water, but where was Derek? Had he gone back to the cottage, thinking they might shelter there?

They staggered into the water, mud beneath their feet, dragging at them. Falling again, but water to cushion them this time. Half swimming, half crawling, saltwater buoying them, bracing for a bullet. where was Derek, where was he—

Her outstretched hand touched the first boat. *Thank You, Father.*

"Easy." She got her shoulder under Trent's good arm, her heart failing. How was she going to get him into the boat?

They that wait upon the Lord shall renew their strength. They shall mount up with wings as eagles—

She surged upward, Trent grabbed the side of the boat, muscles straining, gasping for breath. And then they were in, lying sprawled half on the seat, dripping and exhausted, but alive. Alive.

"We did it." She grabbed Trent, willing him to be conscious. "We made it."

His eyes flickered open, a ghost of a smile touching pale lips. "We did."

"So you did." The voice was cold and deadly. Derek loomed over them, gun steady in his hand, aimed at Trent's head.

Trent managed to pull a strangled breath into his lungs. Now was not the moment to pass out, leaving Sarah to face Derek on her own. His mind struggled to measure the distance to the ignition, the time it would take to start the motor—

Too much. They'd both be dead by then.

He forced himself upright, putting himself between Sarah and the gun. Buy her another moment of life.

She doesn't deserve this, Lord. Maybe I do, but Sarah doesn't. Save her.

"Why?" His voice sounded unfamiliar in his ears, maybe because his head roared with the effort of staying upright. "Why, Derek? I trusted you. You're my brother."

"Brother?" Derek stepped from the dock to the boat, setting it rocking slightly. The tremor made Trent stagger, but Derek stood easily, balanced on the balls of his feet, his smile mocking. "Half brother, you mean."

He let the movement push him down onto the bench seat next to Sarah. Nothing there to help them, but the locker next to it had been left open.

"I always treated you like my brother." Keep his eyes focused on Derek, hope his body hid the hand that fumbled for the locker, groping for anything that might be a weapon. "Why are you doing this?"

"Ask your friend Sarah." Derek wiggled the gun in her direction.

Panic ripped through him. Keep the focus on himself, keep Derek's anger and hatred directed at him. "Sarah's got nothing to do with this. This is about us, you and me. What is it—didn't I give you a big enough salary? Didn't I send you to the right school?"

"Salary. School. Is that all you can think of—the things your money can buy? I wanted to pay you back, you get that?" Derek's face twisted with so much hatred, Trent almost didn't recognize his little brother. "You were the lucky one. You got out. You had the grandparents that got you away from her."

"I tried to help you." His hand closed over a wrench, and hope flared. "I came back for you when I could."

"Too late. It was all too late! I trusted you, and you left me there with her." It was the voice of his little brother, crying in the dark.

"Derek—" His vision blurred, and he felt the strength pouring out of him. "I love you," he murmured.

Derek shook his head, raised the gun. The roar of a motor rent the air. A siren screamed. Derek's face whipped toward the sound. With the last fragment of will, Trent swung the wrench toward Derek, knocking the gun away, feeling his strength gone, plummeting toward the deck.

Sarah cried something, lunged toward him. He tried to tell her to run but he couldn't form the words. Derek moved, leaping to the dock. Then to the other boat. The engine roared, whining from them, away from the approaching police boat.

Sarah's hands, cool on his face. Sarah's voice, sobbing. "Don't you die. Don't you dare die."

Something he had to tell her, but he couldn't. He couldn't. Hold her face in your mind. Slip away into the dark.

"He's going to be all right." Sarah held Melissa against her, praying she was speaking the truth. "Your father is strong."

They waited in the staff lounge at the clinic, huddled together on the sofa, fending off constant offers of coffee, tea, soup, prayer. Everyone wanted to help, and the love that poured out of them was tangible. They almost erased the terror. But not quite.

Images roared through her mind. The gun in Derek's hand, looking like the mouth of a cannon. The grief on Trent's face when he realized that the brother he loved hated him. The blood pouring out of him, staining her hands as she tried to stop it, all her prayers reduced to one word. *Please*.

"He was bleeding so much." Melissa echoed her thought. "I'm afraid."

"I know you are." She stroked the girl's hair. "You saved us, Melissa. Don't forget that. You saved us."

If Melissa hadn't been frightened at seeing her rush away with Derek, seeing her father follow, if she hadn't gone to Geneva, insisted on calling the police—

They'd be dead now, she and Trent. Derek might not have gotten away with it, but they wouldn't have been around to know.

The door swung open. Dr. Sam looked gray with fatigue, but he was smiling. "Lucky for him he had the good sense to have a doctor with him when he got shot. He's going to be fine."

Melissa choked on a sob and buried her face in Sarah's shoulder. "You saved him."

Sarah cupped the girl's face in her hands and looked into her eyes. "You saved both of us. Don't ever forget that."

Melissa's mouth firmed, and suddenly she looked very like her father. "I won't."

"Can we see him now?" She lifted her eyebrows at Sam.

"Sure thing." He held the door open for them. "Go right in. Esther's got the police and the press corralled outside, and she won't let anybody in until you're ready."

She clutched Melissa's hand tightly as they crossed the hall. She suspected the girl's mind was filled with the same song hers was. *Thank You, Father. Thank You.*

Trent lay propped up in the bed, and his face turned toward them the instant the door opened. For an instant no one moved. Then he held out his good hand toward his daughter. With a strangled sob, she ran to him. His arm closed around her.

Sarah's throat tightened, and she strained to hold back tears. Maybe she should leave them alone—

Trent looked at her, over his daughter's head, and he managed the ghost of a smile. "Come. Please."

Her step felt ridiculously light as she crossed the room to his bed. "How do you feel?"

"Like I've been shot and dragged through a swamp." He grimaced, then raised an eyebrow. "Derek?"

The lump in her throat threatened to strangle her. "I'm sorry. He was trying to escape the police launch. He crashed into the bridge piling trying to make it out the intercoastal waterway." She wouldn't say, in front of Melissa, that Gifford said it looked as if he'd done it on purpose. "He didn't make it."

Pain tightened his mouth. "I failed him."

"Don't think that." She clasped his hand. "You did your best for him. That's all anyone can do." Probably only God could understand why Trent had come out of the situation strong and Derek twisted. "It wasn't your fault."

His pain went so deep. He'd reacted to Lynette's death with isolation and bitterness. How would he get through this betrayal from the one person he'd trusted?

Trent shook his head slowly. "I thought I could control everything. Protect everyone. Instead I almost got us killed." He stroked Melissa's hair. "If it hadn't been for Melissa—"

"Fortunately Melissa is smarter than both of us." She deliberately kept her voice tart. "She recognized a trap when she saw it."

Melissa straightened, brushing hair back from her face. "I just knew something was wrong. Uncle Derek was acting so funny. It felt like the day Mommy died."

"You have good instincts, honey."

Melissa managed a watery smile. "I take after my daddy."

They were going to be all right. Something that had been tight inside Sarah eased. Trent and his daughter had come through a turbulent storm that would have swamped some people, but they'd found their way to each other.

And what about her? She'd found the truth she came to St. James Island for. Maybe, someday, that would be enough.

Trent pushed himself up a bit higher. "I suppose Gifford is waiting to see me." He patted Melissa. "Will you go tell him to come in, honey? I may as well get this over with."

Melissa nodded and hurried out, her step assured, her shoulders straight.

Sarah took a quick breath. There was one more thing she had to say to Trent before Gifford came in.

"Gifford is keeping a tight rein on the press." She chose her words carefully. She had to get this right. "He's ready to cover it up, if that's what you want. Write it all off as a regrettable accident."

His face was the tight, controlled mask she'd seen so often since she came back—eyes narrowed, lines harsh, mouth a thin line. Then slowly he shook his head.

"We tried that before, didn't we? It didn't work. We didn't count on a crusader named Sarah."

"I needed to know the truth for myself. It doesn't matter to me whether the rest of the world knows." She was giving him the choice. If he wanted to try and live a lie, she couldn't prevent that. But she would grieve for him.

"Do you think I'm still that foolish?" His hand closed over hers, drawing her near him. "I was wrong. If it hadn't been for you, I'd never have known the truth."

"If it hadn't been for me, Derek would still be alive." She wouldn't soon forget that. "If anyone's to blame—"

"No." His grip tightened painfully. "You were right to begin with. Derek was responsible for the choices he made."

She could only hope he believed that. That he wouldn't go on blaming himself for what Lynette had done, for what Derek had done.

He linked his fingers with hers, so that they were palm to palm, and a wave of warmth flooded through her.

"I thought I could protect my family by controlling everything around them, but I couldn't. You showed me that. The cost of power is too high." His fingers tightened painfully for an instant, and then eased. "Let the truth come out. We can deal with it."

"We?" Her heart began hammering in slow, heavy beats. She forced herself to meet his gaze, and found a warm glow deep in the gray. He looked, finally, at peace.

"I love you, Sarah. You challenge me, and irritate me, and you won't let me get away with a thing."

Hope blossomed, expanding in her soul. "That's not ordinarily what a man says when he's declaring his love."

"You're not an ordinary woman, Sarah Wainwright." He lifted her hand to his lips. "You wouldn't be content with ordinary, and neither would I. I'd rather spend the rest of my life off balance with you than at rest with anyone else."

She saw, finally, what she'd been missing. That was what had been wrong between her and Miles, and she'd never recognized it.

She didn't want a safe harbor, any more than Trent did. They were both better suited to the challenge of the storm.

"I take it that means you won't try to cloister me at Land's End and surround me with armed guards."

"I wouldn't dare." He kissed her fingers. "I love you, Sarah. Do you love me?"

The past was at rest now, all its secrets laid bare and rendered harmless. The future opened ahead of them, filled with challenge and promise. Through all the pain and grief, God had brought them to each other.

"I love you." Her heart swelled with the words. "I love you, Trent, and I will never run away again."

* * * * *

Dear Reader,

I'm so glad you decided to pick up this book, and I hope my story touches your heart. This is the first romantic suspense novel I've written in a long time, besides my work on the Faith on the Line continuity miniseries, and it was such a pleasure to return to it. I've loved romantic suspense since I read my first Phyllis Whitney novel back in junior high.

Land's End takes me back to the Low Country of South Carolina, the setting for my earlier Caldwell Clan series. It's a beautiful area, filled with mystery and romance. Certainly my heroine, Dr. Sarah Wainwright, finds plenty of both when she returns to St. James Island to right an old wrong. She learns, too, as I have, that the only safe refuge in time of trouble is the Lord.

I hope you'll write and let me know how you liked this story. Address your letters to me at Steeple Hill Books, 233 Broadway, Suite 1001, New York, NY 10279, and I'll be happy to send you a signed bookplate or bookmark. You can visit me on the Web at www.martaperry.com or e-mail me at marta@martaperry.com.

Blessings,

Marta Perry

QUESTIONS FOR DISCUSSION

1. Trent Donovan is desperate to protect his daughter, even if he has to hurt Sarah to do so. Can you sympathize with Trent's feelings, even if you don't agree with his decisions?

2. Sarah Wainwright has come through the first year of her grief, feeling as if she's now capable of learning what really happened to Miles, but she finds her grief reawakened by her return to the island. Have you ever been surprised by an emotion you thought you'd overcome? How did you deal with that?

3. Sarah isn't sure there's anyone on the island she can trust to be her friend. Can you imagine feeling that alone?

4. The Scripture theme for the story is from Psalms 18:2: "The Lord is my stronghold, my fortress and my champion, my God, my rock where I find safety, my shield, my mountain refuge, my strong tower." In what ways did you find this theme reflected in the characters' lives?

5. How did Trent try to provide his own "strong fortress" for those he loved? Was he successful? Why or why not?

6. This promise of safety in the Lord is meaningful to Sarah in times of danger. Do you have a favorite verse you lean upon? What does it mean to you?

7. Do you find that the Gullah characters add to the story? What insight into that culture did you gain?

8. Trent doesn't realize that his wealth and power sometimes keep people from being honest with him. How do we see that reflected in the lives of public figures like politicians and entertainers?

9. Trent's determination to protect (or overprotect) his daughter comes between him and Sarah. Have you known about or experienced a situation where this happened? What would be a constructive way of dealing with it?

10. In the end, Sarah realizes that she doesn't want a safe harbor, any more than Trent does—that they're both better suited to the challenge of the storm. Do you feel their relationship will withstand life's storms? How can battling trouble together make a marriage stronger?

And now, turn the page for a sneak preview of
TANGLED MEMORIES by Marta Perry,
part of Steeple Hill's exciting new line,
Love Inspired Suspense!
On sale in August 2006
from Steeple Hill Books.

For twenty-nine years, Corrie Grant had thought she'd never know who her father was. Now she knew, and no one would believe her.

No one, at this point, was represented by a pair of smooth, silver-haired attorneys with Southern drawls as thick as molasses. They looked about as expensive as this hotel suite, where she sank to the ankles in plush carpeting. The denim skirt and three-year-old sweater she usually wore for her monthly shopping trips had definitely not been right for this meeting. She hadn't known Cheyenne, Wyoming, boasted a hotel suite like this.

She slid well-worn loafers under her chair and straightened her back. *You're as good as anyone*, her great-aunt's voice echoed in her mind, its independent Wyoming attitude strong. *Don't let anyone intimidate you.*

"I've already told you everything I know about my parents." Her words stopped one of the lawyers—Courtland or Broadbent, she didn't know which—in midquestion. "I came here to meet Baxter Manning." Her grandfather. She tried out the phrase in her mind, not quite ready to say it aloud yet. "Where is he?"

"Now, Ms. Grant, surely you understand that we have to

ascertain the validity of your claim before involving Mr. Manning, don't you?"

Courtland or Broadbent had the smooth Southern courtesy down pat. He'd just managed to imply that she was a fraud without actually saying it.

She gripped the tapestry chair arms, resisting the impulse to surge to her feet. "I'm not making any claims. I don't expect anything from Mr. Manning. I just want to know if it's true that his son was my father."

Twenty-nine years. That was how long Aunt Ella had known about her mother's marriage and kept it from her. Corrie could only marvel that she hadn't pressed for answers earlier. She'd simply accepted what Aunt Ella said—that her mother had come to Ulee, Wyoming, three months pregnant, at eighteen. That she'd died in an accident when Corrie was six months old. That her mother had loved her.

Pain clutched her heart. Was that any more true than the rest of the fairy tale?

The attorneys exchanged glances. "You must realize," one of them began.

She shot to her feet. "Never mind what I must realize." Coming on top of the struggle to stretch her teaching salary and the meager income from Last Chance Café to pay Aunt Ella's hospital bills and funeral expenses, she didn't think she could handle any further round-around. "I'm done here. If Mr. Manning is interested in talking to me, he knows where to reach me. I'll be on my way."

She was halfway to the door when the voice stopped her.

"Come back here, young woman."

She turned, pulse accelerating. The man who'd come out of the suite's bedroom was older than either of the lawyers—in his seventies, at least. Slight and white-haired, his pallid skin declared his fragility, but he stood as straight as a man half his age.

"Mr. Manning." It had to be.

He lifted silver eyebrows. "Aren't you going to call me 'Grandfather'?"

"No."

He let out a short laugh. "Fair enough, as I have no intention of letting you." He extended his hand to one of the attorneys without looking. The man gave him the copies she'd brought of her mother's marriage certificate and her own birth certificate.

"The birth certificate doesn't name a father." He zeroed in on the blank line, his gaze inimical.

She'd learned, over the years, to brace herself for that reaction whenever she had to produce a birth certificate. *You're a child of God*, Aunt Ella would say. *Let that be enough for you.*

Not exactly what a crying eight-year-old had wanted to hear, but typical of the tough Christian woman who'd raised her. Ella Grant had taken what life dished out without complaint, even when that meant bringing up an orphaned great-niece with little money and no help.

"According to my great-aunt, when I was born my mother was afraid her husband's family would try to take me away. Later, she decided that they had a right to know." She kept her gaze steady on the man who might be her grandfather. "*You* had a right to know. She left for Savannah to talk to you about me when I was six months old. She died in an accident on the trip."

An accident—that was what Aunt Ella had always said. It was what Corrie had always believed, until she'd been sorting through Aunt Ella's papers after her stroke. She'd found the marriage license and the scribbled postcard, knocking down her belief in who she was like a child's tower of blocks.

He made a dismissive gesture with the papers. "Grace Grant never returned to Savannah after my son died." His voice grated on the words. With grief? She couldn't be sure. "If you are her daughter, that still doesn't guarantee my son was your father."

Her temper flared at the slur, but before she could speak, one of the lawyers did.

"A DNA test," he murmured.

Manning shot him an annoyed look. "From what I've learned, that's not likely to be conclusive with the intervening generation gone."

"Nevertheless—" The lawyer's smooth manner was slightly ruffled. Obviously the attorneys would prefer that he let them deal with this situation.

"I have no objection to a DNA test." Why would she if there was even a chance that it would answer her questions?

Who am I, Lord? I know I'm Your child, but I have to know more.

Manning tossed the papers on the table, bracing himself with one hand on its glossy surface. "It doesn't matter. You won't get anything from me in any event."

"I don't want anything." That was what they seemed incapable to understanding. "All I want is to know something about my father. Nothing else."

His mouth twisted. "Do you really think I'll believe that?"

The truth sank in. Manning didn't believe her, and he wouldn't help her.

"No, obviously you can't." She wouldn't offer to shake hands. If her father had been anything like this man, maybe she was lucky he'd never been a part of her life. "I can't say it's been nice meeting you, Mr. Manning, but it's been interesting."

She turned toward the door again, holding her head high.

Aunt Ella wouldn't have expected anything less. But the disappointment dragged like a weight pressing her down, compounding her still-raw grief.

"Just a minute." Manning's voice stopped her again. "I have a proposition for you."

"Proposition?" She turned back slowly, not sure she wanted to hear anything else he had to say.

A thin smile creased his lips. "I won't claim you as a grandchild—understand that. I won't give you anything. But you may come and stay at my house in Savannah for a few weeks." The lawyers were twittering, but he ignored them. "If you mean what you say, that will give you a chance to learn something about my son."

"If you don't believe I'm your grandchild, why would you want me there?" She eyed him, wondering what was in his mind.

His smile grew a bit unpleasant. "Ever heard the expression, 'putting a cat among the pigeons'? I suppose not. Never mind my motives. They are not your concern."

"Mr. Manning, we really don't think this is a good idea." Courtland and Broadbent exchanged glances.

Manning transferred his grip from the table to the back of the chair, leaning heavily, obviously tiring. "You make the arrangements. She can go now, while I'm still out of town. Lucas will take care of her."

"Lucas?" She grasped at the unfamiliar name, trying to make sense of this.

"Lucas Santee. He runs my companies."

"The young woman hasn't agreed to go." And the lawyers obviously hoped she wouldn't.

"She will." Manning sent her a shrewd glance. "Won't you?"

She didn't like his attitude. Didn't like the feeling that he was manipulating her for some reason she couldn't understand. If she acted on instinct, she'd walk right out the door and go back to Ulee. She had plenty there to keep her busy until school started again.

But she wouldn't, because if she did, she'd never know the answers to the questions that haunted her. *I hope this is what You want, Lord.*

"I'll go," she said.

* * * * *

Introducing a brand-new 6-book saga from Love Inspired...

Davis Landing

Nothing is stronger than a family's love

Becoming the makeover candidate in her family's magazine wasn't something Heather Hamilton had planned to do, but she refused to miss a deadline. So the shy auburn editor found herself transformed into a beauty that no one, especially photographer Ethan Danes, could keep their eyes off of....

BUTTERFLY SUMMER

BY

ARLENE JAMES

Available July 2006

wherever you buy books.

Steeple Hill®

2 Love Inspired novels and a mystery gift... Absolutely FREE!

Visit

www.LoveInspiredBooks.com

for your two FREE books, sent directly to you!

BONUS: Choose between regular print or our NEW larger print format!

There's no catch! You're under no obligation to buy anything. We charge nothing—ZERO—for your first shipment. And you don't have to make any minimum number of purchases.

You'll like the convenience of home delivery at our special discount prices, and you'll love your free subscription to Steeple Hill News, our members-only newsletter.

We hope that after receiving your free books, you'll want to remain a subscriber. But the choice is yours—to continue or cancel, anytime at all! So why not take us up on our invitation, with no risk of any kind!

Love Inspired®

Love Inspired®

ALL OUR TOMORROWS

BY
IRENE HANNON

Hoping to heal her shattered life, Caroline James threw herself into work at the local newspaper in her hometown. But then David Sloan walked back into her life. Had the Lord reunited David and Caroline so they could help each other learn to live and love again?

Available July 2006
wherever you buy books

Steeple
Hill®

www.SteepleHill.com

LIAOT

Love Inspired®
SUSPENSE

TITLES AVAILABLE NEXT MONTH

Don't miss these two stories in July

UNDER SUSPICION by Hannah Alexander
Part of the HIDEAWAY miniseries

When her senator father was murdered, Shona Tremaine became the prime suspect—until an attempt was made on her life. As she worked with her estranged husband, Geoff, to solve the tragic mystery, would their renewed commitment be enough to save Shona's life?

MISTAKEN FOR THE MOB by Ginny Aiken

Being mistaken for a gangster and accused of murders she didn't commit turned librarian Maryanne Wellborn's life on its end. And when serious but handsome FBI agent J. Z. Prophet took the case, she could tell he was determined to bring her down. But when the *real* mob got involved, the situation turned deadly....

LISCNM0606